Table of Contents

Chaos in Nanosia

Book 4 of the Nanosia Series

Rhonda Denise Johnson

Rhondazvous Books

Paris, Texas

License Statement

Glossary

Although this is a fictional book and doesn't contain any mathematical calculations or Einstein formulas, so you don't have to be a scientist to follow the story, here are a few terms you will come across as you read.

Boson: a subatomic particle that caries the energy that makes matter move or affects matter in some way.

Dark energy: the place holder name that scientists give to the forces that affect matter but do not interact with the electromagnetic field and therefore cannot be detected by our senses.

Dark matter: a place holder name scientists give to the matter they suspect exist, but which doesn't interact with the electromagnetic field, and therefore cannot be detected by our physical senses.

Electromagnetic field: in the universe, the electromagnetic field contains all the matter and energy that we can detect through our physical senses.

Elementary particle: subatomic particle such as electrons, protons, fermions, and bosons.

Fermion: the subatomic particles that make up matter such as protons, electrons, and neutrons.

Field: refers to an area of study or subject matter.

Gluon: this boson is the strong force that holds the protons in an atom together.

Graviton: the hypothetical boson that contains gravitational energy.

Nano: nine. In the International System of Units, the prefix "nano" means one-billionth, or 10-9. One billion is a number with nine zeroes

Nanotube: a tubular molecule composed of a large number of carbon atoms.

Nanoscope: a microscope whose magnification is strong enough to see subatomic particles.

Nanosia: a fantasy world that is one billionth the size of the real world. Each book in the Nanosia Series focuses on one of the four kingdoms in Nanosia: The Quantum Realm, Atomidon, Cenozonia, and The Realm of Chaos.

Photon: the boson that light is made of.

Quantum (singular) Quanta (plural): subatomic particle such as electrons, protons, and neutrons, bosons, fermions, and photons.

Quantum realm anything that has to do with a subatomic particle.:

Subatomic particle: particles that are smaller than an atom such as protons, electrons, bosons, and fermions.

Chapter 1

Zap was just a normal boy. Just a regular boy doing normal regular boy things like skipping stones off a normal regular forest pond.

He tossed a large stone into the pond, and his eyes grew big as the ripples spread out from where the stone sank. The water was coming for him. The ripples knew who he was. They knew what he had done, and they would drown him.

He yelped and ran for the forest surrounding the pond. He could feel the water lapping at his heels, its gurgling menace urging him into sheer panic. With five trees between him and the pond he stopped and gasped for breath. Then he looked down at the grass under his feet. It was just grass. No water. How could he have felt water through his shoes. How could he have heard the rippling from a skipped stone?

He looked up sheepishly when Lacus, the water mage, laughed. "What's wrong, Zap? It's just water."

Zap brushed his hand across his face and walked back toward the pond. The water was just water. It couldn't come for him. It was just normal water. Nothing abnormal about it. And he was just a normal boy. There was nothing abnormal or irregular about him. He was skipping regular stones across a regular pond. Just a normal regular boy thing.

"So, when are you going to take charge of your element, Zap? You can't use magic over water if you're afraid of it." Lacus held a stone in his hand, pausing for an answer Zap didn't think was normal or regular at all. "You're friends with the journeyman of the earth mage. Will you still be my apprentice when Jawan becomes a master?"

Jawan had moved up to journeyman when he defeated the dreadful Lord Elveston. Zap shrugged the thought away. Even if there was someone else trying to take over the universe, he wasn't the one to defeat any monsters. He was just a normal regular boy with no special powers over water or anything else.

He chose a flat stone and flicked it onto the surface of the pond. It skipped once, twice, then sank beneath the placid water just like a stone should. He didn't need any special power over the water to make it do that.

He flinched at the expanding circles but didn't run. His master was watching him. His master would protect him from any real danger. As long as he stayed near his master, he'd be safe. He could just watch the water and forget all that nonsense about elemental magic.

Lacus reached into a pocket of his robe and pulled out a flask. "You're enjoying yourself. But now it's time for your lesson."

"Lesson?"

"Yes, that's what being an apprentice is all about."

Zap started walking toward their castle. "Oh, well, if we're going to have a lesson, why'd you bring me out here?"

Lacus turned him around to face the pond. "I don't mean a book lesson. You're good at academic learning, but now it's time you got practical experience with water magic."

Zap gulped. "Practical experience? But, master, there's still so much I don't know. I'm nowhere near finished with the book you gave me. I'll just go back now. I even bookmarked the place where I stopped."

"There's only so much you can learn from a book. Some things you have to learn by doing." He gave Zap the flask and pushed him toward the water. "Focus on the water and pull it into your mind. Then divide it into atoms of hydrogen and oxygen and direct them into the flask. That is your lesson."

No! Zap screamed inside. He couldn't touch the water, much less pull it into his mind. "I can't do it."

"Yes, you can. Focus."

Zap bent down and picked up more stones, tossing them into the pond. It was something to do—something normal and safe—until he figured out a way to get out of his master's insane request. He tossed one stone, then two, but before he could toss the third stone, Lacus picked him up.

"In you go!"

Zap couldn't believe that his master had tossed him into the pond like a perfectly aimed stone. "Master! I . . ." Lacus's playful grin was the last thing Zap saw before the water closed over his head.

Water! Water all around him. He flailed his arms in what he thought was a swimming motion that would take him back to the surface. His mouth felt air for a moment. Then he went down again and knew he would not go back up. He wanted to live. To live, he had to breathe. His body knew this. His lungs knew this. What they didn't know was he had to breathe air. Water poured into his lungs and drowned out every thought.

When he opened his eyes, he started to panic again, but the water was gone. He closed his eyes again, breathing in the precious air. Remembering that he was a boy and that he had a body, he sat up and looked around. He was in his room on his bed. It was a perfectly normal room. His books and papers lay on a desk in the corner, his clothes hung on a peg on the wall, and the window opened to a day like any other day. Except it wasn't like any other day. Any other day, his master wouldn't have tried to drown him.

The strange drowned feeling whenever he breathed in told Zap it hadn't been a dream. His master must have put him in his bed, but that didn't mean he wouldn't try something else. It was for this reason that his friend Loby had started the Holy Order of Mice—a group of apprentices and journeymen who got together to protest the way some masters treated their charges like mice to experiment on. Had his master thrown him in the pond to test how long it took him to drown?

Whatever the reason was, it didn't matter. He'd done it. Zap got up, pulled on his clothes, and listened at the door. Hearing nothing, he creaked it open and stepped into the hall. Everything was quiet, but his master might be anywhere. Zap had to get out of his castle and tell Loby—no, Loby would laugh at him. He'd tell Jawan before his master caught him. After seeing the secret passages in Loby's castle, Zap had looked around to see if there were any in his own. Not that he thought he'd ever have to use them to escape his own master.

The passage he found began behind a statue on the floor below his room. He stood at the top of the staircase listening. Something creaked far away. He cocked his head to see if it was coming closer. It was. It wasn't. He couldn't tell. But if it was his master, he'd come soon enough. Zap had to go.

His footsteps sounded like a marching army on the stairs, and he was sure his master would pounce on him any moment to ask where he was going.

He reached the statue and stopped, remembering the dark passage that lay behind it. All he needed to do was get in there and goof up by sneezing in the dust. Or stand there. He remembered that he had a father—a man he'd hardly had time to know, who told him that fear would keep him alive. So, what was he to fear? The very real master Lacus who'd proven dangerous or the dust in an empty passage? He braced himself, pulled the statue away from the wall, and entered.

The passage was dusty and twisting. When he'd come there before, he'd counted twenty paces before he reached the stairs that took him down to the first floor. He held his hand over his mouth and nose against the dust and started counting. After twenty-one paces, he grabbed for the railing and inched his way down the stairs. Fifteen more paces, then turn right and he'd come to an outside door that opened behind a curtain of ivy.

The sun was setting on the other side of the castle. He pushed the ivy aside and stepped out into deep shadow. That didn't mean his master wouldn't see him. He crept along the outer wall until he came to the back of the castle, then ran.

"Where are you going?" his master called from somewhere behind him.

Oh, boy! If his master came after him, Zap couldn't outrun him. Zap ran faster. He couldn't face his master now. What could he say? The man would surely kill him. He reached Jawan's castle and banged on the portcullis. "Jawan! Help!" Zap felt so stupid. The Holy Order of Mice had never actually had to protect anyone from the elemental mages. He had no idea how Jawan could protect him against his master. "Jawan! Please! Help!" Zap expected his master to come up and grab him any moment. If only Jawan would hurry. He banged again and imagined his master laughing at his futile cries.

"What are you doing out here?"

Zap prepared to die. He braced himself for whatever tortures his master had planned for him. But it was Jawan looking at him through the portcullis. "Open up, please! My master! You've got to help me."

Jawan opened the portcullis without asking any questions. When they entered the castle laboratory, he sat Zap down and stared into his eyes. "What's the matter, Zap? What happened to your master?"

"H-he tried to kill me. He might be waiting outside for me right now. He's gone mad."

Jawan shook his head as his master, Myrlo, the great earth mage, entered the laboratory. "That doesn't sound like master Lacus."

"No, it doesn't," Myrlo said. "Zap, calm down and tell us what happened. Why do you think Lacus was trying to kill you?"

"Because he did. He threw me in the pond." Zap wanted to convince them to help him, but this sounded silly to his own ears.

Myrlo and Jawan exchanged glances. "But, Zap, you're an apprentice of water magic. How is throwing you in a pond going to kill you?"

"Because I can't swim."

"Maybe it's time you learned," Myrlo said.

Zap heard someone banging on the portcullis. "That's him! He's coming for me!" Zap ducked under the long wooden table that ran down the center of the laboratory. "Don't tell him where I am." But his master saw him come in here. "Tell him I left."

"I'll go see who it is." Jawan left.

Myrlo stooped down and peered at Zap. The earth mage's penetrating green eyes delved into his as if Zap had no secrets that Myrlo didn't know. "I'm sure Lacus wasn't trying to hurt you. He just wants you to take your place as his apprentice. One day you will be the water mage. But you can't do that if you're afraid of water."

"But he threw me in the pond."

Myrlo sighed. "That may not be the best way to teach someone how to swim, but I'm sure he wasn't trying to kill you."

Zap didn't know. He just didn't know. In truth, he didn't want to believe his master had tried to kill him. But just because he didn't want it to be true didn't mean it wasn't.

Jawan came back looking puzzled. "It's some stranger. He's wearing clothes like someone from Hadley Town, but I've never seen him before."

Zap sighed with relief that it wasn't his master come to get him. He came out from under the table and took a seat.

"Probably wants some magic performed for him," Myrlo said. Tell him I'm busy. He'll have to come back another time. If his need is serious, he'll be back. If he doesn't come back, he shouldn't waste my time."

Jawan left again.

Myrlo turned back to Zap. "Zap, if it will make you feel better, I'll talk to Lacus myself. We'll sort this out."

Jawan returned to report the man said he was there to deliver a message from somebody named Turbatius. Myrlo started as if he'd heard the name of a monster. "What message could Turbatius have for me? I will send this scoundrel away myself." He rose to leave.

Zap panicked. "Aren't you going to talk to my master?"

"Yes, I will. And you should, too. He is your master. Not mine." With that, he left.

"He's right, you know. Your master wouldn't try to kill you. Especially not someone as gentle as master Lacus."

"You would say that." But the idea of his master wanting to hurt him seemed more and more unlikely.

"Look you don't have to face master Lacus alone. Let master Myrlo talk to him first. For now, we could just sit by the pond and watch the moon rise."

Zap thought about that. The water terrified him. At the same time, he was drawn to it.

As they approached the portcullis, Myrlo entered.

"Oh, that man," Jawan said. "Is he still out there?"

"No, he's gone."

"What did he want?"

"I don't know. But he got more than he bargained for. Where are you going?"

"To the pond."

Myrlo looked at Zap and smiled.

They went down to the pond. As the rising moonlight shimmered across the water, Zap wondered why he'd been so afraid.

Chapter 2

The spirit awoke from an eons-long sleep. Or maybe he'd just popped into existence. He didn't know. He only knew that he was here, and here was wherever he was.

Mist swirled around him, parting and coming together again in random eddies that delighted him. Between the swirls, he caught a glimpse of something in the distance. The very idea of distance bothered him. It meant everywhere wasn't here. There were places where he had to go because he was here, and that other place was there.

He was a spirit. Everywhere should be here, and he should be everywhere. If he went where this other thing was—this other place—then it, too, would become here. And so, the spirit moved. But when he came to the other thing, the place where he'd been before became there.

He studied the thing. Maybe he'd find a clue to change this dreadful situation. The thing wore a silver cap with a big blue number nine emblazoned on it. The thing was called Nano, and it was something important in this place. This was the place where everything began—the Quantum Realm.

Bosons and fermions, electrons, protons—all the quanta of which the world was made—gathered around Nano. He knew the thing's name was Nano and pondered what it meant to have a name. The spirit knew this. He knew his own name was Turbatius. He wasn't the ALL in a universe too vast for him to know everything. But he knew he hated Nano. He hated the order Nano kept the quanta in. With the help of nine bosons, Nano ushered the quanta to their proper places in the universe. If Turbatius broke that order, there'd be no difference between here and there and nothing could keep him from being everywhere as a spirit should be.

Nine bosons detached themselves from Nano and accosted Turbatius. Like him, they were made of pure energy, but theirs wasn't sentient energy. They were just things—able to respond and perform the task given them but with no will of their own. The bosons looked menacingly at Turbatius as they moved toward Nano. But he hardly needed this honor guard to usher him in the direction he wanted to go anyway. After all, he was a spirit. Who would dare to herd a spirit?

"Why do you keep such order here?"

Nano glared at him as if he'd asked the most absurd question. "Why would I not? The universe depends on me to keep order and prevent chaos."

Chaos! Another word he liked. Why would anyone want to prevent it? "The universe thrives on disorder. Everything should be free to find its own course."

"There is no beauty in disorder. Without order, there is ugliness."

"I'm not talking about beauty. I'm talking about the way things should be."

"And how should things be?"

"They should be in disorder."

"The very idea of should be implies some kind of order. Disorder means things are not as they should be."

"How dare you!" Turbatius seethed at this insult to his very essence.

He rushed at Nano, but the nine bosons closed ranks to protect their leader, and other forces surrounded Nano with unbearable displays of order—gravity and inertia, strong forces and weak forces—driving Turbatius back until he didn't know where he was.

Furious, Turbatius scouted through the mist. At least it was free of those ridiculous laws of order. So, the whole universe couldn't be a place of order. There had to be disorder somewhere. He'd find that place, and just as Nano kept the order in his place, Turbatius would keep the disorder in his.

That would be his base of power. From there, he'd destroy Nano's hold on the Quantum Realm. Without Nano, there'd be disorder—there'd be chaos—everywhere. Chaos. He liked that word. There'd be chaos everywhere. There'd be Turbatius everywhere. No more here and there. Here would become everywhere. And if he were everywhere, he might even become the ALL.

He looked around and to his delight saw that the Quantum Realm was just one of the kingdoms in Nanosia. He followed the quanta that Nano sent away to the next realm. But here there was even more order than in the Quantum Realm.

This realm had its own version of Nano, but its name was Leeuwen, and it kept a tight rein on where the quanta went. It even read from notes that told it what to do. If spirits could throw up, Turbatius knew he would all over this dreadful place where disarray and confusion never dreamed of entering.

"Twenty-six protons needed in the iron building."

Leeuwen then counted out twenty-six very ordinary-looking quanta and sent them on their way. Turbatius knew Atomidon wouldn't be a good place to start honing his power.

The next realm was criminally organized. The atoms that left Atomidon and entered Cenozonia joined themselves into groups called molecules. Life sprang up when the exact kind and number of molecules came together with a precision that made Turbatius retch. He was ready to despair of ever finding a place when he came to Nanosia's last kingdom.

Turbatius, the spirit of disorder, entered the Realm of Chaos and knew he was at home. Uncategorized swarms of particles zipped here and there. Even the swarms broke up when particles flew off by themselves or joined new swarms. Kaleidoscopes of light and shadow swirled around in every shade of red, green, blue, and yellow. It was as it should be. The entire universe should be like this. It would be.

Turbatius stopped smiling when a castle loomed above the bedlam of this realm. A castle meant a lord. How could there be a lord? The very idea was antipathic to chaos. Turbatius had found this place. It was his, and he would destroy any incumbent who imposed on its disorder. Even if the lord kept the disorder, Turbatius would still cast him out.

I have no partner. Whoever occupied that castle could only be seen as competition, and Turbatius would destroy him. He went to the portcullis, and being a spirit slipped right through. Particles followed him inside. They wanted to play, but he was here on business.

"Lord of Chaos!" his voice reverberated around the cavernous chambers. "Lord of . . ."

"Who are you calling?" a particle asked him.

"Where is the lord of this realm?"

A somber quietness swept through the particles.

"We have no lord."

Turbatius nearly choked with delight. No lord meant the kingdom was already his. "But why are you so sad?"

The particles cast furtive glances at one another. This was something they didn't want to discuss.

"We once had a guardian who loved us. We lost him. Antipan is no more."

"Do not sorrow, my friends. I will be your guardian. I will love you and make you forget all about this Antipan, whoever he was."

"We will never forget Antipan. He never asked to be our guardian. He just was. But who are you?"

Turbatius knew he had to tread lightly. The Realm of Chaos wasn't one he could take by force. Good thing he hadn't found this Antipan here and killed him, or they never would have followed him. "I am Turbatius, the spirit of disorder. My very nature is chaos, and you, my lovely ones, are all that I ever dreamed of. As you were here for me, I will now be here for you."

"To be our guardian—to take on the mantle that was so violently ripped from Antipan—you must form a connection with the Big World."

"The Big World? What is this?"

"It is the world outside Nanosia. But we are two worlds that affect one another. And everything we do in Nanosia is for the Big World."

Why couldn't anything be simple? "I've never been there. How do I even get out of Nanosia to this Big World?"

"You speak of your nature as a spirit. Do you not know that as such you can contact someone in the Big World and work through them?"

Contact someone outside Nanosia in a world he had never known? He was a spirit. He should know how to do it instinctively. Focus. He focused all his attention on finding someone in the Big World. After much strenuous concentration, he brushed across something that he recognized as a mind.

With great excitement, he dove deeper into this Big World mind, searching for a way to connect.

He recoiled from the neatly ordered list of things this mind had to do. Turbatius would have to try again. The second mind seemed promising. It was a happy mind filled with thoughts of bliss.

To Turbatius's chagrin, the mind started cataloguing the reasons why it felt happy—good health, fulfilling vocation, faithful wife, beautiful children, ad nauseam. Before long, everything made so much sense that the feeling of joy sank into the background.

Turbatius ransacked the Big World searching for the right mind. He wondered why the particles even wanted to connect with this world of insufferable organization. But they did, and if he wanted to be their guardian, he had to make a connection with this Big World. He was a spirit. What he couldn't find, he would create. He'd have to create a mind that didn't worry about lists and reasons. He'd have to create a mind of disorder.

He focused again, this time on the material of the Big World. The people were made of the things he'd seen in Cenozonia. He hated to go there, but there was no help for it. If he wanted to create a mind, he'd have to create a body to house the mind, and that meant putting together the components of life. He'd have to do it just precisely. Or he'd end up with a monster at worst, a comatose vegetable at best.

The bodies he studied had far too much symmetry. But he dared not experiment. When he was confident that he knew what to do, he gathered all the materials and set to work creating a man.

Despite everything, the man he created was a thing of beauty. Now for the mind. He dared not experiment too much with that either. He fashioned a brain with all the necessary neurons and synapsis for thought, memory, and function. Then he found a place in the Big World that had something that he wanted—a place of power—and energized the man's mind with the soul of that place. But his man needed a human soul. He searched the place until he found the wandering soul of a man who'd once lived there. A wandering soul was a troubled soul. This one was recently enough departed to be truly troubled. It might not be compatible with the mind of the man he had created, and that would be just the kind of disorder Turbatius loved.

To encourage the element of chaos, Turbatius took some of his own spirit and put it in the man. When his creation opened his eyes, Turbatius smiled.

Chapter 3

"In you go." Lacus thought that throwing Zap into the pond would shock him into remembering that he could swim.

To his horror, the boy succumbed to the panic and began the process of drowning. Lacus recognized it right away—the inability to stay afloat despite obvious efforts to do so, the bubbles as the boy breathed water. But before Lacus could jump in to save his apprentice, a water spirit grabbed the boy and brought him to shore.

"Savorne." He shouldn't have been surprised to see her. This was her pond, and Zap was her son. If she'd been a human woman rising out of the pond, she'd be soaking wet. But she was an undine, so she absorbed the water into her body and was perfectly dry. She didn't look up as she breathed air into Zap's mouth, but Lacus could tell she was angry. "He should not have drowned. He has my gift. It should have saved him." She kept pumping his chest, and water rose from his mouth like a cold geyser.

Lacus said nothing—just kept watching, hoping, and feeling a torrent of guilt and grief.

"I left him with you because I thought he'd be safe with a water mage—someone who could teach him to master his gift with magic. My sisters warned me that even with magic, a human could not be trusted with an undine child—even a half-undine child."

"I . . ."

"Whatever possessed you to throw him into the pond? You should have known he wasn't ready, and now I know that you failed in what I asked you to do."

She breathed into Zap's mouth again, and he coughed but did not open his eyes.

"Breathe, child," Savorne cooed. "Stay with us."

"I didn't know he would give up so easily. I didn't know he was that scared."

Savorne just looked at him like he should have known. And he thought that maybe he should have. Zap had been with him four—maybe five—years, and he should have been paying attention. She glared at Lacus as he bent down to pick Zap up.

The boy's breathing was shallow. But he was breathing, which meant he wasn't dead. He hadn't drowned—at least not in the human sense of the word. "I'll take him to his room. A good rest should revive him."

"It will, but don't do anything like that again. Drowning won't kill him, but he could still be damaged, and I might not be close by next time. I wouldn't depend on my sisters to save him."

Lacus started toward his castle.

"Come back when you finish with him. There is something I need to tell you."

Lacus carried Zap to his room and laid him on his bed. Looking down at the boy's sleeping form, Lacus shook his head. How could he ever make Zap a journeyman? He couldn't even be an apprentice if he was afraid of his own element. What was he afraid of? Savorne blamed Lacus, but she hadn't told him all that he needed to know about this boy. She'd made it seem like Zap would be the perfect candidate for a water mage when Lacus died. Well, she hadn't said as much, but why else would he want an apprentice?

Lacus brushed Zap's cheek, and the boy stirred a little in his sleep. He was breathing better, and his color was back. He'd be all right. Still, Lacus didn't know what he would do now.

He went back to the pond and found Savorne gazing wistfully at the surrounding forest as if waiting for something or someone to emerge from it.

She turned to him. "How is he?"

"Better. Listen I . . ."

But she came right to her point. "There is danger approaching, Lacus."

"Danger. Looks like there's always danger."

"No, I mean real danger. Something has entered the world that doesn't belong here, and I sense that water will factor into defeating whatever it is. So, you must prepare Zap to face it."

Was she kidding? Zap couldn't even face a dip in the pond without panicking, and she wanted him to face an unknown danger. "Look, whatever danger there is, if it has to do with water, I'll handle it. No way is Zap ready."

She looked at him sadly as if she knew something he didn't know. "You can't. This is something Zap must face alone."

"But why? You don't even know what this thing is, so how do you know Zap can handle it at all, much less alone."

"I just know." She wouldn't look at him when she said that. "You must teach him to not be afraid of water. Do it gently, as if water were the friendliest, most natural thing there is. Because it is."

"I don't know." He saw Zap running out of the castle and called to him. He was supposed to be resting, but he was running as if from a monster.

"Let him go. He'll be back. He's going to find what he needs."

Chapter 4

The first thing he heard upon waking was birds singing. But how he knew they were birds and how he knew they were singing, he didn't know. He had no memory of the time before he opened his eyes.

To his astonishment, he knew the name for everything that he saw—trees, sky, the ants crawling up their little hill, his body, his hands, the hair on his legs—though he couldn't recall ever seeing any of these things before.

This puzzled him. Why did he think there should be a before? Nothing should be different from the way it was. So if there should've been a before, then there had to be a before, else how could he think of it?

So many assumptions. He looked around the forest and saw no one who could tell him if his assumptions were correct. The ants and birds certainly couldn't tell him. If he just appeared here, then whoever put him here could tell him why he was here and where he'd been before. He had to start with the assumption that someone put him here. It made sense, and it was the only way he'd get any answers.

A chill breeze brushed across his bare skin. It smelled of water. What was water? He knew what it was, and he knew what to do about the chill breeze.

He closed his eyes and willed himself warm. The breeze caressed him with warmth. He started to feel satisfied until he realized that what he'd done was called magic and it wasn't something people like himself should be able to do.

> People? There were others like himself? He had to find them. Maybe they didn't have magic, but they might know about magic and be able to tell him why he had it and they didn't.

He rose and followed a path out of the forest. A thought occurred to him. If someone put him in the forest, then maybe he wasn't supposed to leave it. Too bad. If there was a someone who thought they had a right to tell him what should and should not be, then they shouldn't have given him the power to do things he wasn't supposed to do and then left him with no directions other than his own inclinations.

As he stepped past the last tree, he saw some people, and they saw him.

"Look, Mama. That man is naked."

"Gracious goodness! I don't want to see that."

He stepped back behind the tree. Clothes. The people wore clothes. That was the difference between people and ants. He was walking around like an ant.

"Well at least he has the decency to hide."

"Maybe he's sick, Mama."

"Or maybe he's mad. Run and get your pa. A man who hides in the woods might need shooting."

"Ain't you coming, Mama?"

"No, I better watch him to make sure he doesn't cause any mischief."

"But, Mama, I thought you didn't want to see him."

"You never mind that. Just run along."

The boy ran off. If he came back with his pa, the man would shoot and not bother to ask questions.

"No, ma'am, I'm not mad. And I don't need shooting. I just need some clothes."

"You really gave me a fright. It's not every day a naked man walks out of the woods."

He doubted she was frightened.

"I've never seen a naked man other than my husband, and he's not tall and handsome."

Uh-oh. This woman was going to get him shot whether he was naked or not. Maybe he should find somewhere else to be. "Ma'am, do you know where I can lay hands on some clothes?"

"I know where you can lay hands on whatever you like."

Poor choice of words. Try again. "Ma'am, I just need some . . . what do you call them? Britches."

"From what I've seen, you don't need them at all." She stepped closer and actually tried to peer around the tree.

What she's seen. He stepped back farther into the forest, putting four trees between himself and the woman.

"Are you afraid of me? I could help you, ya know."

He doubted it.

"Not that any of Jof's clothes could fit you. But I have a neighbor . . ."

21

"Where is he?"

He peered around the tree and saw the boy coming with what had to be his pa. The boy was mercifully carrying a pair of britches. But his pa was carrying a bow and arrow.

"There he is, Pa. Don't shoot him. He has to be sick—running around the woods with no clothes on."

"If I was going to shoot him on sight, I wouldn't have brought the britches."

That was a relief.

"I'll see what he wants first, then shoot him."

"Maylee, you come back over here. I don't want you in my line of fire."

Maylee stepped over to her husband but not before throwing a wink. "Those aren't your britches, Jof."

"No, they ain't. The way Pep described the man, I thought he had to be a giant. So I borrowed some of Lennie's trousers off the clothesline. What's your name, sir?"

"Vordon." He'd never thought of it before. He just knew it, but never needed it before. So he had a name like the ants and the birds, the sky, the trees, and the grass. But he wasn't a Vordon. He was a man. As a man, he had his own personal name. Interesting.

"Name even sounds funny. Well, Vordon, my boy is going to put these britches right here on the ground. Then we'll move off, and you come put them on. When you're decent, you can tell me why you're skulking around in the woods."

Vordon thought about saying he wasn't skulking, but Jof didn't look like he cared for explanations. So, when the family moved off, Vordon stepped out of the trees and donned the britches.

Jof came forward, arrow cocked and level with Vordon's chest. "Now what's your business? And don't give me no crap about being a sleepwalker."

Drat. That would have been a good one. Vordon thought Jof had probably heard all the good ones. In a situation like this, the truth served better. But the truth was that Vordon had no truth. He really couldn't say what he was doing in the forest. He'd probably have better luck with the sleepwalker story than the I-came-here-out-of-nowhere story. Jof was looking at him, but what could he say? "I was hiding."

"Hiding from whom?"

"It's better that you don't know."

"You tell me or I've no reason not to shoot you."

"Jof, no!"

"Pa, give him a chance."

Jof pulled back on his bow string. "A chance to do what?"

Vordon knew he'd better think fast. "Do you think your wife will think highly of you shooting an unarmed man?"

"I'm not ruled by my wife."

"I won't, Jof, and neither will your boy. We'll think you're the biggest coward in Hadley Town."

"You won't be able to tell me nothing ever again, Pa, 'cause I'll know you ain't a decent man."

Jof scowled and lowered his arrow.

Maylee smiled. "You look like you could stand a bite to eat, Vordon. I was just about to go home and fix supper. Why don't you come along?"

"Now see here, Maylee. I ain't said he could do all that."

"So you're not only a coward. You're stingy, too. Won't offer a hungry man a bite to eat."

"I don't work the fields so you can feed every stray that creeps out of them woods."

"Humph." She and Pep turned their backs on Jof.

Jof turned on Vordon. "See what you got the missus doing. Even turned my boy against me."

Vordon tried not to smile. "I didn't do anything. And they're not against you as long as you act like a decent man."

"He's right, Pa."

Jof scowled again, but he started back down the path and gestured for Vordon to come along.

The family lived in a little two-room hovel on the outskirts of town. Maylee kept it clean, so Vordon thought it would be all right to eat the food.

She went over to the kettle hanging over a fire pit and scowled. "Jof, why didn't you remember to bring in some more kindling. I can't start a fire with these great big chunks of wood."

"I just brought in some kindling the other day. You mean you used it all up already?"

"The other day is more like three weeks ago. If we didn't have company, I wouldn't mind letting you eat your supper cold."

Jof stood up. "I'll go fetch some more."

"Wait." Vordon saw an opportunity to make his magic useful. He walked over to the kettle and stooped down. "I'll start the fire for you, ma'am."

"With what? Where'd you get kindling?"

Vordon smiled. "With this." He held up his finger, and a foot of blue fire shot out from it.

Maylee jumped back. "He's a witch."

Witch was one thing Vordon didn't want them to think about him. "No, I'm a magician. I didn't sell my soul to the devil for magic power. I got it from my creator." He was about to say he was born with it but doubted he could prove that he'd been born.

Jof stood up. "You get out of my house, witch. There ain't but one fire mage, and he's up in his castle. I knew something was wrong with you skulking in the woods. Maylee, I know the next time I'll listen to you. Brought a witch in my house."

"One fire mage?" Vordon was puzzled.

"That's right, and it ain't you. One fire mage, one earth mage, one water mage, one wind mage, and one spirit mage. They control all the magic. So, you get out of my house."

Vordon retracted his fire, stood as gracefully as he could, and bowed out before Jof could remember to ask for his britches back.

He followed the path back into the forest away from people. He'd have to figure things out before he dealt with them again. The trees had no answers for all the questions and thoughts buzzing around in his mind, but at least they wouldn't throw him out. Turning down a different path, he encountered a pond and sat down. He tossed his first thought into the water, where it skipped around until it sank deeper. Five mages controlled all magic. Anyone else using magic was shunned as a witch. Somehow, he knew that wasn't right. Yet that was the way it was. What an insane world where things could be that aren't supposed to be. Unless what was supposed to be wasn't necessarily what Vordon thought was right.

But he wasn't a witch. A system that made people think he was a witch when he wasn't one couldn't be right.

Moonlight shimmered on the water. No, that wasn't moonlight but something more corporeal. It shimmered and rose up out of the water into the essence of an intelligent being, if not the shape of a man.

"I am Turbatius, and you are mine." The voice came from everywhere like a thought drifting across his mind. It came from no discernable direction.

"Oh, really? I'm yours? In what way?" Vordon wanted some answers. If Turbatius made this crazy world, then Vordon wanted to know why.

"You are mine because I created you. I had a purpose and brought you into being to fulfill that purpose."

"Was it beyond your control that I have my own purpose?"

Turbatius glared at Vordon. "Nothing is beyond my control. I am your lord. You will have no other besides me. Whatever purposes you may have are ancillary to the purpose for which I created you."

"Did you also create this world?"

"Enough questions! You will not speak. You will listen."

Vordon opened his mouth to protest, but his voice was gone. Turbatius had robbed him of speech and had not answered his question.

"You will not speak. You will listen. The answer you seek lies within my purpose and will lead you to fulfill that purpose."

Vordon shook his head.

"You think you have your own purposes. That which I created, I can destroy and create another more to my liking."

And maybe you'll get it right the second time or the third time, Vordon thought but couldn't say.

"If you want an answer, fool, you will listen. Go to the town library. Your answer is on the forgotten level."

Vordon raised an eyebrow, looking puzzled.

Turbatius sighed. He clearly didn't like questions—not even silent ones. "On the eleventh page of the eleventh book on the eleventh shelf from the top."

Vordon had a zillion questions screaming for vocal expression. But there was only moonlight on the water and a soft breeze like a lullaby singing him to sleep.

He shuddered at the thought of going back into town. This time he'd have to go deeper.

He paused behind the last tree at the edge of the forest. If he went into town, no telling what might happen. But if he stayed there, Turbatius would come for him. So, he followed a path until the grass and flowers were replaced by dingy cottages and derelict-looking buildings.

When he came to the central square full of people, he started to ask the first person he saw where the library was. He opened his mouth, but to his dismay, he still couldn't speak.

The man was too offended by Vordon's mere appearance to notice that he couldn't speak. "Young man, I don't know where you're from, but this is Hadley Town, and here we are decent folks. And decent folks don't walk around the streets with no shirt on."

Vordon slapped his head. Of course, an insane world would measure decency by something as inconsequential as a shirt. He remembered that Jof said he'd gotten the britches off a clothesline. Maybe he'd find a shirt on a clothesline, too. He did, then wondered how he'd find the library if he couldn't ask for directions. He started walking as if his feet knew the way just like he'd known the birds were singing.

The library was the biggest building he'd seen in Hadley Town. It was way bigger than the little shanties the people lived in, and it was made of real bricks. Inside, Vordon caught his breath. This was the first time he'd ever seen a book—and not just one, but hundreds of books on dozens of shelves. Which one held the eleventh book? They all had eleven pages. Then he remembered Turbatius had said it was on the forgotten level.

He descended to the basement sure that if anything was forgotten it would be down there.

The eleventh shelf. But all the stacks had only ten shelves. He walked to the back and examined the last stack. Ten shelves. Of course, if it were hidden, it wouldn't be on something as obvious as the last stack. He moved to the next to the last stack and bent down to the bottom shelf.

But it wasn't the bottom shelf. There was another shelf level with the floor. The eleventh shelf. He counted eleven books, took it out, and read the eleventh page.

If he'd expected to find some profound revelation, he was disappointed. All he saw were children's rhymes. He started to shut the book in disgust. Instead, he read the first line—aloud. To his delight, Turbatius had given him his voice back, but though he intended to read the words he saw in the book, they came out of his mouth in a different language. It wasn't the language spoken in Hadley Town, but he understood it and was astonished. There was meaning behind the words that wasn't meant for children at all. And this wasn't something anyone could stumble upon. If he wasn't meant to find the eleventh shelf, it wouldn't have been there. Interesting.

When he uttered the last word on the page, the wall behind the last stack faded revealing a darkness blacker than a starless night.

Gingerly, he placed one foot over the threshold of the door. Nothing happened, so he felt for the walls inside the door and took another step. Instead of the floor, his foot found empty air. Clinging to the wall, he stumbled down eleven steps before hitting a landing and staggering to a stop.

In the darkness, he dared not take a step. Reaching out with one hand, he felt something that turned out to be a door. But it was locked. No, Turbatius wouldn't bring him down here to a dead end. There must be another way. He slid a foot forward, then another, careful not to shift his weight until he knew his foot was on solid ground.

When he felt the edge of a stair, he stopped. Clinging to the wall, he descended one step, then the next until he reached the landing at the eleventh step. He found the door there, but it, too, was locked.

He found the stairs again and went down and down until on the eleventh landing he came to a door that opened.

At last, he'd find his answer. He was about to enter a room that even the five mages didn't know about and read secrets about magic they'd never dreamed of. He opened the door and was delighted to see that the room was illuminated—courtesy of Turbatius, he supposed—enough for him to read. But the courtesy stopped there.

There were no shelves. Piles of books and scrolls littered the floor as if they'd been dumped down a shaft and landed where they would. Vordon wondered if Turbatius expected him to read every manuscript. Was this a test that would take twenty years to complete?

He knew what he was looking for, and that may or may not be what Turbatius wanted him to find. Too bad if it wasn't. He closed his eyes and focused on information about what happened to magic. Something struck the side of his head. He opened his eyes to see what had hit him. At his feet, a thick tome glowed enticingly.

Pushing the other books out of his way, he sat down on the floor and pulled the tome onto his lap. His eyes bulged as he read about Zelfor and knew it was an ancient place where Romatica and Loorland now stood. He knew also that Turbatius hadn't just brought him into existence a few hours ago. He'd existed before in some way. Zelfor held his earthly roots and was the birthplace of his people. How could that be? Who was he, and who had he been? He'd awakened in the forest, and everything was new. But what he was reading was not new. He'd known all this from before . . .

He knit his brows in outrage reading how his people were slaughtered to create a new order with magic power limited to only a few. At first anyone else with magic was killed. Then the mages decided to take one apprentice to pass on the knowledge.

If Turbatius intended to make him seething mad, he succeeded. He didn't know if the mages who lived today were the same ones who'd slaughtered his people. Maybe they were long lived. Or maybe these today were just the beneficiaries of that slaughter. It didn't matter. He wanted to destroy them and restore the ways of Zelfor. Turbatius would show him how to do it and give him the power he needed. He tucked the book in his pocket and went to confront the mages.

Vordon was a fair man. He'd present his case to the mages and give them a chance to see reason. He stood before the earth mage's portcullis feeling ridiculous. He'd look like some poor supplicant begging for a magical favor. No, he was here on Turbatius's business, and no one could mistake him for a supplicant. He let the anger he felt over the way the mages had treated his people and usurped magic for themselves straighten his back and imagined his countenance would glow like that tome in the forgotten library. With righteous indignation, he banged on the portcullis. A boy appeared from inside.

"My master would know your business, sir."

"Is your master the earth mage."

"He is."

"Then I would speak with him."

The boy looked at him uncertainly, then turned and went back into the castle. Vordon waited.

Finally, the boy returned. "The great earth mage is a very busy man. If you have a message for him, tell me, and I will deliver it."

"How dare you put on airs? Do you not know to whom you speak?" Vordon wished he'd held his outrage in check. Now the boy would include it in his message to his master. "I come in the name of Turbatius the great. I would speak to all the mages to impart what Turbatius has to tell them."

Without another word the boy disappeared again. This time an august man in an earth-brown robe approached the portcullis, which they still had not the courtesy to open. "I am Myrlo. Who are you who comes in the name of the spirit of disorder? Your master is antipathic to all that the elemental mages stand for and would say nothing that we want to hear. Now be gone with you."

Vordon opened his mouth, but his words were commandeered by one more powerful than he was. "Myrlo, the little mage, do you think you can speak thus to my prophet without consequence? You keep order in this world. And I will destroy you—you and all the elemental mages."

Vordon thought Turbatius would destroy this insolent mage, but no lightning flashed, and the mage stood his ground.

Instead, the ground under Vordon began to tremble. It tilted, tossing him away from the castle. Wolves herded him back into the forest, snarling and snapping at him until he retreated deeper in the trees.

If the wolves wanted to bite him, they would have, but they just wanted him to go away. No, the mage wanted him to go away. All right then, he would. But like Turbatius said, there would be consequences. He followed the path, not sure where he would go. Then he heard footsteps behind him and stepped into the trees. He watched Myrlo's boy and another boy go down the path to the pond. The fools! They will pay for rejecting Turbatius. And I know just how to make them pay. I will make them listen.

Vordon gathered rain clouds from all over the Earth. This was dangerous—tampering with the weather. But he only needed it long enough to make the mages yield to his demands. Then he'd put everything back in its natural place. But for now, he'd make it rain so hard they'd do anything he asked if he'd just make it stop.

Clouds boiled in an annoying drizzle, then turned into a serious downpour. The boys came running down the path in a panic.

The fools. Afraid of a little rain. He smiled up at the sky as torrents of rain bathed his face.

Chapter 5

Cintella looked up from her studies and listened—not with her ears. It wasn't a sound she had heard. It was a summons from her master.

Quintessuma, mage of ether, had apprenticed her a year ago, and Cintella was well attuned to the energy of the spirit. Cintella could feel that something had gone wrong in the spirit world—the quintessence. Quintessuma's summons was filled with urgency but no panic. So, Cintella went to see what lesson her master had to teach her.

She entered the tower at the top of the castle, where Quintessuma stood gazing out the window.

"Come closer. I want to show you something."

Of course she did. Cintella joined her at the window and waited to see whatever she was to see.

"Do you see that?"

"What? See what?" She still felt that wrongness in the spirit world, but she saw nothing.

"Your mind is not where it should be. You won't advance past apprenticeship thinking about that boy."

"Sorry, I . . ." She resented the way her master held journeyman status always ahead of her like a carrot in front of a horse to keep her moving forward. If she ever did advance to journeyman, what would her master use then?

But Quintessuma was right. Thinking about Jawan wasn't going to help her understand the fifth element—her element. She'd come so far in her apprenticeship. Why falter now?

She'd been a serving girl at the conclaves the mages held when she'd first seen him—an apprentice himself sneaking around listening at the kitchen door trying to warn his master about the schemes of the fire mage. He wasn't supposed to be there, so Cintella had to sneak him away.

She wound up helping him catch the fire mage. Their victory gave Jawan so much self-confidence that he stopped stuttering. He grew on her. One thing led to another, and she wound up pregnant. She lost the baby, but she never lost her love for Jawan. His master made him a journeyman. But his master was so old that he might die soon. Then Jawan would be a mage, and Cintella would still be an apprentice.

"Cintella!"

There was no use. She had to think about him to think about the reasons why she shouldn't think about him.

"Open the eyes of your spirit and look."

She did, but she didn't see anything amiss. Spirits flitted around here and there enjoying themselves. "I don't see a problem here."

"But there must be something. I felt a strong sense of wrongness—a spiritual wrongness."

"Do you feel anything wrong here?"

Quintessuma paused as if concentrating. "That's odd. I don't."

"Maybe it's not in the quintessence. Maybe it's in the spirit of the physical elements."

Quintessuma thought about it. "That's possible. And if so, then it's for the physical mages to deal with. All I can do is let them know there is a problem."

"They may already know."

Cintella wasn't going to worry about it. If it was out of her master's hands, then it was certainly out of her own. She went to the library in Quintessuma's castle to find a connection between spirit and earth. Jawan was the journeyman of the earth mage. If she could find a connection between earth and spirit, then thinking about him wouldn't take her mind off her work.

She found a promising tome. Quintessence and the Elements. But there was nothing in it that she hadn't seen before. In fact, it only reinforced what she already knew. Her element was different from the other four in every conceivable way, except that earth, being the most physical, was the furthest from spirit on the five-point star that represented the elements.

Still, something connected her to Jawan. She didn't know what. She was determined to find some connection other than the mundane bond between man and woman.

She turned to the chapter on earth and tried to read it, but the words flowed across the page like water.

"Deep in your subconscious mind, there lies a buried crown." The words echoed from the book as the letters continued to flow.

Cintella shook her head. "No! That can't be. I want to find out about the earth element. Tell me about the Earth."

"If we told you about the Earth, the letters would not move, for the Earth is stable."

"That's what I want."

"Are you sure?"

"As ever."

Then the library grew cold as a winter day and as dry as an empty pond. The letters on the page formed a five-point star with the fifth point facing down.

"What are you doing?"

"Your desire is with the Earth, but your connection is with water."

"Water! I love Jawan, not Lacus."

"Lacus is only a mage of water. He will die and another will take his place. The element of water is not mortal. Not a man. Not a woman. You don't understand but will very soon. "

She pushed the book away. What was she thinking about anyway? Magic had its own plans supposedly above the plans of mortals. But she was mortal. She knew what she wanted. She knew what she needed. She couldn't connect to Jawan by burying her nose in a book. She thought about it. Books? They both had to study. Maybe they could study together.

Chapter 6

Zap tried not to think about his master. But the water reminded him of the water mage. There was no use, and maybe Master Myrlo had been right. Maybe his master had just handled him a little roughly but wasn't actually trying to kill him. He picked up a stone and tossed it into the water just to take control of his thoughts. "I'm not afraid of my own master."

"There you go," Jawan said, picking up a stone to throw.

Then something else fell into the water. It wasn't Jawan's stone. It fell from the sky. Plop. Plip. Big drops of rain pelted the pond at an accelerating speed. Soon it fell like a single sheet of water obscuring the far side of the pond.

Zap lifted one foot from the soggy turf, then another. "We need to go inside."

"Why? It's just water." Jawan tossed the stone he was holding into the pond as if it would skip in this downpour. "Why are you afraid of your own element?"

"I'm not afraid, but we need to go." He had to raise his voice over the gurgling and splashing water.

"What's your master doing, Zap? He never makes it rain this much this time of year."

Zap shrugged. "I guess he knows, even if we don't. That's why he's the master." Zap had to keep telling himself that. His master knew what he was doing, and it was all good. "Anyway, he doesn't make it rain. He just lets it rain and keeps it under control."

Zap tried to blink water out of his eyes to no avail. He had to look down. Jawan was blinking, too, and shivering.

Zap shook his head. This wasn't like his master at all.

They headed up the now flooded path that led through the forest and on to home. The forest always threatened to reach out with gnarly claws and scratch Zap's eyes out. But the overcast sky made it even gloomier under the trees, and the rain beat through the leaves so there was no shelter. He stopped. "What was that?"

"What was what?"

"I heard a rustling noise."

Jawan rolled his eyes, then squeezed them shut against what was now a monsoon. "You hear the rain."

But Zap wasn't sure. He heard the underbrush sloshing in the water under him, and he heard the canopy of the forest straining against the water over him. But there was something else. All the sounds of the rain and the trees repeated themselves, but this rustling sounded as if it hadn't wanted to be heard.

"There's nothing, scaredy mouse."

Zap sighed. Of course Jawan would take this time to remind him that he was a mouse.

Jawan opened his mouth as if to drink the rain and raised his voice to the sky.

"Though wind and rain assail us,
Though earthquake and fire impale us,
We are mice."

That was the mantra of the Holy Order of Mice—the mantra he'd had in mind when he ran from his master. But Zap felt like a mouse of a different sort, and he didn't move.

"I'll race you."

"What? No, Jawan, wait!"

"First one out of the forest wins." And he took off down the path, deeper into the woods until the sound of his feet splashing through the water mingled into all the other splashes.

Zap stared after him, not believing that Jawan had actually left him alone. No way was he going to run off into the darkness. He could hardly see the path. And everything he could see seemed preternatural—swaying, dissolving, brooding ominously. No way was he going to run after that boy.

But he was still alone. His drenched skin and clothes could hold no more water. It just poured off him like a waterfall. Water! He couldn't get away from it, but he could get out of the woods. He turned around and went back to the clearing.

The pond had swollen and was almost to the edge of the forest. He shivered—whether from the cold or from the water didn't matter, he was alone and scared more than he could remember ever being. A mouse wasn't supposed to be scared. That's what Loby had said. But Zap remembered his father had said that fear would keep you alive. Fear would keep you from going into dangers that were easier to get into than out of.

Water lapped at his feet, and he backed away. The forest was closer than he'd thought, and he backed into a tree. Water cascaded from the branches joining the rain like someone had poured a bucket of water on him.

Terrified, he jumped back toward the pond only to shrink away when he realized he had nowhere to go.

A glowing mist rose out of the pond. Zap was transfixed. What could it be? The sinking moon didn't shine through the opaque clouds. What then was this glow?

"Help me! I can't swim. Zap, help me."

Zap closed his eyes against the haunting voice of memory as the glowing mist coalesced into the shape of his lost younger brother Ziph's ghost.

"No! I couldn't have saved you. I ran, but you were too far way. Go away, Ziph."

Water! Water! He couldn't get away from it. It was everywhere, and it terrified him because he didn't know how to swim and couldn't have saved his brother.

Ziph cried out so loud that Zap opened his eyes just as a woman rose up out of the water. She wasn't wet. Or she was wet as if she and the water were one, and wet had no meaning for her. "Don't be afraid, my child."

Zap might have found her voice soothing. But there's no better way to make someone afraid than to tell them not to be. And she was the embodiment of water. He had to get away. But the forest behind him was pitch black. The only light came from Ziph and the woman.

"Save me, Zap. I am your brother—your little Ziph. Save me!"

The water woman looked at Ziph with eyes of deep pity. "You could have saved him, Zap. You still can. You can put him to rest in your mind if you enter the water."

Oh, no. No way. The woman wasn't even human. She wanted him to get in the water where he'd be helpless. No telling what she'd do to him. Zap stayed where he was. Not that he could have moved. He was like a rabbit before a wolf and couldn't have torn his eyes away from this vision of horror.

Zap barely noticed when Jawan came up and took his hand. He faintly registered when Jawan said something about an undine and led him into the forest. He was too dazed to be afraid.

They stumbled and splashed along on the inundated path until in the darkness they found that a fallen tree blocked their way. Jawan turned him around and they walked another way. The rain increased, and Zap knew they'd come out of the forest. In the distance, village lights betrayed which side of the forest they'd come out on. He was looking at Hadley Town, which meant the whole forest still lay between them and the mages' castles.

As they walked, townsfolk with covered torches and lanterns approached them. They were as sodden as he and Jawan were, and angry besides.

A man who seemed to be their leader walked right up to Zap and Jawan as if the boys were enjoying this joke at everyone else's expense. "You, boy, what's wrong with your master? Tell him to cut off the water works. We've had enough."

"You tell him we'll storm his castle if he ignores us."

"We don't have big fancy castles in Hadley Town. Our homes are humble and can't take all this rain."

"But don't think you'll be safe hiding behind stone. We'll find a way in or wait until he comes out and drag his ornery face in the mud."

"That we will," they all agreed.

"What are we going to do?" Zap whispered to Jawan.

"You're going to march right up to the water mage's castle and tell him to hop to it. That's what you're going to do."

Jawan was too calm—too quiet. Why didn't he say something? Was he just planning to stare these people down?

"They won't just go away, Jawan. Think of something."

To Zap's amazement, Jawan just turned around and followed the path around the forest. It was a long way, and the townsfolk dogged them all the way.

When they reached the castle, Zap stopped. The people planned to just march right in with him. His master wouldn't be pleased, and Zap would have to answer for bringing them.

"What's wrong?" Jawan asked.

He couldn't tell Jawan right in front of the people. He shouldn't have to. Jawan had a master and knew what would happen if he brought a mob of angry townsfolk into master Myrlo's castle.

"Are you going to get your master, or are we going to storm this rat hole? Open the portcullis if you don't want us to break it down."

At last, Jawan stepped forward. "I know you're upset . . ."

"Upset! I'll show you upset! I thought I was one of the well-to-do folks in town until rain washed my mud brick house away. Upset! I'm outraged."

"But storming the water mage's castle might not be such a good idea. In fact, you should stand outside the portcullis while we go in and talk to Lord Lacus . . ."

"We're not standing out here."

Jawan was the picture of reason. "But if you barge in unannounced, he might think you mean mischief, and there's no telling how he might respond to that. He is a mage, after all, and he doesn't respond well to mischief."

The townsfolk muttered as Zap raised the portcullis, but they didn't move forward.

Zap and Jawan ran through the castle and found his master in the library. "Master! You have to help the people. You have to stop the rain."

Lacus looked up from his work. "Woah, boy. What's all the commotion outside, and why are you coming in here dripping water?"

"The rain, master. It's raining."

"I can see that."

How could he get his master to take this seriously? The people outside could hardly be heard through the thick walls. But Lacus was the powerful water master. He had to sense something. "But it's never rained like this before—not this time of year. There's a mob outside from Hadley Town. You have to help them. They're threatening to take over the castle."

"Yes, I'm aware there's been a disturbance. That's what I'm looking into right now. As for the people, I'll help them if I can, but I don't have to do anything. They can try to break in here. They'll be sorry if they do."

Relief washed over Zap. His master was on top of things as usual. He'd take care of the rain and the people. Zap could go back to being a normal regular boy with normal regular boy things to think about. The abnormal and irregular were for the masters to worry about.

Jawan sighed with relief, too. "Master Lacus, we were just skipping stones on the pond when it started raining like crazy. It's like all the water in the world is pouring down on Hadley Town. I've never seen anything like it."

"Me neither." Zap took one of his textbooks from a shelf and sank down into a chair with it. "I have an exam coming up. I'd better study."

Zap had always been studious about his apprenticeship lessons, but he'd never realized that reading could be so interesting. "See, it's talking about the importance of aquifers. The water actually moves along with the river—but a lot slower."

Lacus came over and plucked the book out of his hands.

"What are you doing?"

"What are you doing? I'm glad to see you're studying for your exam, but there's a time and place for everything. Right now, we have the perfect opportunity for you to get some hands-on experience, and we're not going to miss it."

Zap narrowed his eyes. "Hands-on?" That didn't sound right. That sounded suspiciously like one of his master's tricks.

"Oh, you know what? Master Myrlo doesn't even know where I am. I'd better go." With that, Jawan left.

That was all Zap needed—a fair-weather friend. He looked up at his master. "What are we going to do?"

"We're going back to the pond."

Zap blanched. No, his master wouldn't throw him in the pond again. But what would he do?

"Relax. I'm not going to throw you in the pond. But you need to get over your fear of water and learn to master it."

Zap didn't think he'd ever do that as he followed his master to the pond.

Chapter 7

Savorne stood by the pond to weep, but rain like she'd never seen before drowned out her tears. Shivering, she looked up where the faithful crescent moon had often greeted her arrival. It was the moon that shone that night when . . . How many—ten, eleven years had passed? Many moons traversed the night sky—new, half, full—but only the crescent moon meant anything to her.

But this time, where the moon usually reflected off the surface of the pond that was her home, heavy rain drops now troubled the water. A solid sheet of cloud covered the sky from horizon to horizon. She should see the moon in a clear sky this time of year. She didn't know what this meant. She only hoped it didn't mean she wouldn't be able to see Havlo tonight.

Not that she'd seen him since the day he walked away from her at this very pond. She came here every night to weep for Havlo's loss and hope for his return. Clouds and rain wouldn't obscure him, but they might be ominous. If he didn't return to her soon, she would die, for that is the fate of an undine whose human lover has been unfaithful. She didn't know how much time she had, but it wasn't much.

More ominous still was the closeness of the forest. Had the trees moved? No, the pond had swollen to twice its size and risen one foot in depth.

A male human stepped out of the forest. Savorne's heart swelled in her chest. It had to be Havlo. She opened her mouth, then closed it. She had no idea what to say. If she said the wrong thing in the wrong way, she'd lose him and die.

Fear emanated from him like a perfume. He kept glancing back at the forest as if something horrid were chasing him.

He came closer and she saw it wasn't Havlo but Zap. The last she'd seen him, Lacus was taking him to his room to rest. What was he doing out here? He looked so much like a human boy—so much like Havlo. She hid herself in the rain drops and watched him. She knew him. He might be able to tell her where Havlo was. Would he tell her? She knew him, but did he know her? It had been a long time, so she had to tread carefully.

He was as much afraid of the water as he was of whatever was in the forest, and he ran from one only to face the other. She would've been amused. Except he was her son, and his fear of water saddened her.

A glowing mist on the pond heightened his fear of the water. It wasn't moonlight and she thought maybe she should be afraid too. Though she could hide in water from human eyes, what was taking shape wasn't human. The glowing mist materialized into a boy. She knew him, too, and hated him.

"Help me! I can't swim. Zap, help me."

Savorne felt ashamed of her hatred. He was just a boy—the ghost of a boy to whom the water had not been kind because he didn't understand water. This could be her opportunity to find out about Havlo and help Zap get over his fear. She revealed herself. "Don't be afraid, my child." There. The soothing motherly voice should calm him. Once he was calm, she could ask him about Havlo. But Zap seemed even more unsure.

The ghost boy redoubled his plea. "Save me, Zap. I am your brother—your little Ziph. Save me!"

This broke Savorne's heart. She knew who the boy had been. But what was a ghost? Maybe it wasn't too late for him or for Zap. "You could have saved him, Zap. You still can. You can put him to rest in your mind if you enter the water."

She knew right away that was the wrong thing to say. Now Zap was afraid of her. Why? She'd seen her reflection in the pond and knew that she was comely. But Zap looked at her like she'd just risen out of the underworld. Zap stared at her, so frozen with terror that he couldn't move. Another boy came out of the forest and led him away.

"Undine." The other boy made it sound fiendish.

No! she wanted to scream but knew that would only make things worse. She turned to the ghost. He could tell her about Havlo, but he shrank into the water and was gone.

No! Whatever made her think she could find him? And that would be the easy part. She was an undine. This was her pond. He knew where she was. If he wanted anything to do with her, he would have come back. If he hadn't come back after ten years, he didn't want to come back. Even if she found him, she'd only be trying to get him to do something he obviously didn't want to do.

A wide world, he'd said. More to it than this little pond. Not for an undine. This pond was where she had to be if she lived to be ten thousand years old. And if she didn't do the impossible, that wouldn't happen. She was going to die. Havlo didn't care enough to come back and find out. She wept into the pond as she'd never wept before. The rain ran down her cheeks as if the entire world wept with her.

She wept for the eons she would never see. In what would have been a near immortal life, she would have seen the stars change their courses. She would have seen the sun set where it rises and rise where it set over and over in an endless cycle. Twelve pole stars would come and go, and she would witness it all.

She looked down at her swollen pond. She'd seen it swell before, eons before humans walked the Earth. And now because of a human, she'd never see the pond like this again. She'd wanted an immortal soul. Near immortal was not like truly immortal. But if Havlo did not return and love her, she'd be like the ghost boy—haunting the water but never able to enjoy it the way she did before.

"What do you want with a man?" her sisters had asked her. "He will grow old, ugly, and feeble. Or he will be laid low by sickness. Or some accident may befall him as happens to many humans. Whatever the case and by whatever means, he will eventually die."

Savorne didn't see the point. "We'll die, too."

"Not nearly as quickly as humans do. They barely live long enough to learn the first lessons of life."

"They think the pole star is the pole star because no man lives long enough to see more than one."

"And the men who live during the time the pole stars are shifting don't even know what they are."

"But they do calculations and find these things out," Savorne insisted.

"That's not the same as watching the cosmic dance."

And her sisters danced in the water—creating bubbles, tiny maelstroms, and miniature geysers.

"Be careful," Savorne warned. "This pond isn't supposed to do that. If a human happens by and sees the water doing that, he'll start a commotion."

"There're no humans near here," her sister Remal said. "Besides, they wouldn't believe what they see, any more than they believe the calculations. Most humans believe the Earth is flat, and the stars are just lights in the sky."

"Compared to the human lifespan, you're practically immortal. What more do you want?"

Savorne sighed as rain cascaded off her. What more indeed, she thought. Practically immortal. Near immortal. What difference did it make? The last day of her life would eventually come, and all the eons before that day would seem like the life span of an ant. Death made all time seem short. Without an immortal soul, that would be it. Her earthly life might be long, but her death was final in a way that it wasn't for humans.

She'd known that she was gambling—throwing her dice as the humans liked to say. She had a lot to gain if she won, so she threw them. She ignored her sisters, closed her eyes, and gambled away what she now saw was more than she had to gain.

Stupid! Stupid! She deserved to die for being so stupid. And she had no idea how long it would be before she got what she deserved. But it wouldn't be long. She wanted to stop weeping. She didn't deserve to weep. The rain mocked her. She wasn't weeping, she was crying. Weeping was too noble a thing for one so stupid. She was just crying like the human she'd wanted to be.

"Why do you weep, child?"

"Nexa!" Oh, shame upon shame for my lord to see me like this. "I wasn't weeping. That is just the rain."

"Rain does not contain so much salt. Do you think I cannot feel your heartbreak?"

Of course he could feel it. Her precious lord knew everything. And shame upon shame, he must have known why.

As if in answer to her thoughts, Nexa continued. "You come here each night to weep over a mortal man. Why? Am I not enough for you?"

Oh, he must not think that! "Of course you are, my lord. You are everything, and everything is you."

"But you have never wept for me as you weep for this man."

"No, lord. Because you are always here. There is no need." She knew that was the wrong thing to say as soon as the words left her mouth.

"No need?"

"What I meant was . . ."

"Exactly what you said."

"No! I didn't mean that. I . . ."

"Are neglecting your duties. Look at this pond. It has swept over its boundaries and become choked with the flora of the land. Yet you have done nothing."

Did he expect her to stop the rain? To cast all the excess water back up into the sky and blow the clouds back to the mountains or to the sea? But she couldn't say that—not to her precious lord. Who was she to complain about fairness? He was right in every way, and there was nothing she could say. So, she said nothing.

"This is beyond you. The rain itself is natural but not in this quantity. I do not know where it comes from—this unnatural deluge. It will take more than one self-pitying undine to bring the natural order back—if that can be done. But why do you not weep for this disaster?"

Why indeed. She hardly noticed. This was a disaster. All her sisters working together couldn't turn this around. Her duty was to keep the balance in nature and correct the refuse left by natural processes. But like Nexa said, this much rain wasn't natural. Where did it come from?

"I must go and study this." Nexa began to fade. "Perhaps there is something in the history of the eons that will reveal a slow pattern. Or perhaps, as is true of weather, it is just chaos." He blinked out but left a disembodied message. "Weep no more for mortals, my child. Weep instead for what may yet lie ahead on this Earth."

What may yet lie ahead? A greater disaster than this? This had to be the trouble she'd told Lacus was coming. If Zap didn't get ready to deal with this in time, no one else could. But if Nexa was going to study, that meant he didn't think all was lost. And why should she? She'd do some studying of her own. Find the boy. He's human. He could work outside of nature. If she could just convince him not to be afraid of her—afraid of water—he might be able to do things that even Nexa couldn't. Forgive me, my lord.

Chapter 8

"Why are you smiling, you idiot?"

Vordon opened his eyes to face an irate Turbatius. Why was he angry? "I'm doing what you wanted. Be patient."

"You worthless vermin. What is your life worth to me? I can kill you with a thought. I should."

Vordon looked around desperately and hid behind a tree. Little good that did him. Turbatius's voice boomed around him and Vordon grew weak. "Spare my life, master. It's worthless as you say, but I will serve you if you spare me. I can't serve you from the grave." He fell to his knees in the mud and soggy undergrowth.

"Where is the chaos? Where is the disorder I told you to unleash?"

"The rain will bring disorder. The mages won't be able to control the deluge. They'll need me to stop it. But I won't unless they agree to return to the ways of Zelfor."

"Zelfor! Fool! I don't care about the ways of Zelfor. I want chaos!"

The name had not surprised Turbatius. He knew about Zelfor but, clearly, wanted nothing to do with it. Vordon had to find a way to make his purpose Turbatius's purpose. And if he couldn't, he'd find a way to be rid of it. He had some power of his own. He'd brought the rain. And he had knowledge about things, which was itself a kind of power. For now, though, he'd go along. "There will be chaos. The mages are safe in their castles now, but they'll soon realize they can't do anything in all this rain. It will affect every element. Even the quintessence."

Turbatius loomed over Vordon, filling him with his displeasure. "You are an idiot if you think the mages will care about this. Come with me." He took Vordon to the pond and hid him behind a tree.

Vordon took no pleasure in the rain drizzling onto his face. He shivered and closed his eyes.

"Open your eyes. You must see your failure."

Failure? What did it mean to fail a god? Vordon shivered again but not from the cold.

One of the boys that he'd seen running approached the pond with a man whom Vordon knew was the water mage, and the boy was his apprentice. The mage looked like the rain puzzled him, but he didn't look dismayed and certainly not overwhelmed as Vordon had thought he would be. The mage tried to make the boy repeat some words after him, but the boy was utterly terrified. So, the mage said the words and the clouds dispersed. Just a quick mantra uttered effortlessly, and the clouds carried the rain away.

"You see, you idiot? Anything natural like rain will be under the control of the elemental mages."

"No!" Vordon focused all his power to bring the clouds back. But that didn't change the mage's power to send them away again.

"If you cannot create chaos on Earth, I will no longer preserve your useless life."

Vordon didn't know what he'd do if Turbatius decided his life was worthless. "I'll do what you want. Just show me how. If the mages have power over nature, what else is there?"

"Nature is not all there is. You need Alecto."

"What is that?"

"She is the power of unrelenting fury—just one of the powers of the underworld who, with her two sisters, torments evildoers."

A power? Surely Turbatius would help him summon her and control her. "How do I find Alecto?"

"Why do I need you if I have to do everything for you. This is where you prove your worth to me."

Vordon swallowed hard. How was he going to do this? There had to be a way. And if it would help him destroy the mages, he'd find that way. He just needed time.

He went back to the forgotten level in the library and searched. Alecto, a fury of anger. Yes, she can bring a storm—an unrelenting storm that all the mages together couldn't disperse. They'd have to yield. He read on to find the ritual for summoning her.

The water mage and his boy were still at the pond when Vordon returned. The rain was gone, but the swollen pond still licked the feet of the trees, and the water still ran like a brook on the forest path. They could do what they wanted. It would all be for naught once Vordon unleashed Alecto.

He crouched behind a tree out of their sight and raised his hands to the sky.

The words came out like a melody. He wondered if they could hear it on the breeze. Didn't matter.

The mage and his boy looked up with dismay as black clouds rolled in. Lightning ricocheted across the sky followed by heart-stopping peals of thunder. The tree Vordon stood behind shook as wind tore at its upper branches. Some of the noise wasn't thunder but trees being ripped loose from the ground.

The mage chanted away, throwing all his magic at the storm. But there was nothing he could do. Wind with the wings of a bat and eyes of lightning flew toward the mage.

Chapter 9

Lacus smiled at Zap as they walked out of the castle. "It's time you learned how to control weather instead of just reading about it."

Zap gulped.

Except for the rain, everything seemed quiet outside, and Zap dared to hope the people had given up and gone home. But as soon as he and Lacus stepped through the portcullis, their muttering rose to a clamor. "What kind of water mage are you?"

"You trying to drown us like you think we're kittens?"

The rain-drenched mob surged forward, but Lacus held them with his gaze, and they stopped.

"I am aware there is a problem and . . ."

"That's great that you're aware of the problem, but what are you doing about it?"

A woman in the middle of the mob wrung water from her shawl. It blended with the rain that continued to fall. "Nothing! He's not going to do a blem thing. I told you these mages don't care about us. We could float away like flotsam for all they care."

Lacus narrowed his eyes. "Jaleece, you know that's not true. Yes, I know your name. I know every drop of water in your body by name. Now move out of my way so I can get down here to do something about the rain. If that's really what you want me to do."

They didn't disperse, but they did move aside to let Lacus and Zap pass.

They hardly had to go to the pond. It came to them—swamping the entire clearing. They stood knee-deep in what the day before had been dry ground.

Zap waited to see what his master would do to stop the rain.

Lacus turned to Zap. "I know this seems unnatural, but this is natural rain behaving unnaturally."

"Yes, sir. Will you make it go away?"

"No. You will."

"Huh?"

"Since this is natural rain, it came from somewhere. All you have to do is send it back where it came from."

"But, master, I . . ."

"Close your eyes and focus on the clouds."

"Huh?"

"Don't ask questions. Just do as I say. Focus and repeat after me. Clouds of water, clouds of rain."

Zap couldn't believe his master was trying to make him use magic. The rain was bad enough, but adding magic was cruel. Suddenly, Lacus looked like a monster—the kind of merciless master who threw his apprentice into deadly ponds. "No, master. I can't . . ."

"You can. Clouds are just droplets of water. Focus on sending them back where they came from."

Just water . Zap shuddered as cold water like droplets of his brother's ghost plummeted down on him from a pitiless sky. There was no such thing as just water. "Master, please! Just make it go away." Zap clung to Lacus's robe, but there was no escaping the water. "Make it go away."

And he did. Lacus uttered a short mantra, and the rain obeyed him, of course. He was the water mage. He could make the water obey him. Something Zap could never do. Something Zap could never be.

The rain came back. Zap shuddered. Could his master be losing his power? He couldn't imagine how much trouble he'd be in if that ever happened. But Lacus drove it away again.

Lacus put a hand on Zap's shoulder. "It's gone now. You're not ready. You've been with me all this time, and still, you are not ready."

Zap sobbed with relief, but Lacus only sighed. They stood there for a moment—master and apprentice. The rain was gone, but there was still so much water that Zap was afraid to move.

Lacus pushed Zap away. "Why are you so afraid of water? You have to overcome this fear if you want to ever be more than an apprentice. You can hardly be that."

"Will you get another apprentice, master? Get someone else, and let me go home." Though he had no idea where home was other than the water mage's castle.

Lacus looked at Zap thoughtfully, then shook his head. "No, I can't. I promised your mother I'd take care of you."

"My mother?" Apprentices weren't allowed to have any contact with their parents for the eight years of their apprenticeship. But Zap had no memory of his master taking him away from a mother. There was just that word that Lacus brought up from time to time with no face attached to it. "Where is my mother?"

As always, the answer was, "Never mind. We need to . . ."

A drop of raid slid off Lacus's face onto Zap. Followed by another drop. They looked up. Black boiling clouds rolled over the sky. Suddenly rain fell in torrents, and a dark, vicious wind whipped it through the air. Lacus raised his voice to quell it, but it only got worse.

Zap's eyes widened with terror. "What's happening, master?"

"Nothing. Just calm down. I'll make this go away, too." He raised his hands to the sky and chanted with all his might. He screamed into the sky, demanding the clouds to return to their rightful place.

But the storm only mocked him, punctuating his words with lightning flashes and thunder rolls.

"This storm isn't natural."

The wind blew Lacus's words away almost before Zap could understand them. Not natural. His heart lurched in his chest. Then his master could do nothing about it. It was still water, still wind, but controlled by something not of the elements.

Zap reached out for his master, but the wind blew Lacus up into the air—way up until his body was engulfed in the black clouds.

"Master!"

To Zap's horror, Lacus fell out of the clouds—the wind whipping him this way and that but doing nothing to slow his fall. He hit the ground. Zap watched his master hit water deep enough to splash but not deep enough to make a difference. There was no way Lacus could have survived that fall.

"Master?" Zap tried to run to him, but the wind held him back as if with hands.

"None can save you, little boy. You are mine."

Chapter 10

Everything in the Quantum Realm flowed in perfect order. Nano saw to that. All the quanta in the universe lined up in an endless queue while he inspected each one for regularity.

"Proton. Two up quarks. One down quark. Regular. Pass. Neutron. Two down quarks, one up quark, regular. Pass."

And Nano's bosons escorted them through nanotubes to Atomidon where they'd join other particles to make the atoms of the universe.

Nine bosons stood at his beck and call to handle any irregularities. But there were few. One in particular he tolerated for what reason, he wasn't sure. In the distance, bosons transformed useless positrons into electrons. Nano could never figure out the one W boson that actually gave itself a name—Muto. That in itself was irregular. Nano vowed that at the first sign of trouble, he'd tolerate Muto no longer.

"What is that?" One boson pointed to a particle approaching from outside the Quantum Realm.

Nano couldn't say what it was or what it was made of. It wasn't physical—neither hadron nor lepton. But if it was a boson, Nano had never seen one like it. As it drew closer, Nano realized it was energy—sentient energy. They produced sentient matter in Cenozonia—but sentient energy ? Where was it made? He couldn't let it enter the queen's palace without finding out what it was. So, he sent his bosons to intercept it. It seemed to resist at first. But one instance of sentient energy was no match for nine instances of pure energy. The bosons escorted it back to Nano.

The line of quanta waiting to be inspected stared at the newcomer as if they were as mystified by its existence as Nano was.

"It's a spirit," a photon announced.

A spirit? Now Nano really didn't know what to make of the thing. He knew the names of all the quanta in Nanosia, and there were no spirits among them.

Nano didn't know how to inspect the thing for irregularities. Its very existence was an irregularity. And the first words out of its mouth only confirmed this.

"Why do you keep such order here?"

What preposterous question is this? Nano had kept the Quantum Realm in order for eons—ever since there were such things as quanta. What did the thing expect Nano to do except fulfill his nature? He glared at the thing. It didn't matter that it could talk. And if it could talk, it wasn't a thing. But Nano didn't know any other way to think of it. "Why would I not? The universe depends on me to keep order and prevent chaos."

"The universe thrives on disorder. Everything should be free to find its own course."

"There is no beauty in disorder. Without order, there is ugliness."

"I'm not talking about beauty. I'm talking about the way things should be."

"And how should things be?"

"They should be in disorder."

"The very idea of should be implies some kind of order. Disorder means things are not as they should be."

"How dare you!" The talking thing had the audacity to look insulted. If it was insulted by the truth, what did that say about it?

Suddenly, the thing tried to attack Nano, but the nine bosons stood together in front of Nano. This was so unprecedented that it drew other forces to Nano's defense—gravity and inertia, strong forces and weak forces. The thing had no choice but to flee before such irresistible force. To Nano's dismay, the thing slipped through a nanotube that would take it to Atomidon. Leeuwen would wonder what Nano's problem was sending him such a thing. But it was Leeuwen's problem now.

He had to inform the queen. Like his bosons, Nano could be in more than one place at a time. So, while one instance of him resumed inspecting the quanta, another appeared before Queen Quanta in her throne room.

Nano was the queen's right-hand man and didn't have to prostrate himself before her as her other subjects did. He stood beside her while she enjoyed her courtiers dancing around her in their appointed orbits. None was out of step, too slow, or too fast. When he'd given her the proper amount of time, he leaned over and whispered into her ear. "Your Majesty, there's been a disturbance that I think Your Majesty should be made aware of."

"A disturbance?"

"Not to worry. It's been taken care of or at least driven out. But it may return, and for that reason, Your Majesty should be informed."

Queen Quanta looked around. "We see no disturbance. What could threaten our peace and order?"

"That's just it. Something came into the Quantum Realm that I've never seen before. An instance of sentient energy that the photon called a spirit."

"We've heard of spirits. They exist in the quintessence."

"I've never heard of such a realm. I know of only four here in Nanosia—the Quantum Realm, Atomidon, Cenozonia, and the Realm of Chaos. Please don't tell me this is one of those make-believe realms outside of Nanosia. There is nothing outside Nanosia."

"We speak only of what we have heard. And your disbelief doesn't make it an impossibility. But why should we feel threatened by this spirit? From what we've heard, they are quite benign."

"Not this one, Your Majesty. It actually suggested that I stop keeping order in the universe, claiming that disorder is beautiful. Then it attacked me, but my bosons drove it off."

"Attacked you!"

"With what intention, I can only imagine. How can anyone think there is beauty in chaos?"

The queen looked like she knew she was about to say something Nano disagreed with—but she said it anyway, to Nano's horror. "We've been to the Realm of Chaos, and yes, it is a beautiful place. There is order in the chaos."

Nano pressed his lips tight. She was, after all, the queen. To tell her to her face that she was wrong bordered on treason. He just shook his head imperceptibly and blinked.

Nine bosons rose from the mist that pervaded Nanosia and prostrated themselves before the queen.

"Rise and speak," she ordered.

One did rise. "Your Majesty, the spirit that came to Nano earlier has now declared itself as the monarch of the Realm of Chaos."

"Monarch of the Realm of Chaos." The queen actually looked bemused.

But Nano was stunned. No monarch had reigned in the Realm of Chaos since Antipan met his gratuitous end. "What does this mean?"

The boson looked perplexed. Not that he would know. "I'm only reporting what's being said, Your Majesty. The spirit goes by the name Turbatius, and the particles in the Realm of Chaos seem to love him as they once loved Antipan."

Nano nearly choked with horror. "The nine of you must go to the Realm of Chaos. Find out all that you can about what's going on and what this Turbatius intends to do."

Chapter 11

Jawan wanted to stay and urge master Lacus to take the rain seriously. But he figured Zap probably didn't want Jawan to be a witness to whatever his master was planning.

Like all the other mages, Master Lacus had a portal that would take him just about anywhere instantly. All he had to do was think about where he wanted to go. Jawan stepped through the window-like portal. Well, maybe not instantly. No matter how often he used it, Jawan would never get used to the queasy stretched and squeezed feeling the portal gave him as it did whatever it did to get him from one place to another.

He stepped out into the laboratory of his own castle and found his master in a trance. Jawan was eager to tell him about the rain. With no windows, Myrlo wouldn't have been able to hear the rain through the thick walls of his castle. He'd know about it. The great earth mage knew about everything. But he couldn't experience it. He hadn't been out there, so Jawan had to let him know how bad it was. Still, trance state was do-not-disturb state. So, Jawan waited.

"I know that you are here, Jawan. You cannot disturb me. I come out of the trance when I am ready."

"Oh. I mean, yes, sir. I want to tell you . . ."

"About the rain. Yes, I know. But that is Master Lacus's affair."

"I've never seen it rain like this before, master. There's something else going on. Master Lacus never lets it rain like this."

Myrlo hadn't shifted from his trance posture. He hardly seemed to move. Only the sound of his voice told Jawan he was present in the laboratory. "No, he doesn't. I don't know what's causing this rain. But it is rain, and Lacus will handle it."

"I just left him, and he doesn't understand how bad it is."

"Then maybe it's not that bad. More important for me to think about is what I learned in trance. The Earth is disturbed."

"Disturbed, sir?"

"Yes, disturbed—under great pressure. It may have something to do with the rain. I must study it further."

That was master Myrlo. The whole world could be threatened with destruction, but he would get all his information before he made a move.

"I feel the torrents of rain and the distress of the earth. It's as if the rain is angry. But that's impossible. Whatever's going on, I hope Lacus can do something about it. Water is his element, and none of the other mages can deal with this if he can't. Prepare the fire cubes."

"Why? We can't go out in all this rain to create a volcano." It made no sense, but Jawan couldn't think of any other reason Myrlo would want the fire cubes.

Myrlo raised an eyebrow. "No, we > can't."

"I didn't mean . . ." Jawan hoped his master didn't note the sarcasm in his use of the word we > . He hadn't meant to be sarcastic. But more often than not, Myrlo stayed here and studied earth theory while Jawan went out to do the actual work.

"You didn't mean to say it, but you know as well as I do that I'm getting old. The fire cubes aren't for volcanoes. They're for me. I feel a draft."

The Earth master feels a draft? > Jawan hated to think about it, but his master was mortal and would one day die, and Jawan would take his place.

That's what Myrlo had been preparing him to do all these years. There could be only one Earth mage, but there had to be one. Jawan frowned. Just when he needed to be out there keeping the balance in the Earth, he was trapped in this castle by a force that even Myrlo didn't understand but had to study. Jawan pulled out the box where they kept the cubes, but it was empty. "There aren't any cubes. I'll have to go get some from Loby." Jawan shuddered at the thought of going back through the portal, but that was better than going out in the rain.

He pushed the box back under the table and turned to the portal. Before he could step into it, someone came out of it. First a foot, then a leg, then a very pretty face and shoulders. "Cintella! You picked a great time to come."

"I love you, too, dear."

"Sorry, I didn't mean to be sarcastic." Not that dear > wasn't on the sarcastic side. "There's just a lot going on here. A lot of stress."

"Well, we did have a date to study together." Cintella entered the laboratory and dropped her books on the central table.

Jawan slapped his forehead.

"Don't tell me you forgot."

"All right, I won't tell you that. But like I said, there's so much going on here today that I didn't even think about it." Oops, wrong thing to say. Why couldn't he remember there were some truths a girl just didn't want to hear—like that he hadn't thought about her. The world could be coming to an end, or he could be breathing his last, but he'd better be thinking about her.

"You weren't thinking about me? That's nice to know."

Jawan sighed. He should've remembered. If he loved her, he would've remembered. But he did love her. So, why hadn't he remembered? "I was out with Zap, and it started raining really bad. I've never seen so much rain. It was incredible." Incredible, yeah right > . Should he tell her about the undine? Why doesn't he just shut up?

"I was just out this morning, and I saw no sign of rain. Must have come up really fast."

"It did. Believe me."

But she didn't.

Myrlo cleared his throat as if they'd forgotten about him. Jawan was forgetting a lot of things lately. "Hello, Cintella. I'm afraid you've come at a bad time. Jawan, are you going to get the fire cubes?"

"On my way now, sir." He turned toward the portal, glad to have an excuse to get away.

"You're leaving?"

"Well, yes. Master Myrlo wants me to get some fire cubes from the fire mage." Way to go, Jawan. Blame it on your master. He can take it.

Cintella folded her arms and leveled a look on Jawan that reminded him she was the alias of Queen Quanta in the Quantum Realm. She'd tried to go with them to Nanosia once and got trapped in the portal because she couldn't exist in the same world with the queen. They looked exactly alike, and a blind man—who could see more than he was supposed to—had predicted Jawan would one day marry a queen. He supposed Cintella was that queen. But what was she the queen of?

Myrlo cleared his throat again. The woman would just have to understand. He looked at her, knew that she wouldn't, but walked toward the portal anyway.

The floor tilted enough to throw him off balance. "Cintella, what are you doing."

"I didn't do anything."

Indeed, she was holding on to a table while the whole castle shook. The bottles rattled on the shelves, and dust sprinkled down from the ceiling.

"What is this?" Jawan ran to catch the bottles before they fell.

Myrlo rode the bucking floor like an old sailor on the high seas, but he looked puzzled. Jawan knew a mage wouldn't tell his journeyman that he didn't know what was going on. Still, Jawan could see it in his eyes, and that scared him. "Is this the disturbance you were talking about? It's getting worse."

"Calm down. I'll summon Lacus to find out what he's doing about the rain. I'm sure he has everything under control—or is getting it under control." He reached for the summoning bells by the portal and stopped.

"Master, what is it?"

Myrlo made a shushing gesture and picked up the bell with the inverted triangle that symbolized the water element.

"Why is it dull like that?" Jawan asked.

There was only one reason why Master Lacus symbol didn't glow like the others. But instead of answering Jawan's question, Myrlo shook the bell. It didn't chime. It was supposed to chime, but it clattered in confirmation of what Jawan and Myrlo already knew was true.

Cintella shifted uneasily. "Is everything all right?"

"Yes." Myrlo rang the bell to summon Quintessuma, the mage of the fifth element—spirit.

They waited, knowing that it took time for a mage to answer a summons.

A melodious but distressed voice filtered through the portal. "Myrlo, I know things are just as distressing for you as they are for me. I don't know how I can help you. I'm so busy."

"Quintessuma, it's Lacus. . . We are worried about him. Is he . . ."

"I'm afraid so. Our dear brother Lacus arrived in the quintessence moments ago. I must go. There is drought and inclement weather everywhere. People's spirits are down with the weather, and I must comfort the living and transport the dead to the quintessence."

Jawan shook with terror. "How can we stop the rain without master Lacus?"

"In quintessence? That's impossible," Cintella said. "How can mages die?"

"We can," Jawan said.

Myrlo turned to Jawan. "Take my hands. We will focus on strengthening the castle stones."

Jawan took his master's hands and closed his eyes. As the castle continued to shake, he focused on the stones and timbers—tightening and strengthening them. But the shaking didn't abate. If anything, it shook even more. The chandeliers swung dangerously like the pendulum on a clock.

Myrlo opened his eyes. "Rain alone cannot do this. This isn't natural. We need to go outside and see what's going on. We won't find out by sitting in this windowless laboratory."

"But without windows, at least we'll be safe." Cintella didn't seem sure.

A shower of dust fell down from the ceiling to belie their words. They headed for the portcullis. Thunder pealed through the halls as they ran for the castle's entrance. Wind blew them back as they approached the portcullis. They grasped it and held on. Rain lashed Jawan like a whip. He could hardly breathe as air went everywhere except his nostrils.

Cintella gasped. "We can't go out there."

"No!" Myrlo agreed. "This is not natural. Look!"

They saw faces in the wind. Horrid faces with lightning coming from their eyes and bats' wings churning the wind.

"It's Alecto! What is she doing here?" Myrlo screamed above the thunder. "I must close the gates, or she will enter the castle itself."

Jawan's eyes widened with astonishment. "No! wait!" He pointed, and beneath the flying debris, they saw Zap hugging the ground for dear life.

"We've got to save him," Cintella said.

But Myrlo shook his head. "We can't go out there. We have to close the gate."

Jawan and Cintella stared in amazement as Myrlo chanted a spell to close the gate.

"The tunnel!" Jawan shouted at Zap. "Take the tunnel to Loby's castle. I'll meet you there."

Myrlo nodded at Jawan as the gate shut and Alecto beat against it. "I will summon Volvo to see what he can do about the wind, though I doubt that he can do much." He picked up the bell with a horizontal line running through a triangle and rang it. Its moist, masculine chime made the dull clatter of Lacus's bell sound all the more melancholy.

They waited. Mages didn't just drop everything and step through the portal when their bell rang. Dust continued to fall from the ceiling, and the floor continued to buck as they waited. Jawan and Myrlo paced the floor. Cintella sat at the long wooden table. Visions of hopelessness danced before all their eyes.

"Why would you call me at a time like this?" Like Quintessuma, Volvo sent his voice but did not come in person. "I can do no more with the wind than Lacus could have done with the rain."

Myrlo sighed. "I didn't think so. But I had to see if there was anything you were trying to do."

"I'm trying to stay alive. I've no scroll or tome in my library that tells me how to banish Alecto."

Jawan shuddered at the thought that there was nothing the mages could do.

Then Jawan and Cintella took the portal to Loby's castle.

Chapter 12

Zap feared to raise his head. How could he survive the storm that had killed his masterthe furious storm that hadn't even let him go to his master? If he tried to stand up, it would do to him what it had done to Master Lacus. Better to stay still and wait for help to come.

Help? Who would come to help him when no one knew he was out here? He shook off his fear just enough to realize that he was lying in water. With his head down, he'd soon exhale and breathe water.

Water!

He jerked up only to be pummeled by relentless rain. He couldn't escape. He had to. He had to get to one of the mages and tell them about his master. But he needed a mage to help him get to a mage. His lungs burned for air. Fear wasn't going to keep him alive if he lay here and drowned.

He lifted his head and tried to rise to his knees. A gust of wind slapped him onto his back. He sat up only to be blown down again.

Ziph's face loomed over the water. No, this wasn't right. When his brother's ghost appeared, it was always in the water or rising out of it. The faces he saw were in the wind. To his horror, monstrous faces flew through the wind. Lightning flashed each time the monsters moved their eyes. Bat's wings carried them at astonishing speeds.

Zap shook his head.

I'm hallucinating

, he thought.

I swallowed muddy water, and now I'm seeing things.

This was something beyond the horror of his brother's death. It was beyond the horror of a ghost. At least the ghost had once been human. But these monsters . . .

Out of the blowing wind, voices cackled and roared at once. One voice rose above the cacophony of the others. "I am Alecto, the unceasing wrath of retribution. I punish evildoers. If you have done evil, I will destroy you."

Impossible

. Master Volvo controls the wind, and he would never create a wind like this. This wasn't a natural storm.

"I'm not an evildoer."

"That's what they all say. Evildoers wouldn't tell me the truth. They're all as innocent as newborns in the face of death."

Zap gulped.

No, no, this can't be real.

Hallucination or not, he had to move. Alecto, or whatever she was, was up there, but the water was down here, and it wasn't a hallucination. He wiped his eyes, but that only smeared more mud on his face. Turning over, he rose just enough to keep his face out of the water and crawled.

"Trying to get away? You are mad."

Zap thought,

I must be mad to think I can do this.

The forest loomed above him. It lay between him and the mages' castles. Zap trembled with sheer terror. He couldn't go in there.

"See how menacing the forest is, little boy? You're just a little boy, and you can't do what needs to be done. There are monsters in the forest. If you crawl, the snakes will get you. If you walk, the wolves will get you. If you climb a tree, I will blow you away."

Alecto was right. Zap thought,

I'm nothing. I'm insane to even try this.

He buried his face in the sodden turf, hoping to lose his tears in the water. Water! He shrieked and jumped up. Alecto blew him down. He crawled further into the forest, his hands and knees splashing water.

"By the way, snakes can climb trees."

Zap gasped. There was no wind in the forest. She couldn't get to him in here. But the trees could. They brooded above him. Daring him to enter their domain. They hated hima walker. They wanted him dead. Why had he run from one fury to another? Escaped Alecto only to let the trees have him? He was insane. A branch reached down and pulled at his hair, trying to get him. He shrank away from it only to be ensnared in the roots of another tree. They had him. He would die.

He tore loose, leaving part of his cloak. Inch by torturous inch, he followed the forest pathsplashing through the water over roots and broken branches. His knees ached. His palms were raw. If he kept going, he'd be out of the forest. And then there'd be Alecto again. She knew him. Knew he was evil. He'd killed his brother. Failing to save him was as good as killing him. He was evil and he couldn't get away from her. Couldn't get away from water. Couldn't get away from trees. He was so overwhelmed by fear that he froze.

"Scaredy cat. Scaredy cat. Afraid of a little water. Shame on you."

From right behind him and in his ear, Ziph rose, bearing the bloated face of the drowned. Zap's fear unfroze his limbs. He jumped up and ran out of the forest.

He would have sighed with relief at the sight of Master Myrlo's castle, but Alecto had focused her storm on it. What now? Zap looked back at the forest. He couldn't go there. He couldn't do anything. Ziph flew out of the forest straight at Zap's head. He fell to his knees and crawled again with Ziph ever behind him.

And Alecto in front of him. The fury wasn't paying him any attention. But the ghost was. Maybe if he stayed close to the ground, he could sneak around to the back of the castle . . . No, the storm would be back there, too. It was a storm, not an army. Why would it attack the front of the castle and not the back? He didn't know how he would get in. With the ghost behind him, Zap knew only that he had to move.

Incessant flashes of lightning revealed that the castle was swaying in the wind like a treetop, and Zap wondered if he'd be safe there. Two silhouettes stood backlit in the castle's portcullis. Lightning flashed and Zap saw that they were Master Myrlo and Jawan. Zap caught Jawan's eye in the blinking illumination and realized Jawan was yelling something at him. Zap tried to understand, but what the thunder didn't drown out, the wind blew away. One word made it through tunnel.

Jawan was telling him to go through the tunnel under Loby's castle. Zap remembered when they were battling Loby's former master, they'd used a tunnel to sneak into his castle. And Jawan wanted him to go there? Alone? Zap looked around. From darkness to darkness. But at least at the end of the tunnel there'd be a mage who could help him in a castle that Alecto wasn't attacking . . .

To Zap's horror, Alecto looked around to see who Jawan was yelling at and saw him. "Fools! Do you think you can escape me? Neither stones nor trees will save you from my undying wrath."

A gust of wind blew Zap off his knees into the muddy water.

"Where are you, little boy? You can't hide from me." Bat-winged monsters flew in the wind. Lightning eyes searched for him.

Was he safe? Had she lost him? He hardly dared to hope. He hardly dared to sit up again but knew he had to. The fury would find him, and he needed to not be there. So, he crawled.

From Myrlo's castle to Loby's castle wasn't too far if he'd been walking. But on his knees, it seemed like he'd never get there. Finally, he reached the copse of trees that hid the secret tunnel behind Loby's castle and crept inside.

He lifted the trap door that led down into the tunnel. It was pitch blackblacker than pitch. And Jawan expected him to go down there? He remembered that at some point the tunnel forked off into two tunnelsone leading to Loby's castle and the other leading to the fire pit. He stared into the darkness trying to remember whether to turn left or right.

"Scaredy cat! Scaredy cat!"

Zap was so startled by the ghost's voice booming out of the gloomy silence that he tumbled down into the hole, and the trap door snapped shut above him.

A hand touched him. He knew it was a hand. It felt like the hand of someone or something. Zap shrieked.

"It's me, Jawan."

"Why didn't you say something before scaring me like that?"

"You'd have still been scared one way or the other."

***

Zap used what seemed like his last little bit of strength to climb the stairs into Loby's laboratory.

"You look terrible." Loby's eight-months-pregnant wife, Prenda, heaved herself out of a chair when Zap entered.

Zap shook water out of his face and tried in vain to wring it out of his clothes. If he looked as terrible as he felt, he must really be a frightful sight.

"I was already boiling water for hot cocoa. Let me get you a cup." She went to the side counter to do just that.

Zap sat shivering at the long wooden table that ran down the center of every laboratory in the world. He felt thankful but not much better when

Prenda wrapped him in a warm blanket and placed a cup of hot cocoa in his trembling hands. He should be warm and cozy, but the fire in Loby's hearth reminded him so much of Alecto's wrath that he couldn't stop shuddering. He envied Crisp, Loby's pet salamander, lying snug under a table like all was well in his little world.

"It doesn't make sense," Jawan was saying. "How can there be so much rain if master Lacus isn't here. He brought the rain like my master creates volcanoes and earthquakes to relieve pressure in the Earth."

Zap shook his head. "No. Master Lacus didn't bring the rain. He regulated it. But this isn't a natural rain. Not a natural storm. My master tried to stop it and it killed him."

"You're right." Loby stoked the fire. "Master Volvo wouldn't send wind with monsters in it."

Crisp stared at Prenda when she sat down. There wasn't much room for him in her lap anymore, so he jumped into Cintella's lap, and she stroked his back. "It's chaos. Anything this wild outside the control of the elements has got to be chaos."

Loby smiled a smile that Zap didn't like. "That's exactly what it is, Zap, and you have to go to the Realm of Chaos to find out what's causing it to spill out into our world."

Zap blanched. "The Realm of Chaos was Lord Elveston's domain, so you should go."

"It was my master's domain, but I had nothing to do with it. I'm the mage of fire. This storm is bringing rain, so you should go."

Logic. Too much logic. "There's wind, too. So we should get Master Volvo."

"Master Volvo already told us he can't do anything about this storm," Jawan said. "He's as helpless as Master Myrlo. You have to go. Come with me."

"Where to?"

"Just come. I think I saw something in the laboratory that might help."

"In the fire mage's laboratory?"

Jawan took Zap's arm and led him into the laboratory. It looked like all the mages' laboratories with a long wooden table down the middle, except here was the door to the fire pit. Zap wondered what Jawan could have seen, but before he could ask, Jawan pulled him through the portal.

Zap gasped as the portal's magic pulled him out of Hadley Town and put him back together again in Nanosia, a world one-billionth his normal size. He and Jawan stumbled through the mist, trying to catch their steps and their breath. It was just as disorienting for Jawan as it was for Zap.

"You tricked me. You knew I didn't want to come here."

"Well, go back."

Zap turned to do just that, but the swirling mist of Nanosia obscured his vision. He stepped forward. Maybe if he kept walking straight, he'd find the portal. But they hadn't come straight. All their stumbling left him with no idea where the portal was. The thought of wandering around in the mist until he lost Jawan, too, made him stop.

Jawan brought him here. Jawan knew how to get back to Hadley Town. He'd better stay with Jawan. And Jawan knew why they were in Nanosia. All Zap had to do was follow Jawan. "So, what now?" But he knew where Jawan wanted to go, so staying with him may or may not be the best of two bad choices.

"Oh, no. This is your quest. You take the lead."

"Fine. We'll go back to Hadley Town."

"After you then."

Zap gulped. If Jawan didn't want to take the lead, what could they do?

"Zap, you know where we have to go. Stop pretending."

"I'm not pretending. I don't know the way to the Realm of Chaos. Which path should I take?"

"It doesn't matter. All roads lead there if you follow them long enough. See the darkness in the horizon over there?"

Zap looked where Jawan was pointing. A brooding darkness hung over the far horizon like it was the end of the world.

Jawan nodded. "That's where we have to go. Now picture in your mind a road under our feet that will take us there."

"You make it sound that easy."

"It is. I've done it. Loby did it. Since you're a mouse like us, you can do it, too. That's the way things work in Nanosia. Just do it."

"Suppose I just conjure a road back to the portal?"

"Won't work. The roads only go to places native to Nanosia. The sooner you do this, the sooner we can finish and go back home."

Zap sighed. He focused on the mist under their feet and imagined it was a road to the Realm of Chaos. He paused to let Jawan take the first step. But Jawan gestured for him to go ahead. "It's your road."

Zap stepped forward, and Jawan fell in step beside him.

"The Big One!"

"It's the Big One returned to us, and he brought a disciple."

Millions of quanta orbited Zap and Jawan—electrons and neutrinos, protons and neutrons, groups of quarks of every shape and size. Photons flew out of the electrons, then watched from a distance, too elite to share the fermions' sense of awe.

Zap shrugged. He'd forgotten about the crazy quanta. They thought Jawan was the answer to some prophecy in Nanosia. The Big One from the Big World who would come to save them from Antipan.

"Why do you come, Big One? Antipan is dead. What doom do you come to save us from now?"

Zap looked at Jawan, waiting for him to answer. "Say something. They're waiting for you, Big One."

But Jawan just looked away.

It was up to Zap to say something. He swallowed. "There . . . there is something going on," he stammered. "Something in the Realm of Chaos."

"There, that wasn't so bad." Jawan made Zap want to throw up sometimes.

The quanta moved in perfect order in concentric orbits around the boys.

"What is it?"

"What's coming?"

"Another monster?"

Nine bosons marched through the cloud of quanta and surrounded Zap and Jawan. Zap gulped. He'd forgotten about them, too. The big beefy bosons. Pure energy that he couldn't escape in Nanosia any more than he could escape the water in Hadley Town.

"What's going on?"

"What's the commotion?"

"This is highly irregular."

The boson squad leader glared at Jawan. "You again!"

"It's the Big One."

"From the Big World."

"And he brought a partner."

The leader scowled. "There is no Big World. I don't know where you came from. But I know where you're going."

"We . . . we have to go to the Realm of Chaos."

"The Realm of Chaos? Come to take Antipan's place, have you? We heard there's a new monarch in the Realm of Chaos."

Zap and Jawan exchanged glances.

"I guess you know all about it. But you won't be joining him. We're taking you straight back to Nano. You'll tell him what you know."

Chapter 13

Elemental particles of all sorts flew around Turbatius in a frenzy of caprice. He didn't know if that was good or bad that they had so completely banished all thoughts of the previous monarch of the Realm of Chaos and accepted Turbatius as their new ruler with glee.

A particle alighted on the palm of his outstretched hand while others orbited his head, singing, "Turbatius the king! Turbatius, Lord of Chaos!"

He decided it was a good thing.

"Lord, trouble approaches."

Trouble? What could trouble the Realm of Chaos? Where all are free, how could anything be wrong? He followed the particle to the gate and got his answer. Nine bosons were approaching the Realm of Chaos, marching in such orderly lock step that Turbatius felt sick just looking at it. They stopped at the gate glowing with energy. Turbatius thought they must also be bursting with the desire to break loose from their mad adherence to order. But when the leader raised his hand, they stopped as one and did not move.

"They cannot enter," a particle said.

"They don't belong here," said another.

Turbatius laughed. This was his domain, and Nano couldn't touch him. He caught the leader's eye and smiled. "It is time for us to dance."

"Yay!"

Being denizens of the Realm of Chaos, they were free. He couldn't make them do anything. But so many wanted to dance that it seemed they had planned this as a show just to entertain the bosons. Particles zipped this way and that, up, down, diagonal, perpendicular, and parallel. They never got in each other's way, but near collisions resulted in gales of laughter.

The bosons glared at them, which only made them laugh all the more.

In the midst of the bosons, two things marched as if the bosons were their honor guard. What kind of things could have that much power? But they weren't things—weren't particles or quanta. They had minds like Vordon. Turbatius had seen one of them outside the pond near Vordon. What were they doing here?

This had something to do with Vordon. Was his creation fraternizing with other minds in his world and Nanosia? But Vordon had never been to Nanosia and wouldn't know Nano except through these things. He couldn't have sent them here to join Nano. But he'd clearly sent them here as spies and now they were joining forces with Turbatius's enemies. If Turbatius didn't still have some use for Vordon, he'd kill the traitor right then and there. He would keep an eye on Vordon and find out what was what.

The particles continued to dance. Turbatius gasped at the beauty of light and color, of unexpected shapes and patterns. But there was something wrong. He sensed a rhythm to their dancing. How could there be rhythm in disorder? The rhythm was so complex that the bosons couldn't detect it. But Turbatius could, and he didn't like it. He wanted disorder in everything—plain, inexplicable, chaotic disorder. He was Turbatius, after all. The spirit of disorder. The Lord Monarch of the Realm of Chaos. And he would have it. He must stop the dance. But dance was just movement. He must dismantle the laws that combined matter and movement, time and space, to create rhythm. Vordon had just begun, and Alecto held the key to stopping this orderly madness in the big world. Destruction would trickle up and down. "Children, follow those things. Find out where the bosons are taking them."

He'd created Vordon, so all he had to do was close his eyes to appear to him. The man was still in the forest, the perfect place for him to carry out his master's will.

"Summon all the furies and pit them against the elemental mages."

The man was startled to see his master. "How will I do that?"

"Fool! Have you not studied the use of your tools?"

Of course not. A mortal would never dream of using the furies as a tool. But Turbatius would, and he commanded his servant, "Tell the furies that the mages have committed great crimes against the joy and freedom of humanity. Tell them the mages have been the cause of the shedding of tears and grinding of teeth. Tell them the mages deserve punishment."

"Do you think they will believe that?"

Turbatius rolled his eyes. "They are furies. Their place is not to believe or not believe. Their place is to punish evildoers. And your place is not to question your master."

Vordon raised an eyebrow. "Master?" The challenge in his voice was unmistakable.

Turbatius raised a wind that blew Vordon against a tree. "Master. Do you question that as well?"

"No!" Vordon groaned as his head banged against the tree.

"No, what?"

"No, m-master."

Turbatius imagined what disorder he'd create smashing Vordon's head. But that would wait until Vordon finished his task. "Make the mages look as evil as the blackest soul in the universe."

The particles had told him that the world above was connected to Nanosia in some way. So, destroying the mages would take care of Nano. As above, so below. Turbatius would find the spies and make them tell him Vordon's plan of treachery. No point asking Vordon—for he would only lie.

Chapter 14

Muto wondered why he was doing this. Well, it was his job—a thankless job turning positrons into electrons. They looked just as miserable as he was bored. But Nano wanted it done, so he did it.

At least he wasn't the only W boson Nano had snatched out of Atomidon to do this. But he was the only one who survived after the transformation. He shook his head as another W boson touched a positron and winked out of existence, leaving a neutrino that another W boson would die to turn into an electron. What happened to them, and why was he the sole survivor? He'd touched billions of positrons with the magic touch of transformation, turning their positive charge to neutral so that another unfortunate W boson could turn it negative.

"He's surviving." One of the W bosons still waiting to perform his fatal task pointed at Muto. "He's not supposed to be here. It's irregular."

Muto laughed. That was what Nano liked to say. So, he was irregular. Wouldn't have it any other way. If he could do something about the boredom. Those other bosons didn't live long enough to get bored. But maybe he'd live long enough to do something about it. If only he could turn the positrons into something other than electrons. That would be fun. But they were leptons. They had no smaller parts that he could manipulate.

Nano wanted him to work with positrons, but there were other particles in the Quantum Realm. He looked around. Protons orbiting toward Nano's nanotube caught his eye. They'd be perfect. Each proton was made up of two up quarks and one down quark. If he could just turn the down quark into an up quark, he'd create something that Nano would definitely call irregular.

One of the protons fell slightly behind the others, curious about the W bosons and especially about Muto. He winked at her, and she smiled, slowing down even more. He gave her a come-hither smile, and she did.

Muto smirked. This was going to be so easy. He'd have to add a little spice so it wouldn't be more of the same old, same old. "May I ask your name, little quantum?"

She actually blushed—her up quarks taking a little bow—and her one down quark shivered delightfully.

"I don't have a name of my own. I'm just a proton—one of trillions."

Muto put a sad look on his face. He did feel sad that this sweet little quantum devalued herself so much. But he wanted her to know just how sad he was, so his face grew long and sorrowful. "Don't you want to be different? Don't you want to have a name all your own that I can call you by?"

She looked puzzled. "But I'm already a proton. What else could I be?"

"Yes, but that's not a name. If I call you proton, I could be calling trillions of others just like you. I have the power to make you special."

"Nano won't like it."

"Who cares what Nano likes. Nano can go to the Realm of Chaos for all I care. Let's have some fun, you and I." Before she could think to protest further, he turned her down quark into a strange quark.

"What have you done? This feels odd."

"It's a two-step process. Hold still. I'm almost there." He turned the strange quark into a charm quark. "Ah, my lovely, charmed lamb. Now we can play."

The other W bosons looked over with alarm. "That's not right. A charmed lambda has one down quark, an up quark, and a charm quark."

Muto laughed. "I told you you'd be special. Who wants a down quark? And I didn't say lambda. I said lamb." He beheld her. "My little lamb. My creation. There is nothing like you anywhere in the universe. I shall make your name Amaki."

All the other W bosons stared at Muto aghast.

"This is not proper."

"It's irregular."

"There goes the universe."

Even the positrons waiting for Muto to change them into electrons trembled with uncertainty wondering what he would do to them.

"I can't do anything to you sniveling leptons. You're fit for nothing but electronification."

"But that's supposed to be a good thing." The positrons protested. "You say it like it's a bad thing."

"It's a good thing. Trust me. My Amaki, how do you feel? Better?"

"I feel wonderful." She didn't look like she felt wonderful. She looked worried. "But how will Nano accept me now. I'm so irregular. He's sure to reject me."

"Don't worry about Nano. He's nothing. I accept you, and that's all that matters."

"You can't send me to Atomidon."

Muto rolled his eyes. "Why do you need to go to Atomidon?"

"That's where all the protons go to create atoms."

"You're not a proton anymore. You're a charmed lamb. Very different."

"Aren't there any charmed lambs in atoms?"

"No," he lied. If she got into an atom—into what they called a hyper-nucleus—she'd be even more tightly glued into the strong force than the protons were. He wanted her for himself. He'd created her. Anyway, there weren't any lambdas with two up quarks, so no.

"Then I'm doomed!"

"No, you're free. You can have fun." He reached out to dance with her and show her what a joy life could be as his charmed lamb.

She pulled away from him. "I'll just wonder around Nanosia with nowhere to go, nowhere to belong, and no purpose. Why did you do this to me?"

"You mustn't take it like that."

But Amaki flew away. He watched her fly past the protons and disappear into the mist of Nanosia. The other W bosons cast reproachful eyes on him. Why? He hadn't done anything wrong. She was just flighty. Maybe if he could get one of the other protons to come closer. But they saw what he'd done to Amaki and kept their distance.

Even the positrons had the nerve to get restless.

"What will he do to us?"

"I don't want to be a lambda."

"It was bad enough they wanted to turn us into electrons."

"Maybe I like being a positron."

"Enough!" Muto didn't care about Nano and his orderliness, but he still didn't want to lose his only reason for being in the Quantum Realm, where he had unlimited access to quanta of all sorts. "Get in line!"

Chapter 15

Nine bosons assisted Nano at the gate to Atomidon. They were capable of being in more than one place at a time, so when they shimmered, he thought they were returning with their report about what was going on with the new monarch of the Realm of Chaos. To his surprise, they returned ushering two highly irregular particles with them.

Irregular particles were rare in the Quantum Realm, but Nano had seen them before, so he raised an eyebrow when the quanta took this as an opportunity to make an irregular commotion. "Line up. Get back into your orbits."

"It's the Big One!"

"The Big One is here."

"Why? Antipan is no more. Is the Big One here to save us from another calamity?"

Now Nano knew he had to put a stop to this. "Fools! There is no Big One."

"But there he is. You see him yourself. You put him in the queen's dungeon when he was here before."

"That was just an irregular particle." He looked at the two the bosons had brought in. It was the same nuisance and his sidekick come to vex Nano once again. "And it's still irregular, so I will deal with it the same way."

Some of the quanta glared at Nano. "He's going to put the Big One in the dungeon?"

"He did it before."

A billion quanta raised their murmuring voices, and Nano knew he had to put a stop to it. He'd bring things back to regularity by doing what was regular. "You, there!" He pointed to the nearest quantum. "Come forward. I must inspect you."

The quantum came forward trembling with excitement. "To think, I arrived in the Quantum Realm just in time to see the Big One!"

Nano grunted. "No, you arrived just in time to go to Atomidon."

The quantum looked crestfallen. "Do I have to?"

"If you pass inspection." He examined the quantum carefully. Two up quarks and one down quark—a perfect proton being held together by the strong force. "You pass. Next."

The bosons led the quantum into a nanotube while Nano turned to the next quantum in line.

"It is the Big One!"

"He's here!"

"And he brought his disciple."

Quanta rushed forward to bow at the particles' feet. Nano glared at them, and they returned to their proper places.

Nano rounded on the bosons that brought the particles. "Where did you find these irregular particles? You were supposed to be finding out what's going on in the Realm of Chaos."

The boson leader stepped forward. "We couldn't get into the Realm of Chaos, but we found these two claiming to be on their way there, so we figured you might want to interrogate them."

"Is that what you figured? They've been here before. I didn't like them then, and I still don't. What do you mean, you couldn't get in? Anyone who's either brave or stupid can enter the Realm of Chaos."

"Some force blocked our way."

Nano's eyes widened. "You are bosons. Pure energy. What force could be strong enough to keep you out?"

"Some force the new monarch of the Realm of Chaos is wielding."

"The new monarch of . . ." Nano turned a furious eye on the particles. "You're in league with this upstart. First you joined Antipan in his schemes. Now you're scheming with this Turbatius. What are you up to?"

One of the particles gestured to the other, but neither of them seemed ready to answer for themselves.

The boson leader spoke instead. "As I said, they said they were on their way to the Realm of Chaos. Maybe it just arrived and hasn't seen Turbatius yet. So, we caught them before they had a chance."

"A chance to do what? Arrived from where? Wherever they came from, it was somewhere here in Nanosia. They know Turbatius just like they knew Antipan."

One of the particles started whispering frantically to the other. Then one of them spoke. "We didn't come here to do mischief. In fact, we want to find out what's going on in the Realm of Chaos just like you.'"

Nano scowled. "I'm sure you do, but your reasons are very different from ours."

"Not really. We're just boys. I'm Jawan, and this is Zap."

Nano and the nine bosons looked at each other. "There is no particle in the Quantum Realm called a boy or a Jawan or a Zap," Nano said.

"Then maybe they really did come here from the Big W . . ." the boson leader started to say.

But Nano glared at him, and he fell silent. Nano was tired of this nonsense. There was no Big World. No Big One. There was nothing but Nanosia, and everything that existed was here. "These particles are lying about what they are and what they plan to do." He glared at Jawan and Zap. "You seem to be all of one piece, so you're not hadrons. But I've never seen leptons like you either. You must have come out of the Realm of Chaos. Anything could come out of that place."

"I told you, we're boys."

"Nonsense. I've had enough of this. I have work to do. Take them to the dungeon."

The one called Zap blanched. "The dungeon! But we haven't done anything."

"And you're not going to do anything."

The one who called himself Jawan looked around like he was fishing for something—anything. "I noticed you're still using the W bosons I showed you before to turn positrons into electrons. See, I helped you when I was here before. Have you forgotten?"

Nano shook his head. "An irregular particle may have its uses, but it's still irregular and has no place in the Quantum Realm."

"We weren't trying to come here. Your bosons brought us here. Now just let us go and we won't bother you anymore. In fact, we're on our way to the Realm of Chaos. Can't get any farther away from the Quantum Realm than that."

"The Realm of Chaos!" Nano had heard enough. "What more evidence do I need?" He gestured to his nine bosons. "Take them."

The nine shimmered, then they and the irregular particles were gone.

The eye of every quantum in the Quantum Realm was fixed on the spot where their savior vanished as if expecting him to defy Nano and come again.

Nano scowled. "Next!"

"You just sent the Big One to the dungeon." The next particle stared at Nano as if for the first time. "How could you? The Big World sent him here to save us. How could you send him away? To the dungeon of all places?"

"Save you from what?"

"We don't know. There's been no prophecy. But there must be something bad on the way, or he wouldn't have been sent."

"Nobody sent that irregular particle. For the last time, there is no Big One. There is no Big World."

The quanta murmured at this. "If there's no Big World, where do the atoms go? What is the purpose of the Quantum Realm? What does it matter if we're regular or irregular? Everything came from the Realm of Chaos, so maybe everything will go back there and what's in between doesn't matter."

"It matters." Nano examined the particle before him. "I make it matter. I'm the queen's right hand, and if I say you need to be regular, then that is what you need to be. You're irregular. Two up quarks and a charm quark! A lambda. And not even a proper lambda at that. Turbatius is doing something already. Where did you come from?"

The lambda particle shrank back in dismay. "Muto made me."

"Muto?"

"The W boson you put in charge of transforming the positrons into electrons. I was a proton just passing by to see what he was doing when he transformed my down quark into a charm quark."

"I know what Muto is. So, you were just passing by." Nano scowled. "Now you see what comes of being out of your proper orbit. One good thing about W bosons—they can only work mischief once, then they're annihilated." But this Muto was still here, and he'd create more lambda. "A W boson that can survive an interaction!" This was more horrible than a mere irregular particle. "I won't tolerate anything like that in the Quantum Realm."

"Will you put Muto in a dungeon like you did with the Big One? He came to save us. You have to let him out, or we're all doomed."

Nano shook his head. There couldn't be a Big World. He only knew what he knew, not what he imagined to be just because others had no other answers. But he had an answer to this—Turbatius. He was the answer to all mischief just as Antipan was before him. "Come with me. I'll show you what I do with bosons who create disorder in my realm."

"What will you do with me?"

"What I do with irregular particles."

But before he could grab her, the lambda ran away. He stopped. Why was he chasing after irregular particles? His bosons would get her. He'd see to this Muto, then he'd see what he could do about Turbatius.

Chapter 16

"What's going on?"

Muto looked up. To his dismay Nano's nine bosons were bearing down on him. But they were addressing all the W bosons, not just him, so he turned back to his positrons as if this had nothing to do with him. Who knew? Maybe it didn't. Why assume guilt before he knew why the bosons were there? But the other W bosons glared at him—marking him with their eyes.

The bosons turned on Muto, pushing Amaki in front of them. "Is this the one who transformed you into a charmed lambda?"

Muto was astonished. Were they actually trying to turn his little Amaki against him? He looked at her. Through his eyes he conveyed the message I created you. You owe me your life . Then he remembered how distraught she'd been over the transformation. But still . . . she was his.

" Lambda? What's that? I'm a lamb. You said I was your lamb."

"He's the one." Then she slipped away. His little lamb was no dummy. She had to know Nano had just one plan for an irregular particle like her. So she just left Muto to his fate. No dummy but no angel either.

They surrounded Muto, but he hid his fear behind a smile. He had to get out of this. "I meant no harm. I was just having a little fun to break the boredom. That's all."

The boson leader scoffed. "We didn't bring you here to have fun. If you're bored, you don't belong here."

"Come on. It's not like I did anything permanent. I can change her back into a proton easily enough."

"You wouldn't be talking about changing her back if you hadn't been caught. A little fun. We found her weeping her heart out."

This was really bad. But maybe not. So Nano would screech and scream about keeping order. Muto would promise whatever and go on about his business.

"Nano doesn't even want to see you. You're going to the dungeon."

The other W bosons shook their heads as the nine bosons led Muto away.

"We told him he has to keep order like the rest of us."

Muto muttered, "Why would I want to be like those kiss-ups?"

"What was that?"

"Nothing."

"What about us?"

The nine bosons looked at the positrons who'd been lined up for Muto to transform them into electrons as if they'd just as well been forgotten. In the space of a nanosecond the nine bosons dispersed the positrons among the other W bosons. Then they gathered power around Muto and shimmered.

As a boson, Muto could shimmer, too, and be in two places at once. But he was a weak force—not one of Nano's elite nine. When they took him, he felt like he was being torn apart from himself, then hurled back together again. He looked around and found himself standing in front of the Quantum Realm's infamous dungeon.

He was horrified. The walls of the dungeon were made of quarks—hundreds of miserable quarks stacked together with no room to move.

"This is an outrage. This is an abuse of their right to find joy in existence."

"They're doing what they're supposed to do. If they can't take joy in that, then they don't exist for joy. In you go." They opened a cell door and pushed Muto in.

"Wait, I . . ."

They shut and barred the door.

Muto narrowed his eyes. He didn't have to stay here, no matter what Nano wanted, Muto was still a W boson, and he could pop out just like he popped in. He'd work his mischief in the Quantum Realm and be gone before Nano's bosons could catch him, and he'd destroy Nano.

He closed his eyes and willed himself elsewhere. But when he opened his eyes, he was still there. He tried again, but nothing happened. He ran to the door and tried to pass through it. But the door was solid, and he stayed where he was. He slumped against the door. He couldn't get himself out. He'd have to wait for Nano to let him out, and when would that be? "How long am I going to be in here?"

The bosons were gone, but a quark near the ceiling corner answered. "We've been here for eons and will likely be here for eons more. Can't say about you. Maybe you should make yourself comfortable. An eon is a long time to pace the floor."

They're sentient enough to talk and be aware. "Don't you feel outraged at how Nano treats you? Don't you want to be free?"

"Oh, it's not Nano. He just keeps order in the universe. He doesn't decide what order is. And besides, free to do what?"

"Free to . . ." Muto had to stop and think. Did there have to be a purpose for freedom? Wasn't freedom its own purpose? "Free to be."

The quarks looked puzzled. "Free to be what?"

Muto sighed. Why did he have to justify freedom to them? If they saw no value in it, then maybe they didn't deserve it. They wouldn't know what to do with it. Still . . . "Aren't you tired of being miserable? I'm miserable enough, and I just got here."

"You should see the particles in the other cell next to you. They call themselves boys. There's nothing else like them anywhere in Nanosia."

"But they were here before. We hear it's the Big One and his disciple who saved Nanosia from Antipan. Why Nano would put them back in here, we don't know."

"But we're just quarks. Nobody listens to us. So, here they are, and here you are."

Here he was. He wasn't going to stay here for eons. He put himself into a state of rest, dreaming of escape and putting Nano in a black hole.

Chapter 17

Zap hung his head, but Jawan looked embarrassed as millions of quanta orbited the bosons escorting them to the dungeon.

"It's the Big One."

"You see, even Nano has appointed him an honor guard."

"The Big One is worthy."

"To be praised."

Honor guard? Zap snuck a peek at the nine beefy bosons surrounding him and Jawan. They had to be kidding. But quanta didn't kid. They were seriously in awe of Jawan, their one-time savior, whom they believed had come to save them again from some unknown danger.

The orbits of the quanta grew smaller and smaller like a noose tightening around Zap's neck. Protons, neutrons, and electrons—all types of fermions—zoomed in and out for a closer look, a touch. It made Zap sick. He was just a disciple of the Big One—the big nothing who'd gotten him into the mess in the first place.

"Make way! Make way!" Their boson escort pushed the quanta back.

The orbits of quanta widened, but they stayed with Zap's group.

"Where are you taking the Big One?" the quanta asked. "We thought you'd be going to see the queen, but you're headed the wrong way."

The boson leader snarled. "Queen Quanta doesn't want to see this irregular urchin. We're taking him to the dungeon."

"To the dungeon?"

"The Big One has come to free some poor particles wrongly imprisoned."

"Isn't he wonderful to stir himself for the least of us?"

Even the bosons shook their heads in disbelief. Zap sucked his teeth. Why doesn't Jawan rally all those quanta to help them? If they all banned together, a million quanta should be able to overpower nine measly bosons. But Jawan looked so embarrassed by all the attention he was getting, there was no way he was thinking about using that attention to help them. And the bosons exuded pure power. Even if the quanta had power, the bosons were power. Zap saw no hope.

The dungeon loomed before them—dark and foreboding. The trapped quarks that made up its walls attested to the hopeless state of anyone trapped inside. Zap knew that once he entered, there was no way he was coming out—not if it depended on Nano. Jawan had been in there before and come out. Lucky Jawan—the Big One. And he'd had help, which they didn't have this time. They weren't coming out.

The bosons push them into a cell. "Make yourselves comfortable. You'll be here for a while."

"A long while, boys."

The boson leader shook his head. "There's no such particle as a boy. Not in the Quantum Realm—not anywhere." He slammed the cell door with an ominous clank.

Make himself comfortable? Millions of eyes gazed at him piteously. And they wanted him to get comfortable? So, bosons could joke if fermions couldn't.

"You take the cot," Jawan said. "I can't sleep. I'll just dream some crazy dream."

Like Zap could sleep? What else was there to do? Sleep away the rest of his life? Wake up to eat. Did Nano even know they had to eat? Was there even any food in Nanosia? Zap lay down and closed his eyes. His mind drifted into a state of semiconsciousness that might have been sleep.

He's sitting in his master's laboratory poring over a tome about a world where there is no water. Lacus tugs his arm, trying to get him to go to the pond. "No, I don't want to go. We can't go there. Something terrible will happen there. Something . . ."

The tugging gets harder, more insistent. Lacus fades out, but the tugging continues.

Zap felt himself being yanked out of his dream and cast onto the floor. "Jawan, what are you doing? You told me I could have the cot. If you want it back, just ask. Don't . . ."

"Silence!" a venomous voice hissed. It wasn't Jawan. Zap opened his eyes and wished he hadn't.

"I am Turbatius, and you are mine."

Jawan cowered against the wall as if he wanted to fade into it and hide among the quarks.

To Zap's horror, Turbatius focused on him. "Why Vordon would send such a sorry excuse for a spy, I don't know, but it doesn't matter. You're mine now, and I will get the truth out of you."

"Truth?" Zap stammered. "Vordon? Who is that?"

"Don't be foolish enough to pretend he didn't send you. Do you think I am a fool?" He slammed Zap against the wall. "Just remember, I am a dangerous fool. Don't play with me."

"We won't," Zap assured him.

"I know you won't. But I will play with you until you tell me what Vordon is up to."

Zap gulped with terror as Turbatius dragged him and Jawan out of the cell.

As they passed the door of the next cell, a voice pleaded with them, "Don't leave me."

Nobody would want to be left in this dungeon. But Zap wasn't sure having Turbatius come for you was what he'd call being rescued.

Turbatius sneered. "This place is full—perhaps another spy. I must see to him."

"I'm not a spy."

"Silence!" Turbatius glared at his newest victim. "Who are you?"

"I am Muto."

"A transformer. I could use you. But if I take you from this place, you must obey me."

Why didn't he think he could use Zap and take him out of there? And Jawan. He'd been so scared, he'd almost forgotten about Jawan. Maybe the two of them could make themselves useful to Turbatius and he'd forget all that nonsense about a spy. They didn't even know who Vordon was.

"Anything you say."

That's the way , Zap thought. Whatever Turbatius said. He thought about his father. Fear will keep you alive. That wasn't cowardice. That was just staying alive.

Without touching it, Turbatius swung the door open with sheer power, and Muto walked out.

"Goodbye, Muto!" Even the quarks liked this person, so he couldn't be bad.

Muto looked like a boson, but he was smaller, weaker than Nano's bosons. And Zap had never seen just one of them. There were always nine—one-billionth.

Zap never got used to the magic of Nanosia that made roads just appear before you and take you wherever you wanted to go. He guessed they were like portals, which he didn't like either.

Muto looked wistfully toward the Quantum Realm, which angered Turbatius. "So, you love the order they keep there."

"I hate it. I want to destroy it. I will destroy it."

"Yes, we will. But you, little weak force, must stay with me, and together, we will do away with everything that Nano holds dear."

Nano was no friend, but if Turbatius didn't like him either, Zap didn't know what to think. His enemy's enemy wasn't his friend. But maybe he could use this all-around hostility to stay alive. He abandoned even that little hope when he saw the darkness at the end of the road they traveled. The Realm of Chaos. His heart pounded with terror. "Please, let's go back."

"Back where?" Turbatius scowled. "To the dungeon? To Nano, who put you in the dungeon?"

Back where? Not back to Nano, who would just make the whole thing start all over again, and he'd end up with Turbatius in the Realm of Chaos anyway. Back to Hadley Town, trapped in Loby's castle, unable to go out in the storm? Back where? He looked toward the Realm of Chaos and shuddered with sheer hopelessness.

Muto was just overjoyed. "We're going to the Realm of Chaos—a wonderful place where anything can happen."

Zap sighed. Muto definitely was not going to be an ally.

Jawan shuddered, too. "Well, we wanted to go to the Realm of Chaos, but not as prisoners. Still, maybe we could look around and find out what's causing all the rain."

Zap didn't see what good that would do if they couldn't escape and go home. He glanced at Turbatius and knew they'd never escape. "I never wanted to be here anyway."

But Muto overheard him. "You're scared of the Realm of Chaos? Turbo, they're scared of the Realm of Chaos."

"What did you call me?"

"Turb . . ."

Turbatius lashed out with power, and Muto went flying through the air. "You will show respect. I don't care if they're afraid of my realm. That's where they're going."

Chapter 18

Amaki ran as fast as she could. If Nano had the gall to put the Big One in the dungeon, he might put her in there, too. She had to get away from him. That meant getting away from his bosons. They were pure energy and could jump out right in front of her even as she ran away from them.

Everywhere she looked—everywhere she ran—lambda orbited or just flitted about in no particular order. Muto had been busy. Amaki shuddered thinking of what Nano would do to her creator now that they'd caught him. Muto may be mischievous, but he hadn't truly meant to harm her. While Nano tried to put her in the dungeon. So who was most dangerous? Nano would do something. No way would he allow the Quantum Realm to fall into such disorder.

She made her way to the dungeon, not sure how she'd help the Big One, and maybe Muto was in there, too. But she had to do something. She had to see if there was anything she could do to make the Big One more comfortable, if not free. Though she wanted him to be free.

"Let him go!"

"Let the Big One go!"

"When you put the Big One in the dungeon, you put us in there, too."

Millions of quanta gathered around the dungeon protesting the arrest of the Big One. But the bosons fell in among them, arresting many.

"Break it up!"

"Break it up!"

"Get back into your orbits!"

More bosons arrived. Amaki thought they were reinforcements, but they were half dragging, half pushing Muto toward the dungeon. He was a boson, too, but W bosons carried a weak force while Nano's bosons were strong. Saving the Big One was impossible enough. Adding Muto to her geas made it downright hopeless. And it was a geas. No way could she get one out and leave the other.

She moved closer to a group of quanta who'd been there before her. "Did they say what they'll do to the Big One?"

"Leave him in there until he rots."

"Or we get him out."

"Say, aren't you that lambda that Nano rejected." One of the quanta looked at her too intently.

"No, they all look alike," another quantum said.

"I tell you, that's her."

Amaki backed away and hid behind the nearest cloud. It turned out to be a cloud of protons. With her charmed quark, this was a bad hiding place, but it was the first thing she could find. At least the bosons might not detect her charmed quark from such a distance.

"Release him!"

"Amnesty for the Big One!"

"Annihilation for the infidels!"

Amaki teetered on the brink of despair. The quanta kept protesting, and the bosons kept arresting them. They weren't helping the Big One, so why didn't they just all go away? Maybe she could sneak in if they all just went away.

The cloud of protons started moving closer to the dungeon entrance. She moved with them but knew she could only move so close, then she'd have to jump to another cloud before the bosons saw her.

"You're not a proton." One of the protons glared at her.

"No, but I . . ."

"Where's your down quark? You have to have one if you want to hang around with us."

She couldn't tell them she was a lambda. They might forget about the Big One and march her straight to Nano.

She looked around and saw a cloud of lambda far away. She'd have to cross an empty space where she could be seen by any quanta or boson looking that way. She held her breath, looked around, and made the crossing.

The lambda surrounded her.

"What were you doing with those protons?"

"Did Muto create you from a proton? You know you'll never be a proton again, and they'll never accept you no matter what you used to be."

"You know Muto?" Some of the lambda had a charm quark like hers. But some had a strange quark. Charming or strange, they were her own people. She belonged with them. They'd never send her away. "I wasn't trying to be a proton again. I was just trying to hide from the bosons."

"Well, hide with us."

"You see what they did to Muto. They'll do the same to us."

"We can't protect you if they attack us, but at least we'll be together."

At least? Everything was at least . But for now, it was the most she could get.

The bosons weren't letting anyone near the dungeon, and one by one—cloud by cloud— the quanta drifted away. Amaki and her lambda family moved in orbits so the bosons wouldn't pay them any attention. After making sure all the quanta were in their proper trajectories, the bosons went away, too. Going back to see what Nano wanted them to do, Amaki supposed.

A charmed lambda flashed her a brilliant smile as he passed by in his orbit. Moving around in an endless circle was what quanta did. And yet, it seemed unnatural to Amaki. It was a waste of time. And she couldn't waste time while the Big One languished in Nano's dungeon.

"Where are you going?" the lambda asked.

They weren't going to let her just slip away. "I want to see what I can do for the Big One."

"And Muto. Don't forget Muto."

"We owe him our existence."

"Maybe we can help you."

She shook her head. "No, if a bunch of us go, we'll just attract the bosons. I'll figure something out." Though she had no idea what.

"What's that?"

Amaki turned to see what the lambda was pointing at. Moving toward the dungeon was a massive something. It exuded energy, but it was unlike any boson she'd ever seen.

"That's the spirit of disorder."

The lambda drew back in horror as the spirit entered the dungeon. Soon the spirit emerged with Muto, the Big One, and his disciple.

"What will happen to them?" she asked.

"If we knew, we might wish we didn't know."

"They're headed for the Realm of Chaos. They're going to die."

She turned to the lambda. "Forget about the bosons. We have to go help the Big One and Muto. Who'd going with me?"

None of the lambda came forward. If anything, they moved back. "We're not going anywhere near the Realm of Chaos. There's nothing but darkness there, and anything could happen."

Amaki looked around hoping for some brave particle to come with her. But no one did. So, she turned and went after the Big One on her own.

Chapter 19

They entered the Realm of Chaos and were immediately surrounded by a swarm of particles. No protons or neutrons—just loose particles flitting here and there with no thought of orbiting anything. And yet their dance created a symmetry—a symmetry of chaos—a chaotic symmetry. It terrified Zap because whatever it was, it was chaos, and anything could happen.

Jawan looked awestruck. "I forgot how beautiful this can be."

Muto chortled. "This one likes it." He slapped Jawan hard on the back and petted one of the particles that alighted on his shoulder. "Lovely darlings you have here, Turbatius."

Zap's eyebrows rose in disbelief. "You're crazy."

"Fools!" Turbatius turned on them. "I didn't bring you here to play." He looked pointedly at Zap. "And I know Vordon didn't send you here to play. Whatever he thinks he's doing doesn't matter. You're under my mercy, and I have no mercy. You will tell me what he's trying to do, or you will die."

Fear > , Zap thought. Fear would keep him alive. "But I never heard of Vordon."

"Liar! I saw you there when Vordon brought the storm. How could you have survived if you weren't a part of it?"

He seized Zap and gestured for Muto to follow him. "Come and see what I do to liars. See how I get the information I want."

Zap thought he'd grab Jawan, too, but Jawan wasn't there in the storm, so Turbatius had no need of him. Zap didn't know if that was good or bad for Jawan. Particles swarmed around Jawan as Turbatius dragged Zap away, and Muto followed them to the castle.

This castle was an exact replica of the castle the late Antipan had in Hadley Town, where he had been known as Lord Elveston. So, Zap knew where Turbatius was taking him. Turbatius entered the castle's laboratory and dropped him on the floor. When Turbatius turned to get the fire cubes, that might have been a good time to run, but Zap looked up at Muto and didn't move.

"Why are you looking at me, boy thing? I'm not here to help you. I'm here to enjoy myself. That's a good enough reason to be anywhere."

Turbatius came back with a fire cube in each hand. "Are your lips still sealed?"

Zap knew he had to speak—to say something. But he didn't know what to say. Who was Vordon? Zap wanted to open his mouth, but he couldn't take his eyes off the fire cubes as they seared his chest. He opened his mouth then—to scream. Muto laughed.

"Vordon is my greatest masterpiece, but I didn't know he was worth suffering for—dying for. Tell me why he sent you here." Turbatius plunged the fire cubes into Zap's shoulders.

Fear will keep you alive. Tell him something—anything. "Vordon sent me here to make sure you weren't planning to hurt him." That was so lame. Turbatius wasn't such a fool to go for that.

And he didn't. "Will you insult me with a lie like that?" Outraged, the spirit that was Turbatius filled the laboratory and slammed the fire cubes into zap over and over—his chest, his back, his forehead, his arms. Zap had never known it was possible to feel this much pain. And for his mind, it wasn't. He fell into unconsciousness.

It seemed like he'd only blinked before shocking sensations jolted him off the floor.

Turbatius pulled him close until he was face-to-face with the spirit of disorder. Zap didn't know which was worse, the fire cubes or the horror inspired by Turbatius chaotic visage.

"I can hurt you in your sleep. I can do things to your body that will last long after the pain is gone. Is Vordon really worth it? I think not."

Fear will keep you alive > . That had to be true. That was his only hope. "Vordon is planning to take over the Realm of Chaos for himself. He's going to use the storm. He didn't tell me how. But the monsters in the storm will obey him. That's why I didn't want to tell you. I was afraid of the monsters." Was that enough detail to make Turbatius believe him? Poor Vordon. Had Zap just condemned an innocent man? Poor Vordon? > Hmph. Poor Zap. This lie might end the pain only to bring something worse.

Muto had cowered into a corner when Turbatius's wrath filled the laboratory, but now he grinned. "Guess you know what you're doing. They always play innocent until you apply a little pain." He sneered in Zap's face. "A little pain to loosen the lips, eh, boy."

"Silence!" Turbatius snarled. He was satisfied but not appeased. If anything, he was angrier than ever.

He glanced at a tank in the corner and smiled at Zap thoughtfully. Zap didn't think it was good when Turbatius smiled, and whatever the spirit was thinking about couldn't be good. Turbatius picked Zap up and put him in the tank. "Watch closely, Muto and see what happens to those who plot against the spirit of disorder." He turned a valve, and the tank began to fill with water.

Zap watched in horror as water covered his feet and ankles. He cast around desperately, but the sheer glass walls of the tank offered nothing to climb on.

"Our boy is afraid of water. It's his own element, but it terrifies him as much as the Realm of Chaos."

The tank filled slowly—covering Zap's waist and chest. He pounded on the glass with his fists. "Don't leave me in here. Please!"

Turbatius and Muto waved goodbye and left.

Zap pounded on the glass again, but his little fists couldn't break it. The water rose above his chin, and he panicked.

"Brother, brother, now you know. Wish I could save you." Ziph floated in the inches of space between the water and the top of the tank.

Water soon filled even that space. Zap saw no point in holding his breath. He had already drowned. His body's instinctive need to breathe drew water into his lungs. He didn't feel his unconscious body bump against the top of the tank as he drowned.

Chapter 20

In the rain drenched forest, Vordon surveyed his sorry lot. How could his master, his creator, have left him so miserable? Vordon had tried to do what he asked. Turbatius wanted Vordon to summon all the furies, but Alecto was about to kill him all by herself. No way was he going to bring them all to torture him.

"You are the fool who summoned me to beat on stone walls." Alecto screeched through the storm raging above Vordon's head. "I exist to punish men, not stones. You are a man, and I will punish you. Don't think you can hide in the forest."

Vordon flinched as winds of fury uprooted the trees around him. Alecto laughed. The wind laughed. It came at him with bat's wings and lightning eyes. He ran. "You can't escape me, little man."

She was right. She was everywhere. Laughing, howling. As inescapable as the wind. Bat wings buffeted his face, covering his mouth and nose so he couldn't breathe. He had to breathe. He had to escape. He ran from tree to tree. She uprooted each one before he touched it. The wind had it in for him. Was chasing him. Knew him by name and hated him.

What was he thinking? The wind was just the wind. It knew nothing. But there was something in this wind, and Alecto would drive him mad if he didn't find shelter.

Through the rain and mist, he barely made out the silhouette of a castle. It wasn't the earth mage's castle but one of the other cursed elemental mages. If he could make it to the castle. He ran toward it.

"No! you will not find safety in stone walls."

Rain and wind beat him back toward the forest. He fell to the ground out of the wind and pulled himself toward the castle by grasping at grass. The grass was underwater and slick, but he pulled. Slipping and pulling, he inched his way under the storm—under Alecto.

"Where did you go? I will find you, little man."

Just as he had known so many things, Vordon knew the mud in the water hid him from her. Earth was the opposite element of wind, and as long as the mud covered him, she couldn't see him.

He reached the stone foundation of the castle where there was no grass to pull himself forward. He rolled onto the stone and lay gasping. Alecto raged around, looking for him. As rain washed the mud from his body, she saw him and screeched. "You will not get away! You are mine!"

Wind knocked him to his knees again, but it pushed him against the portcullis. It began to rise, and a hand pulled him into the castle.

A man guided him down the corridors of the castle. "What were you doing out there? You're soaked."

"I was trying to get in here."

As they moved deeper into the castle, Vordon felt the madness of Alecto ebb away. They turned a corner and entered some sort of laboratory. The man sat Vordon down at a long wooden table running down the center of the laboratory. Vordon sneezed.

A woman Vordon hadn't seen at first rose and headed toward the door. "We'd better get you some dry clothes before you catch cold."

Vordon pulled off his sodden boots and laid his head on the table, exhausted.

"Why did you want to come to the fire mage's castle?" the man asked.

"Is that what this is?" Vordon thought for a minute. Maybe he could get through to the fire mage what he couldn't get through to the earth mage. Fire was more open to change. Then the fire mage could persuade the others. Kill five birds with one strategically tossed stone. "Where is the fire mage? I'd like to speak to him."

"At your service. I'm Loby. This is my wife, and this is my castle." A young man, who looked to have just come into being a man, pointed to an obviously pregnant woman then swept his arm about as if to take in the entire castle.

Loby

. With a name like that and a pregnant wife to boot, the fire mage couldn't be as closed-minded as the great Myrlo. But a man doesn't choose his name like he chooses his actions. Vordon noticed the instruments of fire magic. Loby was young, but Vordon didn't think he'd gotten his position as fire mage by being a fool. Vordon would have to be subtle, keep his eyes open, and wait for the right moment. And when that moment came, the magic of the elements would be spread abroad just like they'd been in Zelfor.

He was finished with Turbatius and his madness. Zelfor wasn't about chaos and disorder. It was about freedom and joy. Vordon could only hope that Turbatius was finished with him.

The woman shook her head. "You must be freezing cold." She went through a door and emerged carrying what looked like blocks of fire held away from her body with tongs.

Loby grasped her arm. "What are you doing with those? My fire cubes aren't something to dabble with."

"I'm not dabbling. I'm just doing what any decent human being would do. Something that wizards apparently don't think to do." She dragged a large stone basin from under the table and filled it with water and set it near Vordon's feet. Then she placed the fire cubes around the basin. "Take off your shoes and put your feet in the water to warm them."

Vordon did as he was told, but Loby did not look happy. Jealous? The woman was lovely, and her condition didn't hide her voluptuous curves. Vordon knew he'd have to be careful. He just hoped the woman wouldn't go so far as to massage his feet. Loby's unhappy look might escalate into violence. At the same time, Vordon didn't think he'd be the unhappy one if she did.

To Vordon's relief, the woman left him to tend to his own feet. She placed a mug of hot cocoa on the table in front of him. "You'll want to get out of those wet clothes." With that, she left the laboratory.

Vordon's feet grew warm and cozy. He sat back and closed his eyes.

"So you like the tender loving care of women. Well, don't get used to it. That one is taken. You'd have to be blind not to notice that."

"I wasn't thinking about . . ." vordon looked up as another lovely one entered the laboratory.

"Prenda had to lie down and rest, she's doing way to much for a woman about to burst." She dumped a bundle of clothes on the table. "So, you're what blew in with the rain. Well, I'm Cintella, and these are for you."

"Cintella?" Vordon didn't know how he knew, but that name harked from Zelfor. Maybe he read it in the library, or maybe it was one of those things that he just knew.

Loby rolled his eyes. "Don't mess with her. She's the spirit mage's apprentice and the earth journeyman's girl. Not to be messed with."

"I wasn't planning to mess with her."

"Just so you know."

No, he wasn't going to

mess

with someone named Cintella. But he'd find out everything he could about the lass. Maybe she knew where she'd come from and would provide the opening Vordon needed. He looked into her eyes and knew at once. Zelfor!

"You can go into this room to change." Cintella handed him a towel and directed him into a side room.

He changed quickly and emerged, eager to get to the bottom of this mystery. He confronted Cintella immediately with what he suspected. "You descended from the queen of the ravaged land of Zelfor."

Cintella stepped back—puzzled. "I don't know what you're talking about. I never heard of such a place." But she looked unsure, as if she'd recognized something in the name.

"The place where we stand now—in fact, all of Romatica—was once known as Zelfor. It was a great kingdom with its own kings and queens."

"Where we stand now?" Loby stared doubtfully at Vordon. "Looks like I would have heard of such a legend."

Cintella pursed her lips. "I remember when I was a child my grandmother used to tell me that we descended from a royal family. But it was in a land so far away that it wasn't even on any map the Romaticans have."

Vordon shook with glee. This was what he'd been waiting for. Now if he could just move them forward. "There's more than one way to be far away. Was it far away in space or in time? Of course, it wouldn't be on any of the maps Romaticans drew. They don't want anyone to remember. Especially not people like you, Cintella."

Loby shook his head. "I don't know. It sounds too convoluted for credibility."

But Cintella—darling queen Cintella—disagreed. "Maybe not. Maybe there's something to this. This could answer some questions."

Chapter 21

Particles danced around Turbatius and Muto as they emerged from the castle.

"Did we do well, lord?"

"Are you pleased, lord?"

"Did we make you happy, lord?"

Lord

. Turbatius turned the moniker over in his mind and liked it.

The lord of the Realm of Chaos

. Something the realm has needed for a long time. "Yes, you did well. I am well pleased with you."

They'd kept an eye on Nano, his enemy, and uncovered Vordon's treachery. Now because he trusted Vordon, the hapless boy would soon be dead. Nanosia didn't need a boy. Where was the other boy? It didn't matter. If he hadn't the sense to leave the Realm of Chaos, he'd soon be dead, too. "But you must go back and keep an eye on our friend Nano—make sure he doesn't do anything unfriendly. I have business in another place, but I'll be back soon."

"Oh, lord, can we go?"

"Not this time. The business I have isn't pleasant."

At least it wouldn't be pleasant for Vordon. Turbatius turned to Muto. He must show the W boson what he did with traitors. Too bad Muto wasn't a spirit, or they could both close their eyes to menace Vordon. "We cannot get where we must go from here. The portals don't work in the Realm of Chaos, so we must go out into Nanosia."

"Back to the Quantum Realm?" Muto's eyes gleamed with anticipation. "So, we will kill Nano."

The enemy of my enemy . . . sometimes Turbatius wasn't sure, but he liked Muto's attitude. "I don't know if Nano can be killed. But he can be destroyed. Today, though, I have other quarry."

They left the Realm of Chaos and walked away in the mist of Nanosia.

"Here." Turbatius stopped in front of a hole in the mist. "Brace yourself. This will take some getting used to, and it's possible that you never will."

With that he took Muto's hand and pulled him into the portal to Hadley Town. Apparently, Muto hadn't braced himself, or he had but it did no good. When they came out on the other side, Muto fell to the ground and retched.

Turbatius cocked an eyebrow at the sight. Muto was round. He couldn't be mistaken for a human. But he had appendages that served the purposes of a head, arms, and legs. "I hadn't known quanta could do that."

"I hadn't known either. I've never done it before. I never felt torn apart and put back together like that either." Muto kept his head lowered as if he planned to stay there on the ground for a while.

"Get up. I don't have time for foolishness." And really, he didn't. Already he could feel the physical world ebbing away his strength. He glared at Muto. But for wanting to teach that fool a lesson, Turbatius could have just come in the spirit and done away with Vordon now that the furies were in place, then he wouldn't feel their chilling bite. But his flesh felt it. There was no help for it. The spies had just been tools. It was Vordon who sent them, and Turbatius had no use for traitors who sent spies. He'd take only a moment to kill Vordon and then return to Nanosia, the world where he was strong.

Alecto still raged in her storm, flying about looking for some miscreant to punish. But where were her sisters? Where were Megaera and Tisiphone? If Vordon hadn't summoned them as commanded, Turbatius had no more use for him.

For a while, Turbatius could ignore the wind and the cold rain. But Muto shivered and held himself as if his freezing arms could keep his body warm. Turbatius knew if he stayed in this world too long, he, too, would feel the cold. He tsked in disdain. He'd just have to suffer until this business was done.

They approached the castle where Vordon was hiding and slipped through the bars of the portcullis. A familiar voice drifted down one of the corridors, and Turbatius stiffened with rage.

Turbatius boiled with anger at the sight of Vordon sitting in some sort of laboratory reading a book to humans.

Does he feel so comfortable in his deceit? We shall see!

"You!"

The three humans jumped back. One had enough sense to flee—not that that would do her any good if she were the object of his wrath.

103

Vordon just stared at his creator—surprised but not yet comprehending the trouble he was in. "Master?"

Turbatius sneered. "There's no point playing innocent with me. Did you think I wouldn't come for you? Did you think you could plant a spy in my world, and I wouldn't discover it?"

"Spy?"

Turbatius had had enough. He picked Vordon up and dashed him against the side counter. Something broke, but Turbatius didn't care what it was.

"I sent no spies, master. Believe me. I did not."

Vordon cowered against the wall, still clutching the stupid book in front of him as if it were a shield. That was the book he was reading to the humans. Turbatius would find out what could be so important to Vordon. Despite his protestations of innocence, this book held proof of his treachery.

"What is that book you're holding?" Turbatius snatched the book from him. "

The Last Days of Zelfor.

How did you find out about Zelfor, and why is it so important to you that you would betray your creator?"

Vordon shook his head. "I didn't betray you. I would never. But Zelfor is the kingdom of my ancestors. It holds the secret of magic—of my magic. It's the reason I agreed to help you."

The man had found the secret of his creation. Maybe he didn't know everything, but he knew enough to find out the rest. Not that Turbatius would let him live that long. Vordon had already done enough to warrant death. "The secret of your magic lies in me, not in any book. You help me because I created you—not too long ago, in fact. So, how can you have ancestors?" The man had become like his master. He knew that there was more to him than Turbatius had told him. He knew about Zelfor, but did he know Turbatius created him not out of thin air but from the spirits of Zelfor that were already here—from the soul of a Zelforean man? How much did he know? He knew too much. His curiosity would make him useless in Turbatius's plans. He already thought he could make his own plans. "Tell me one good reason why I should not destroy you where you lie?"

"You need me. That's why you created me."

"Idiot!" The man saw his weakness. He had to destroy him before Muto saw it as well.

Turbatius lunged for him.

"In here." One of the other humans opened a side door for Vordon.

But in his present form, Turbatius was not as fast or as strong as a spirit should be, and Vordon slipped through the door with the human before Turbatius could reach him.

Muto chortled. "Looks like he got away."

Muto must never see his weakness. "You are getting close to making a pest of yourself."

"Oh no, I just meant . . ."

Turbatius didn't wait to hear his nonsense. He yanked open the door where Vordon had disappeared and dashed in after him. A blast of heat knocked Muto back, but Turbatius plunged into it just as Vordon and the human disappeared around a bend at the bottom of the pit. Turbatius raced after them. He had to pause when he reached the bottom of the stairs where his momentum almost drove him into a wall of fire.

He turned but didn't see them. It didn't matter. Unless they were stupid enough to plunge into the fire, they had to go straight. And he would catch them. With Muto scampering after him, Turbatius flew down a long passage after his quarry.

A door at the end of the passage left them outside the castle in a copse of trees.

"Stay where you are." Turbatius couldn't allow Muto to see him catch his breath.

This must not be seen as a failure to catch his enemy, but the physical world was telling on him. Icy wind and freezing rain vexed him more than it ever had. He wouldn't be able to withstand this for long.

Muto passed under the trap door of the passage. "Are you all right?"

"Yes, I am always all right, but I want you to stay there for a moment."

"It's cold down here."

"If I have to come down there, I will take you back to the fire pit and make you beg for cold."

Muto wisely kept his tongue, but another voice rang through the wind. It was the wind.

"You are nothing." Mocking faces flittered through the air.

Turbatius closed the trap door, so Muto couldn't see or hear Alecto. "I am the spirit of disorder and lord of the Realm of Chaos."

Laughter like the wind rattled the trees. "Chaos is not disorder. You see the wild dance of particles in the Realm of Chaos and think it's random. It only looks that way to you. The pattern in chaos is so intricate, it is beyond your simple linear comprehension."

Was the wind now questioning the intelligence of spirit? "There is no pattern in the Realm of Chaos. That's why they call it chaos."

"You betray your ignorance. The dance of chaos follows initial conditions that are varied and innumerable. Any little thing can change these conditions—even the flapping of a butterfly wing."

Turbatius recalled the particles of the Realm of Chaos. Their movements did seem to have the symmetry of a dance. But if that were so, then it wasn't disorder. No! She had to be wrong. He only thought he saw symmetry because he looked for it. "If there was no disorder in the Realm of Chaos, then where?"

"You've never been to my home."

"No, I've never been to the underworld. And even I would rather not go there."

"Why not? You won't find more disorder than in Tartarus. You call yourself the spirit of disorder, then you should go there. You should live there."

He'd never heard of such a place. It wasn't in Nanosia or on earth. But if he destroyed the dance in the Realm of Chaos—destroyed order in the Quantum Realm, then all would be Tartarus. He felt a surge of strength against the pull of the physical world. There'd be no physical world—no difference between here and there. He'd be in his element in every place. An omnipresent lord of all.

"Come to Tartarus! Come to Tartarus!" the wind howled.

But Turbatius knew what he had to do. He opened the door to let Muto out and started to walk away.

"You know where they went? Did that monster wind tell you?"

"Forget Vordon for now. I have business in Nanosia."

"Aren't you going to punish him after what he did? Getting soft, are you?"

Turbatius threw Muto to the top of a tree, where he fell until he hit a branch that could support his weight. "Never think that."

Turbatius continued walking and left Muto to find his own way out of the tree. "Vordon is by no means forgiven, but he will keep. I have a greater task."

Covered with scrapes and scratches, Muto finally caught up to him and they went through the portal. This weakened Turbatius more. He'd returned just in time, but Muto didn't need to know that. He debated whether to dismiss the little W boson so he wouldn't see his weakness or keep him on hand as an important part of his plans.

As they entered the Realm of Chaos, his strength returned. His darling particles swarmed around him, and he saw that Alecto was right. They never collided or made a move that wasn't beautiful and complete. All of Chaos was one grand choreography.

Muto clapped his hands with glee as a string of particles formed a pink, purple, and blue rainbow that undulated across the sky then exploded in a brilliant cascade. "Now this is what I'm talking about. Particles are spectacular when not tied down by strict regulations."

"I will not have this in my kingdom!"

Muto kissed at particles taking turns alighting on his shoulders and didn't notice Turbatius's anger.

"There will be no more dancing in my kingdom." Turbatius's voice dripped with such menace that all of the Realm of Chaos seemed to stop and take notice.

"Is our lord unhappy?"

"We've displeased him."

"Yes, you have. I want disorder. You have given me order hidden in intricacy. There will be no more dancing in the Realm of Chaos. I am your king, and you will serve me."

"No more dancing?"

"But the whole universe dances."

"Our dance is only a part of that."

"We can't stop."

Turbatius raised himself until his spirit filled all Chaos. "You will stop. You will move only to carry out my will. And my will is to fill all Nanosia with disorder."

"Then you cannot be our lord."

"You're asking the impossible."

"Nothing is impossible for the spirit of disorder." And the spirit seized all the particles in the Realm of Chaos and locked them in his castle.

"What are you doing?" Muto ran from particle to particle trying to save them.

"Are you questioning what I do?"

Muto stepped back. "N-no, of course not."

"This is my kingdom, and I will have my way. I have a task for you, and you will do it."

"Anything you say."

"You will go back to the Quantum Realm, and you will intercept every proton and neutron before it reaches Nano and use your power to convert it into something Nano can't send through the nanotube to Atomidon." In case the little W boson thought he could get out of the Realm of Chaos and do what he wanted, Turbatius added, "You will do this, or I will convert you into oblivion."

Chapter 22

Zap felt a pressure pulling him out of darkness. His eyes fluttered open, and he knew he was in a different place—though different from what, he didn't know. A face loomed over him. It took him a moment to realize it was Jawan, who lowered his mouth onto Zap's, sucking water out of his lungs and pumping his chest. "Sssss!"

"What's the matter? Oh, you're burned." Jawan moved his hand, trying to find a place on Zap's chest where he wasn't burned.

But Zap hurt all over. His mind was foggy. He didn't know why he was hurting.

Burned?

He'd been burned? The place wasn't Hadley Town. It was . . . then he remembered. Turbatius, the water tank, the dungeon, the Realm of Chaos.

He grasped Jawan's arm. "Jawan, we've got to get out of here."

"But we're where we wanted to be. We can find out what's causing the storms in our world. Then we can go home."

Zap cast around him—searching the darkened corners for dangers. "How? Turbatius isn't going to let us out of here. How did you even get in here?"

"Turbatius and his W boson sidekick left the Realm of Chaos. I don't know where they went, but if we're quick, we can look around and be gone."

"You don't know where they went or how soon they'll be back, but we probably don't want to be here when they get back. So let's go."

"We have to find out about the rain. That's why we came here."

"That's why you dragged me here. If the storms came from the Realm of Chaos, and Turbatius is in charge here, then he must have caused them. That's all we need to know. We can't do anything to stop him, so let's go already before he gets back."

Jawan sighed. He didn't want to be here when Turbatius got back any more than Zap did. He stood up. "We have to go back, but to tell you the truth, I'm not sure I know how."

Zap blanched. "You brought me here and don't even know how to get back?"

"I can help you."

Zap stared at the strangest particle he'd ever seen. He couldn't say what it was about it, but it was surely something that Nano would think was irregular. "Who are you?"

"Oh, sorry," Jawan said. "Zap, this is Amaki. She followed us when Nano threw the Big One in the dungeon."

"She's a . . ."

"Lambda. I'm a lambda, and you are hurt."

"I'm all right." Though he didn't feel all right. He just didn't know what getting tender loving care from a lambda would feel like.

Amaki smiled like she didn't believe him but wasn't going to say anything. "Well, I'm going to help you get out of here."

"Why?" Zap looked at Jawan.

"Jawan is the Big One, and he tells me you came from the Big World."

"If only you could come to Hadley Town, too," Jawan said. "If you stay in Nanosia, Nano will catch you sooner or later, and you'll wind up in a dungeon yourself."

"But in Hadley Town she'd be as small as . . ." Zap started to protest.

"Maybe not." Jawan rose to his feet and pulled Zap up. "We shrank to her size when we came to Nanosia, so maybe she'll grow to our size when she comes to Hadley Town. Anyway, we have to go."

But Amaki shook her head. "No, Nanosia is my home. There may be things worse than Nano in the Big World. I'll help you get back to your world. But at least here, I know what to look out for."

Zap squeezed his eyes shut. Every move tore at his burned skin. Eerie silence met him when they left the castle. He'd braced himself for Turbatius's particles to stop them even if Turbatius himself was gone. But no particles intercepted their progress as they marched out of the gates of the Realm of Chaos.

"Right here. This is the portal." Amaki stopped before a spot in the mist that Zap would have walked right by.

Zap balked. "Portal. I really don't want to go through that again."

"Then stay here," Jawan said. "Maybe Turbatius will let you sleep in one of the bedrooms in his castle tonight. And who knows. He may have a secret, so you'll never have to go through a portal again in your life."

Zap pushed past Jawan and Amaki and entered the portal. Fear might keep you alive, but you had to choose what to be afraid of.

***

"Jawan!" Cintella hugged Jawan like he'd been gone a million years, and she thought he'd never come back. She looked up. "And Zap! What did they do to you?"

Prenda surveyed the charred marks on his clothes. She couldn't help but see the pain in his eyes, though he tried to act like it was nothing. To his utter dismay, she lifted his tunic to view his chest. "Why are you even walking around? You should be laid out in shock."

He pulled his shirt back down. "I'm all right. It's not as bad as it looks." Or as bad as it felt.

"Well, at least let me put some kind of salve on it."

Zap winced as if the very thought of being touched hurt. He was hoping the wounds he'd gotten in another world would stay in that world, but he was out of luck and had come back to Hadley Town burns and all.

She went upstairs and came back with a salve that was painful but cooling. "What did you do? You were gone so long."

Jawan shook his head. "We were detained by a couple of Nanosians who loved our company so much they didn't want to see us go."

Cintella sighed. "Sounds like you had as much trouble as we did. Wish I could've come with you."

Zap didn't think so, but he said nothing.

"What happened?" Jawan asked as he and Zap plopped down at the long wooden table running down the center of every castle laboratory he'd ever seen.

"We had a visitor from Nanosia. A spirit. It filled the whole laboratory demanding that our guest confess to sending Zap to spy on him."

"Guest?"

"Oh, a chap from Hadley Town came in to escape the storm. The spirit chased him and Loby into the fire pit. I hope they escaped."

Zap and Jawan blanched in unison. "Turbatius is in the fire pit!"

"How long ago was this?" Zap stared at the fire pit door. "I hope he didn't chase them into the fire. Maybe that's why they haven't come back yet. Turbatius wouldn't give up before he caught them."

"It has a name?" Cintella asked.

"Everything in Nanosia has a name. I mean everyone," Jawan said.

Zap pointedly turned away from the fire pit door as if looking would summon Turbatius.

As if Zap's mere thought of the spirit summoned him, the fire pit door creaked open.

***

Vordon wondered what Loby thought they were going to do. Was the man crazy putting them in this doomed position? Blazing fire in front of them, enraged spirit behind them, and treacherous stairs under their feet. Vordon had handled fire in a small quantity. But they were racing toward an inferno. Why had he followed Loby? He didn't know the man, and for all he knew, the man had a death wish and brought Vordon along so he wouldn't have to die alone.

At the bottom of the staircase, a passage veered off to the right, but Loby didn't turn. Instead, he headed straight for the fire. Vordon paused. The man was mad. Maybe as fire mage, Loby could withstand the flames. But Vordon only played with fire magic. He was no mage. He heard Turbatius descending after them and thought he was about to die.

Loby grabbed his arm and pulled him into a space hidden behind the fire. "Be careful. The fire spills over the lip of the pit, so you can't tell where the pit begins. Stay close, and be quiet."

Like Vordon could go anywhere. Flames licked at his toes, and he tried to back away, before realizing that he wasn't burning. He felt the heat, but it was a pleasant sensation. He turned and watched Turbatius speed down the other passage. The spirit would have caught them by now if they'd gone that way. Hidden behind the flames and smoke, they were safe for now—until Turbatius realized his mistake and came back even madder than before.

Vordon was so close to the fire. Without knowing why, he turned to face it and felt a strange attraction. He stretched out his hand to touch it.

112

"What are you doing?" Loby pulled Vordon's hand back. "That's real fire. Nothing to play with."

"Actually, I kind of like playing with fire." He reached out again and passed his hand through the flames. To his delight, it felt like he was passing his hand through a current of warm air. He stepped forward and buried his face in it.

Loby pulled him back and pushed him against the wall. "I don't know what you think you're doing, but there can be only one fire mage, and that's me."

Vordon blinked at the rage in Loby's eyes. It made no sense. "All right. I'm not trying to take your place. I just wanted to see what I can do. This is new to me."

"You can't take my place," Loby hissed. "Let's go."

Careful not to make a sound that Turbatius might hear, they crept back up to the laboratory only to see the boy he'd seen before in the forest dart under the table and Queen Cintella laugh her head off.

Prenda rushed to Loby and threw her arms around him. "Loby, don't scare me like that. Don't make me think our baby will be born fatherless."

Loby sighed and patted her arm. "It's all right. We got away from it."

When the boy picked himself up and sat at the table, Vordon got a good look at him and caught his breath. He'd seen that face before. It was his memory, and yet it was not his. Where had it come from?

Pond water dripping off the undine couldn't hide her tears from Havlo. He didn't want to see her cry. He'd feel bad, but he still had to do what he had to do, so he turned away. He couldn't help her. He had to get on with his life—he and his son. He'd take a wife and Savorne would die. That wasn't his fault. That was just the way things were. She wasn't even human. Close enough to human to give him a son. But still not human. His life was more important.

He had to hold his nose when he entered the relic of an orphanage in Hadley Town where the undines had left his son. It smelled like the caregivers had a once-a-week schedule for changing the children's clothing and sheets no matter how often they lost control of their bladders.

He found his son alone, swimming in a water hole. Havlo looked about, but there was no towel to dry him with. And no one watched him to see or care if he drowned. Havlo seethed with anger. But when he pulled the boy out of the hole, he was dry—naked but dry and not shivering from the cold that Havlo himself could feel.

This boy was special. The word magic popped into Havlo's head. He didn't believe in magic, but he knew this boy was special in some uncanny way. He deserved better than to grow up in filth and poverty.

Havlo took his son to Romatica, where he set up shop as a silversmith and married a beautiful—and very human—woman.

Tillian was beautiful outside. He thought she'd be beautiful inside, too. But she resented every moment that Havlo spent with his son. He dug a pond and filled it with spring water imported from a nearby mountain. If his boy loved water, he'd get the best.

Tillian hit the ceiling. "But you wouldn't build an indoor bath house for me."

"What's wrong with the public bath?"

"Oh!" She threw a skillet at him. "You spend more time with that boy than with me." Then she sank down at the kitchen table and cried. "I don't ask for much."

Actually, she did. But she was his wife, and he needed a wife to run a respectable shop. If he left her, it would cause a scandal, and no one would do business with him. So, he picked up the skillet and placed it back on the stove.

She bore him a son and their life together turned peaceful. Until their son got old enough to follow the boy into the pond.

"Why aren't you wet?" their son asked.

The boy shrugged. "I swim so fast, the water doesn't have time to make me wet." And he dove back into the pond, sat cross-legged on its very bottom, and blew bubbles to the surface.

The boy was collecting firewood for the smithy when their son decided he could do what his big brother did. He jumped into the pond and kicked his way to the bottom of the deepest part. He opened his mouth to blow bubbles, and water rushed in. When they heard the son's mother scream, Havlo and the boy ran to the pond, but they were too late.

"Help me!" They were the cries of a ghost that haunted Havlo's dreams every night.

"You drowned my son!" Tillian screamed.

"No, I tried to . . ."

"You hell-spawned bastard. My son was human and you're not. For that you drowned him!" Tillian dragged the boy to the pond and held his head under water. "You unnatural imp. Water won't drown you because your demon mother is keeping you alive."

Havlo grabbed Tillian to keep her from bashing the boy's head with a rock. "Woman, what are you doing to my son?"

"Your son. Not mine."

Yes, he was his son. Not just a boy but a boy with gifts that Havlo didn't understand. He couldn't leave his wife. He couldn't leave his business. But he had to get his son away from her. So, he sent him back to Hadley Town, had another son, and tried to live a normal human life with his normal human wife.

Vordon blinked. Was Turbatius sending him these visions? Were they memories about some man he used to know? If so, what did they mean for him? He had no idea, but though the vision had spanned several years, it had all happened in the blink of an eye, and he was still standing in front of the fire pit staring at the boy.

At least Loby seemed happy. "Oh, Jawan, Zap, you're back." He sat beside the earth mage's journeyman. "How are things in the good ol' Realm of Chaos? I don't guess you stopped whatever's causing the storm."

Whatever's causing the storm.

Vordon shuddered. They must never find out, or he'd never win them to the cause of Zelfor.

"No," Jawan said. "That's still a problem. We haven't even had time to think about the storm."

"Well, I hope you had time to get something to eat. We're under siege here. Can't go out in the storm and our victuals are running low."

They had no food? Vordon blamed Turbatius for this. Turbatius's plans had nothing to do with Zelfor. He picked up the precious book that Turbatius had cast away. It was Turbatius who'd led him to the knowledge of Zelfor, but Vordon owed him nothing.

"Why don't we go see if the storm has let up a little." Jawan rose and stepped out of the laboratory.

"If it hasn't, we'll just have to use the bell to summon Myrlo. The earth mage should be able to help us find food."

The earth mage! Oh, that was the last person Vordon wanted to meet right now. Myrlo wasn't amenable to his cause, and Vordon doubted he ever would be. But he couldn't object, or they'd want to know why. He bit his lip.

Wanting to disappear but having no other choice, Vordon followed Jawan and the others to the portcullis.

Loby pressed close to the portcullis to look out at the rain. "I wonder if we can go out there."

Alecto answered his question with fury. Vordon stepped back lest the monster see him and point him out.

Loby jumped back. They all did. "Guess we won't be going out there tonight."

Zap was terrified. "This is Turbatius. He brought this storm. He killed my master, and he's coming back. Close the gate, Loby. No, that won't keep him out. We are doomed."

That was his master that Alecto killed? Vordon was glad the boy blamed Turbatius. He'd do nothing to make him think otherwise. He smiled, trying to help Zap feel reassured. But Vordon was saddened that Zap feared Turbatius. The boy could help him, but he must not be afraid. "We must defeat Turbatius."

"I've seen Turbatius," Jawan said. "He can't be defeated—not by any of us. Not by all of us."

"Oh, but he can." He had to make them understand that—especially Zap.

Then his precious Queen Cintella asked the one question he dreaded most. "What makes you so sure? What's your relationship to Turbatius?"

"Yes." Jawan put a finger on Vordon's chest. "Why did he come after you personally? Sending a spy is an act of betrayal. Only a friend can betray you."

"Spy?" Zap glanced at Jawan. "You're the reason Turbatius came after me."

Vordon was astonished. He didn't know if it was good or bad that the boy had met Turbatius and survived. Good that he did survive, but was he now so scared that he'd be of no use to Vordon? "Turbatius came after you?"

"In the Realm of . . ." Zap stopped as if not sure if he should say any more.

The boy really was scared, making up some make-believe place. A realm? But where did Turbatius come from? He shrugged. Maybe he'd have time to deal with the boy's fear. But it was too much—all of them jumping on him. If he told them about Turbatius, they'd soon figure out that he sent the storm, and it would all be over. He had to think of something believable yet innocuous. "Trust me. I'm no friend of Turbatius. Never was. Turbatius came after me before . . . well, it's a long story."

"Loby looked out at the storm. "We're not going anywhere anytime soon. We'll listen to your story even if it's long. But it better be good."

"Turbatius captured me. But I escaped and think I know a way to defeat him. He . . . he wanted to control me. To make me do something. Obviously, I'm not under his control. I escaped. I found out some secrets about him, and now he's afraid I'll use it against him, which I certainly will." And again, he smiled at Zap.

They went back into the laboratory. Loby picked up a bell and rang it. "We'll have to summon Myrlo."

"Will he come through the portal? You know he likes his horse," Jawan said.

"He won't be riding any horses tonight."

"Myrlo?" Vordon didn't want to be around if Myrlo came.

"I hope he's not busy. If only I could put some urgency in the bell. We really need some food," Loby said.

Vordon had to disappear before the earth mage stepped through that portal. Speaking over his shoulder, he made for the laboratory door. "I'm tired from all this excitement. Think I'll find a bed somewhere and lie down."

Chapter 23

Muto gasped. Why would Turbatius attack the particles in his own realm? They just wanted to dance, and they did it with such freedom and grace. What was wrong with that? "What are you doing?"

Turbatius plucked the particles out of the air where they danced and flung them into the castle. They cried out. Muto tried to save some of them, but Turbatius was determined there'd be no dancing in the Realm of Chaos.

"Are you questioning what I do?" the menace in Turbatius's voice alone drove Muto back a step.

"N-no. Of course not."

"This is my kingdom, and I will have my way. I have a task for you, and you will do it."

"Anything you say."

"You will go back to the Quantum Realm, and you will intercept every proton and neutron before it reaches Nano and use your power to convert it into something Nano can't send through the nanotube to Atomidon. You will do this, or I will convert you into oblivion."

Muto didn't doubt it. He remembered how easily Turbatius had tossed him into a tree in Hadley Town. There were no trees in Nanosia, but there were worse predicaments a W boson could get into.

He left the Realm of Chaos and conjured a road to the Quantum Realm. Then he chuckled. What did he care what Turbatius did in his own kingdom? He was going to destroy Nano and have a little fun with all the quanta in the Quantum Realm while he was at it. Wasn't like Turbatius wanted him to do something he didn't want to do.

Nano stood in his usual place in front of his nanotube, declaring who was regular and who was not. Quanta came at him from all directions, so Muto wouldn't be able to convert them all like Turbatius wanted. But he could do enough to keep Nano so busy he wouldn't be able to keep any kind of order in the Quantum Realm, and that would destroy him.

With the mists of Nanosia shrouding him from Nano's view, Muto set up shop. He turned the down quarks in a cloud of protons into charm quarks.

"What is this?"

"I feel so delightful."

"And you look so cute."

The protons squealed with glee.

Muto noticed something that he hadn't seen in Amaki. The color charge of these lambda particles was different. If they'd been normal lambda particles, they be red, or green, or blue. But his lambda darlings were purple. Muto laughed. Purple! Old Nano was going to have a fit.

"Run along, my darlings, and present yourselves to Nano. You'll mesmerize him. You're so charming."

The newly transformed quanta looked uncertain, but he shooed them along and turned to the next cloud of protons. For a change, he turned the down quarks into strange quarks. To his delight, they turned maroon.

He sent them on their way and approached a cloud of neutrons, turning their up quarks into charm quarks. "Who would have thought that a baryon with two down quarks and a charm quark would have a pink color charge?"

A commotion came from Nano's direction. So Muto moved to keep the bosons from zeroing in on his position. He turned the up quarks in another cloud of neurons into strange quarks and they turned orange. He decided to do something really bizarre with the next batch of protons that came his way. He turned two of their quarks into charm quarks and burst with glee when they turned psychedelic.

"What's going on?"

"What's causing this?"

Muto heard Nano's bosons long before they reached him and slipped back into the mists. Circling around them, he settled down in a place where he could watch Nano's consternation.

"Irregular, irregular, irregular. They're all irregular. I can't send you to Atomidon."

Muto's lambda looked at each other in dismay. "But there are lambdas in Atomidon."

"We'll just make hypernuclei."

"That's perfectly normal."

Nano stared at them. "There's nothing normal about lambda with quarks and color charges like yours. And even if you were normal, it would disrupt the balance of the universe to send so many lambdas to Atomidon. There's not a regular proton or neutron among you."

"Well, turn us back into protons and neutrons."

Muto knew Nano could do that, but it wouldn't mess up his plans.

Nano looked troubled. His nine bosons looked utterly perplexed.

The boson leader stepped forward and shook his head. "We've never seen quanta with such unusual color charges and aren't sure what to do with them."

Nano sighed. "I'll just get the W bosons to change the quarks back to the normal flavor. I hope that will take care of the color problem, too."

He could hope all he wanted, but Muto still wasn't worried. He set to work changing more and more quanta into spectacular lambda the likes of which the Quantum Realm had never seen. Soon Nano's bosons were so busy undoing what Muto had done that they had time for nothing else. Regular protons and neutrons stood by the wayside waiting for the bosons to usher them through the nanotube, but the bosons were busy elsewhere. Muto snuck in and turned them back into lambda particles. When the bosons reached the place where he'd been, he was somewhere else laughing his head off.

But he couldn't keep this up indefinitely. He had to disable the W bosons. And he knew how to do that. He went to the nanotube where the W bosons entered Nanosia and sealed the carbon sheets of its mouth with gluons. He smiled, listening to the weak little W bosons trying in vain to loosen the strong force of the gluons. Muto faded into the mists when Nano's bosons came to see what was holding up the W bosons.

"How did this happen?"

"I don't think this is just happening. There are laws governing the Quantum Realm. This has to be deliberate."

"Turbatius!" all nine of them said in unison.

That's right, Turbatius—not Muto . By the time Nano's bosons loosened the gluon, the W bosons had decayed into quarks and antiquarks—further blocking the nanotube. Beautiful. If only he could get close enough to Nano to see his face. The sight would be priceless.

Instead, he went back among the lambda and watched them dance. Free from the constraints of regularity and the so-called Pauli exclusion principle.

The lambda danced with abandon, following no orbits but their own individual trajectories. There were billions more of them than had been in the Realm of Chaos. And Muto had created them. He had turned the Quantum Realm into a second Realm of Chaos. No, not second. His would be the first—Chaos Primis.

With Nano's bosons busy elsewhere, Muto snuck up behind Nano and knocked him over the head. He dragged the unconscious prig to the dungeon and left him in the same cell where Muto had been not long ago.

Chapter 24

The mist coalescing over the pond wasn't something Savorne noticed as her tears mingled with the rain falling into the water—until it began to speak. "Why do you cry, Mother?" The form of the boy—translucent and ghostly—hovered before her, a look of concern on its face. What concern have the dead for the living?

Savorne narrowed her eyes. "I am not your mother."

"You are the mother of my brother. A woman whom my father once loved."

Once

. If the ghost came to comfort her, he should choose his words more carefully. "But now he loves another. That's all I need—confirmation that I will soon die."

"Not necessarily."

"Will you bring your father back to me? Make him abandon his wife and pledge his undying love to me?"

"You don't need his love to live. Win the love of your son. Teach him to overcome his fear of water. Then I will be released from the bondage his fear creates, and you will live."

Savorne signed. "Oh, is that all I have to do? Win the love of a boy who is afraid of me?"

"You are beautiful, and winning Zap's trust and love will not be hard for you. If you believe in yourself, he will, too."

For a moment, she dared to let hope into her heart. Her lips spread into a smile, and she closed her eyes under the weight of what could be. But when she opened her eyes another weight fell upon her, and she winced. She couldn't leave the pond. Zap was far away. How was she ever going to win his love when she was trapped in a place where he was not? "So, I must wait for him to return here and hope that I don't frighten him away?"

"No, you don't have to wait. He is in yon castle." The ghost pointed out one of the mages' castles. "Go there and you will find him. He won't be able to run from you inside walls."

"What makes you think that IIIIIIII can go inside walls?"

"Oh." He had the nerve to look abashed. "It will be hard for you and a little uncomfortable. But my father will not come back. If you want to live, you must bear with a little discomfort and meet Zap where he is."

If she wanted to live

. "Of course I want to live." Then she knew what she had to do. It would be hard, but not impossible. She wasn't, after all, a fish-tailed mermaid or a dryad trapped in a tree. She wasn't trapped at all. She could walk away. But it wasn't as simple as taking a step—a step she'd never taken in the millennia of her existence.

She turned to the pond. "My sisters, are you near? Come and bid me farewell, for I must go."

For a moment, there was no sound above the rain. Then a mournful melody wafted from the water. Bubbles and ripples, then five other undines surfaced.

"Go? What do you mean go?"

"You can't go."

"Have you found another pond?"

"Have you found your human sweetheart?"

"But this is your home."

Indeed, it was. Her sisters were going to make this harder than it had to be. "I am going to the castle."

The mist and rain made the castle look farther away than it was. Savorne smiled at her well-meaning sisters. "I'll be back."

"No, you will not!" To Savorne's horror, Nexa rose out of the water in all his terrible glory and glared at her. "You have a duty to this pond—an eternal duty. If you leave in pursuit of your human lover, you may not return. The water will not welcome you ever again."

Savorne swallowed hard. She was going to tell him it wasn't for her lover but for her son that she was leaving. That would only give him the opportunity to say it didn't matter. And it didn't for Nexa. They were both human.

Her sisters wept. They knew she would go no matter the cost. They wept for the cost she'd have to pay. "Don't go, Savorne."

"You will miss the pond."

"You will miss us."

They were right. Saying farewell to the pond meant saying goodbye to them, too.

"And we will miss you."

Nexa continued to glare. "It is your choice."

The ghost drew himself up over the pond. "Yes, it is your choice. What will you do, Savorne? I hope you want to live as much as I want to be free."

Nexa and the five sisters stared at the ghost.

"What is this?"

"This is not natural."

"As unnatural as the storm."

"Did you bring the storm?"

"I did not. But if I were unnatural, then I could not exist, for everything that exist in nature is natural."

"So say you." Nexa growled at the ghost, having no idea what he was growling at. "Be gone, thing outside of nature."

"If I were outside of nature, how could you see me? How could we be having this lovely conversation unless you were outside of nature with me?"

"Blasphemer!" And the five sisters sank under the water.

But Nexa trembled with fury. "Do not leave the pond, Savorne. This is not a threat. This is a promise."

Savorne turned her face to the wind, and the wind laughed.

"Which mage owns that castle? It's not the water mage's castle."

The ghost shrugged. "Does it matter? You must go."

She didn't understand why that would be a secret unless the ghost just didn't know. She sighed and set her feet on the path to the castle. The forest was cold and gloomy, the water under her feet was comforting, but she missed the pond already.

Stop it, Savorne

. She shook her head and did not turn back.

But when she emerged from the forest, the storm redoubled its strength, whipping her back and forth. Vicious laughter echoed across the sky. "You are not human, but you resemble the humans. I am tired of punishing the trees. I will punish you."

"Alecto, let me be!"

"Why should I? I know what you are, undine. I know that you shed tears for a sinful man. That makes you an accomplice to his sins, worthy of punishment."

"You are insane." Savorne raised her arms to shield her face from the wind.

But for every step she took toward the castle, it blew her another way. So, she pretended to be going another way, and it blew her toward the castle. She was airborne. The wind was so fierce. It blew her around and around the castle—orbiting it like a star. She couldn't breathe, for Alecto blew the wind away from her nostrils. The wind slammed her into a turret. She banged her head against the side of a window and fell in.

She sensed water, but she couldn't see the water or the sky. As if on a canopy of darkness, Nexa appeared before her. He slipped her into her pond. "All is forgiven. All is forgotten. You are home, child. The human has pledged fealty to the water king. He has grown fins like a merman and is bound to the pond. This will keep you here, and you will both be my children."

Her five sisters danced around them in the water, singing the melody of happy sirens.

But the water didn't feel right. She was sitting, not swimming. The bottom and sides of the pond were hard, and the water came only up to her chest. She opened her eyes and blinked.

Where was she? She'd been in a storm. Something about Alecto, a ghost boy, and Nexa. Then she remembered but had no idea where she was or how she'd gotten here. She must be inside the castle. She certainly hadn't walked in, so someone must have found her and brought her into this place. The water soothed and strengthened her, though it still was not her pond.

A human woman entered. For some reason, that surprised Savorne. She'd never seen a human woman. She knew that when a human man was unfaithful to an undine, she would die. But it had never occurred to her to think of a human woman.

Yet there she was. Not as beautiful as undine but not grotesque. She was passably comely. "Good, you're awake and not drowned. Vordon said you wouldn't drown if we left you in the water. How do you feel?"

"Battered, but I'll live."

"You're a strange one. We heard a racket up in one of the turrets and went up to investigate. And there you were as naked as you please. Here, I brought some clothes for you." She put a bundle on a thing made of wood.

Savorne shuddered to think of what had been done to that poor tree. "Clothes?
"

"Yes, clothes. You can't run around a castle full of men with nothing on. But I suppose if you were running around outside a castle with nothing on, it doesn't matter. But you can't do that here."

Savorne looked at the bundle. It was made of the strange things Havlo put on his body, and she thought she remembered him calling them clothes. But though he put them on himself, he never insisted that she put them on as they lay in the forest listening to birds and dryads chattering.

Savorne rose out of the water, and the woman handed her another piece of cloth, wanting her to take it and do something with it. Savorne had no idea what she was supposed to do.

"Dry yourself off." Her eyes widened with astonishment as the water rolled off Savorne. "What world did you come from?"

"This world."

"No way." She threw the cloth she was holding into a corner and picked up the clothes. "I don't suppose you even know how to put these on. By the way, my name is Prenda. Do they have names in the world you come from?"

Savorne rolled her eyes. She was beginning to not like Prenda. "I told you, I am from this world, and my name is Savorne."

"I'm sorry. I didn't mean . . . It's just that you look like a real woman, so I expected you to know what real women know."

"I am a real woman. What you mean is you thought I was human."

Now Prenda really did blanch. "Ah . . . yeah. I never talked to someone who isn't human." She held up something that Savorne remembered seeing on Havlo. "Here let me help you put on these britches."

Savorne thought about how awkward and intimate it would be to let Prenda help her put on the britches. "I can do it myself." She took the britches and examined them, trying to picture in her mind how to put them on. She knew how they looked when they were on Havlo. She sat down and pulled them to her, putting one foot in each leg. She pulled them as far as her thighs

126

and had to stand up. The britches pulled her off balance and she fell. Glaring when Prenda reached out to help her, Savorne shimmied the britches onto her back side and made sure her feet were free before standing up.

"This is a tunic." Prenda handed her a cloth very much like the one she was wearing.

Savorne took it and pulled it over her head. "You humans go through so much trouble. We undines wear the water."

"Right."

"Why must I wear clothes just because there are men in the castle?" Savorne pulled her arms through the holes in the tunic.

"Because . . . well. Because it's something that we do. We don't want men to see our nakedness."

"And you don't know why?"

Prenda seemed to think about it. "Men act funny when they see a naked woman. It does something to them, and they do things like they own the woman. She's his possession."

Savorne thought of Havlo. He had seemed possessive when he saw her. His eyes glazed over as if Alecto had taken control of his mind. "So, you put on clothes to keep men from going crazy."

"Ah . . . yeah. You could say that."

Human men do crazy things? And what about human women? Could she trust Prenda? No, if the woman intended to hurt her, she'd had her chance. Savorne paused at that thought. Prenda might not be as fluid as water, but circumstances might shift, and she'd change her mind. Savorne would stay on guard. But she'd come here to find Zap. Until she did, she'd need Prenda. "Is there a boy here?"

Prenda looked at her—weighing her. "Yes. In fact, there are two boys here."

"I need to speak to him."

"You know Jawan and Zap?"

"I know Zap."

Prenda raised an eyebrow as if waiting for an explanation, but Savorne offered none. "Wait here." Then she disappeared down the hall.

Was she going to get Zap? Savorne wondered at the secrecy. The hallway was so quiet and the air so dry. It was very dry, and her skin began to itch.

She heard two pairs of feet coming and thought it must be Prenda and Zap, but she turned to come face-to-face with Havlo.

"Savorne?"

"You two know each other?" Prenda gaped at them. "Woman just falls out of the sky and already knows everybody."

"Hello, Havlo." Savorne reeled inside but wasn't about to let him see it.

Prenda looked relieved. "Oh, well then, that's one person you don't know. His name is Vordon."

For just a moment, Havlo looked like he wanted to crawl off somewhere and hide. But he caught himself and smiled. "That's a long story. But, Savorne, you've come to see Zap?"

Prenda turned on him. "You should be a writer because you are full of long stories."

"Writer?" Savorne didn't know if the woman had insulted him. She made it sound horrid.

Havlo smiled even brighter. "Never mind. We'll take you to see Zap."

"The monster!" Zap shrieked the moment he saw Savorne and ducked under something long that must have cost the death of many trees. "The monster wants me, and you brought her to me!"

Another boy—the one she'd seen at the pond—glared at her. "An undine!" He came at her with fire that he had trapped in some way—some form of magic. "Stay away from Zap! Leave! What are you doing in the fire mage's castle, water witch?"

Fire mage's castle?

Savorne remembered how evasive the boy ghost had acted when she'd asked him whose castle this was. He'd tricked her. She'd have never come near the castle of her elemental enemy—not even for Zap—and the ghost boy had known that. But now that she was here, and Zap was here, how could she leave?

Chapter 25

Water witch! She was a water witch. And Zap was a coward. But he didn't care. Fear would keep him alive—protect him from water and witches.

From his safe perch under the long wooden table, he watched legs and skirts scattered about the laboratory floor. Weren't they afraid with a witch—a monster right there in the chamber? No telling what she might do to them. Why didn't they run? Jawan thought he could just tell the witch to leave. Well, the legs that were hers just stood there, so she wasn't taking orders from him.

"Put those down, Jawan. This is no way to treat our guest." That was Prenda.

Guest?

Didn't they know what she was? She may look like a woman, but that was no human. Her disguise fooled them. Zap shuddered to think what she was underneath—some hideous monster.

"I guess not." At least Jawan didn't sound convinced that she wasn't a water witch. Good. He'd be watching her, even if Prenda wasn't.

But Zap's heart sank when Vordon spoke. "I think I know her. Her name is Savorne. But I've no idea how I know this."

She bewitched you, you moron. That's what witches do

. Zap wanted to thump Vordon on the head. But he stayed where he was. No telling what Vordon's relationship to Turbatius had been or might still be.

"Then she's not a complete stranger. Even if you're still a stranger, Vordon. But she's a woman. She doesn't look dangerous."

So, she bewitched Vordon, Prenda, and Loby. And was trying to bewitch Jawan. He was the earth mage's journeyman. He shouldn't be stronger than Loby. The fire mage himself. But maybe strength had nothing to do with it. Maybe strength made people even more vulnerable. But if that were so, then Zap would be invincible. Who knew? But Zap would stay where he was.

To his horror, the witch bent down and peered at Zap under the table. He was the one she'd come for. Would his friends give him to her to save their own skin? The same fear he felt would keep them alive, too. But no, they weren't scared. They were bewitched. And Zap was cooked, for sure. The witch smiled. All Zap saw were teeth.

"You don't have to be afraid of me, Zap. I just want to talk to you."

Yeah right. That's what all monsters say. Zap scooted deeper under the table. The monster frowned as her next meal got away from her.

Behind him Loby's salamander, Crisp, hissed.

Hiss at her, not me, you crispy cat. Hiss at the witch.

But Crisp ran at Zap, hissing and spitting fire. Zap bolted out from under the table and ran. He didn't care where he was going—knocking into chairs and walls. He just ran—sure that witch and fire cat were right behind him. He didn't stop to check. He ran until he banged into the portcullis.

"You!" Alecto howled with glee as wind and rain lashed Zap through the bars of the portcullis. "Want to come out and play, little boy? Mind you now. I play rough."

Zap stared in horror. How had he come here? He hadn't meant to come here. He hadn't meant to go anywhere except away from the witch, and now he was here. Monsters within and monsters without. No way to escape.

He felt hands—more than two—pulling him gently away from the portcullis. He recoiled. The touches were meant to be gentle, but they only reminded his burned skin that it was supposed to hurt. When he saw that two of those hands belonged to the witch, he knew he was dead. Fear was supposed to keep you alive, but that was only if you had room to run. He didn't, and he knew he was dead.

But Cintella was standing right beside the witch, a look of urgent reassurance on her face. "It's all right, Zap. Savorne won't hurt you."

Savorne. Monsters didn't have names. Did they? And such a pretty name—not a monster's name. He released his death grip on the portcullis and followed them back to the laboratory.

Vordon was flipping through the book he'd been holding. He looked up and smiled. "I know just what we need—a little history. Not long ago, I dreamed about a man named Havlo, a native of Hadley Town who sought his fortune in Romatica. Havlo is one of the few surviving descendants of the people called Zelforeans who lived in this land long ago."

It sounded interesting. Zap liked history. Under Lacus, he'd studied the history of water magic. It got scary when his master described rivers of water pouring down from mountains and carving out paths through the land as it wound its way to the sea. But Vordon wasn't talking about water. He was talking about something Zap had never heard of before.

"It turns out, I am Havlo. That's why I take an interest in Zelfor. The history of that land—of this

land—is my history."

Zap gasped. "You mean this is Zelfor?"

"Not just Hadley Town but all Romatica before the Romatican army conquered the Zelforeans. Listen to this." Vordon read from his book. "The field of Hadlon ran with blood as the Zelforeans made their last stand against the invaders. It was in that field that they hid their great treasures lest they fall into enemy hands. Though the Zelforeans fell, they could never let their treasures fall, for then they truly would be lost." He closed the book and raised an eyebrow as if to say,

Don't you get it?

But Zap didn't get it. He could only wait to see if Vordon would tell them. Maybe this was why Turbatius was after him, and he still wasn't ready to confess some horrible secret.

"The pond in the middle of our forest is the field of Hadlon. The field filled with water and the town was named Hadley Town. That's why Turbatius placed me near this place. It is a place of power. If he works his will here, it will affect the entire Earth."

Cintella popped up. "But did they ever uncover the treasure? Is it still there?"

Vordon smiled. "Yes, my queen. It is still there, waiting for the rightful heirs."

Zap didn't know why Vordon and Savorne both were looking at him.

"Now I remember this pond was not always in this place," Savorne said. "We came with the rain. The undine came in a powerful monsoon, and Nexa was given charge of a powerful secret, which he wouldn't divulge to us. It must have been the Zelforean treasure."

Zap recoiled from her. She might not be a wicked witch or a ferocious monster, but she was still associated with water. Everything about her screamed

water

, and he couldn't bear it.

She noticed and took his hand gently. "You don't have to be afraid of water, Zap. You are my son and have power over water."

No! She's lying.

Son of a water witch? "No! No way! You're not my mother."

She reached for him. "You don't understand, son. You . . ."

"Get away from me, water witch!" He turned and picked up a fire cube and brandished it at her like a mace.

She backed away. "You would threaten me with fire?"

Zap realized what he was holding, threw it down, and ran out of the laboratory. In a blind rage, he cranked the portcullis open and raced out into the storm.

Wind and rain, bat wings and lightning lashed at him, but he didn't stop long enough to be terrified of Alecto. He just ran until he slipped in the slick grasses and lay there submerged in water—sobbing and not caring.

A ghostly coldness drove him to his knees. The mist coalesced into Ziph.

"She's telling you the truth, you know."

"Shut up. I'm no water witch. I have no power over water."

"No, you're not a witch, but you do have power over water."

Zap shook the horrid thought away. "I don't! I don't! I had no power to save you."

"The power was there before our father brought you home. Then you learned to be afraid of water. Maybe it was my mother's fault. She wasn't a nice person, and she envied you."

"I don't remember any of that. I only remember not being able to help you. I had no power."

"No, not as long as you were afraid. But that had nothing to do with me. The undine brought you to the orphanage. The people there hated the powers of your mother, were afraid and jealous of them. They tried to drown you, but you wouldn't drown. They tried to burn you, but you wouldn't burn. So, they made fun of you. Every time you came into the pond where they swam, they would leave. They took every chance to make some remark that made water seem bad. Only bad people didn't drown. When you came to us, you tried to overcome your fear, but it was already there. My drowning solidified it."

His drowning. He made it sound like a perfectly normal thing that happened to perfectly normal boys all the time. Do you remember when you drowned? I remember my drowning. Too bad it only happens once. Otherwise, I'd love to do it again. Wouldn't you?

Zap remembered sliding through the water like a fish—not having to hold his breath the way other boys did.

"It's unnatural." A huge matronly woman clucked her tongue at him as she ushered the other boys away from the pond.

The younger Zap reasoned that if nobody understood how good the water felt, then maybe they were right. It wasn't good. He wasn't good. He was bad. He became afraid, and his fear kept him from getting in the pond when the other boys were there. They'd hold him under the water for hours and pelt him with rocks. Fear will keep you alive.

The older Zap shook the memories away. He ducked his head in the water, trying to remember how good the water felt. He did remember and he didn't drown. A cool sensation washed over his chest, arms, and back like water better than any salve. He dared to breathe deeply, and it didn't hurt.

Ziph glowed brighter in the mist. "I am free now. But you still have need of me, so I will stay."

A hand touched Zap's shoulder. He looked up, and Savorne smiled at him.

Chapter 26

Zap looked around as the rain slowed and then stopped. The clouds stopped boiling, and the wind lay still. He couldn't believe it. "The storm is gone."

Savorne shook her head. "Not gone completely. While fear controlled you, Alecto saw your fear as guilt, which allowed her to attack you."

"But why is she here, attacking me now? I'm just a boy, and she never attacked me before."

"I don't know exactly. There are a lot of things coming together now, but it all hasn't come together yet. This is about Zelfor. You are Zelfor, Zap. When Alecto attacks you, all Romatica feels it."

Zap gulped. That was a big responsibility on his little shoulders. "I'm not sure I want to accept that responsibility."

Savorne shrugged. "It's going to be true whether you accept it or not."

Yes, it would be. If only it didn't have to be. Master Lacus would have known what to do. Master Lacus would have taken the responsibility. He would have . . . Zap tried to look away, but everywhere he looked, his eyes landed on water. He shivered. Lacus was gone, and now the world was left with all this water.

Savorne followed his gaze. "Why do you look so upset? There's a lot of water, but it's still just water. You can easily get rid of it."

"No, I can't. But maybe Volvo can blow it away."

"You mean you apprenticed with the water mage all this time and don't know how to make water evaporate?"

"I know how." But reading about it in a book was one thing. Taking the actual water into his mind was something else. Truth was, he'd never really done anything with water. Whenever Master Lacus tried to make him practice water magic, Zap found a way to let his master do it. "Maybe we could just leave it. Won't it sink into the ground?"

"No, we can't. You know we can't. This water doesn't even belong here. It was taken from all over the world. It has to go back where it came from."

Zap gulped again. She didn't have to say it, but he guessed it was his responsibility.

Send it back

. "How can I do it? I don't know where all this water belongs."

Savorne put a hand on his shoulder. "When the water is in the sky, the wind will send it to its proper place. But only if you're not afraid. If you are afraid, Alecto will come again."

Only if I'm not afraid.

Then he might as well get ready for the monster to return, because he was petrified.

"Focus."

Zap drew in a breath. If his mother thought he could do this, then maybe he could—even if he was afraid. He was going to be afraid, and Alecto would come back whether he tried to send the water back or not, so he might as well try.

He focused his mind on all the water that was not supposed to be on the ground, in the trees, and flooding the ponds of the world. Each drop separated into molecules. This was what his master had tried to get him to do, and though he'd never planned to actually do it hands-on, he remembered his lessons. Like a black hole, his mind drew in the molecules of water and separated them into the atoms of hydrogen and oxygen. The reality of what he was doing hit him, and he remembered that he was supposed to be afraid of water. But it was too late. He cast the atoms into the sky, where each oxygen atom naturally combined with two hydrogen atoms. They became clouds. The entire earth was overcast. No, some places had no clouds. Pine trees and tomatoes withered in deserts that were supposed to have plenty of rain. But the clouds looked like natural clouds—the kind of clouds that Volvo would blow back where they belong.

Then he walked with his mother across the damp grass into the castle.

"We need food." Loby entered the laboratory, patting his empty belly. "Somebody ate the last of our stores. My stomach says it wasn't me."

Crisp squealed innocently in the corner.

"Now that the storm is gone and the land is basically dry, we can go to town and buy some victuals." Loby busied himself with his fire paraphernalia, signaling that he couldn't possibly go.

Prenda caressed her tummy as if anyone were thinking about asking her to go.

"I thought Myrlo was going to bring us something," Cintella said.

"I don't think the earth mage likes being summoned," Jawan said.

Loby smiled at him. "But you don't have to be summoned. You're right here. A little fresh air and exercise will do you good."

Jawan looked like he wished he'd kept his mouth shut. "Come on, Zap, Cintella. You can help me carry the groceries."

They hitched three horses to a wagon and started down the road.

Cintella shivered. "The clouds still look dark."

Jawan shrugged. "I guess Master Volvo will blow them away when he gets around to it sooner or later."

Zap glanced at the clouds. They did look dark. Was Alecto really gone?

Thunder rolled directly over them, and sheets of rain cascaded to the earth.

"Did you think you'd gotten rid of me?" Alecto roared through the wind. "I was just gathering my strength."

Lightning crackled and thunder crashed. The three friends ducked under the wagon.

"We can't stay here. It's only going to get worse."

Jawan was right. Still Zap didn't know what to do. If they left the shelter of the wagon, Alecto would get them for sure. Fear. Overcome your fear and she'll be gone. Thunder boomed enough to reset his heartbeat. Overcoming fear was easier said than done.

Jawan crept forward, so low to the ground he was nearly crawling. Cintella and Zap followed him. The storm raged around them, but they kept their heads down. Maybe if they didn't look at the lightning, it wouldn't strike them. A less than comforting thought. They kept going until they reached the copse of trees that concealed the tunnel to the castle.

***

Zap flopped into a chair and laid his head on the laboratory table. "I had her. I had her. If only I hadn't been afraid this one little time. All it took was a moment of doubt."

"There was nothing you could have done." Cintella wrung water out of the hem of her tunic. They hadn't even dressed for rain. "We were all scared."

Jawan cocked an eyebrow. "Did you think you were the only one who wasn't supposed to be scared?"

"I'm the only one whose fear caused the storm."

"You could hide from her," Vordon said. "She's of the wind. Wind and earth are opposites, so even muddy water will hide you from her."

"I remember when she lost me. But no, she wasn't just attacking me. People in town felt it, too. All over Hadley Town. Even if I hide, she'll still be attacking everything else, and how long can I hide?"

Savorne put a hand on his shoulder. "She must have been waiting for you. She must have been right there waiting for the smallest opportunity."

"And like a big dummy, I gave it to her."

"Not a dummy. You just have to try again."

"And she'll be waiting again."

"And you banish your fear again."

"Back and forth. When will it stop?"

"She won't give up for you, so why should you give up for her?"

Vordon stood and banged his fist on the table. "No! You don't have to go back and forth. You can defeat Alecto."

Jawan, Cintella, Prenda, and Zap just looked at him. "How?" they asked in unison.

"I am Vordon. If you're Savorne's son, then you are also mine. Fire and water. Two opposites, but you have the power of both."

"That's impossible," Savorne objected.

"No more impossible than me loving you. Fire and water came together, and now Zap is our son. He is also the son of Zelfor. He is the heir the undines have been waiting for."

"I've been around that pond for years, and the undine never came to me."

Vordon smiled. "It's one thing to be
around
the pond, shrouded by ignorance and fear. Now you can go
in
the pond, confident in the knowledge of who you are."

Chapter 27

Vordon had to make the boy see. This was his son. His son! Savorne and his son. Though his love for Savorne was only something he shared by proxy with Havlo, it was something to cultivate if it meant making the boy see.

Zap sat up straight. "Yeah. I guess I can do it again. I made her go away once, and I can do it again."

"As many times as it takes." Vordon beamed with anticipation and shining visions of a restored Zelfor. "Once you've subdued Alecto, then you can be all that a son of Havlo was meant to be." A son of Havlo was a son of Zelfor, and the boy had a way to go to be all that, but the road was clear. Vordon knew exactly what to do.

"A son of Havlo. I do remember him a little. He was a big man—it was you. You're not as big as you were then. But you're Havlo—the man who took me out of that terrible place. But Havlo had no magic. He never talked about Zelfor. And he never read books. He wanted me to be a silversmith like him."

Vordon struggled to keep a frown off his face. Clearly, the boy admired Havlo, which meant Vordon had to be Havlo. He had to make that connection. But if Havlo had no love or even knowledge of Zelfor . . . Vordon would deal with that. But for now, he had to be Havlo.

Vordon blinked. Havlo blinked. He looked around him. A long wooden table, glass and fire, a strange looking cat, and people he didn't know. But here was Savorne, and there was the boy. But he'd sent the boy to Hadley Town. He'd left Savorne there. Which meant

the man

had brought him to them. Of all places, he didn't want to be in the backwoods of Romatica. Unvarnished wood and stone. These people knew nothing of the rich tapestries and sumptuous cushions in the queen's palace.

He headed for the door. The boy looked at him quizzically as he passed by, but he didn't care. He made his way to the portcullis. At least they had one of those. He cranked it open and stepped outside. He'd steal a horse. He'd walk if he had to—anything to get back to the bustle of city life. He'd stop in the King's Inn and drink himself silly. The man wouldn't know where he was or how to get back here. Havlo went around the castle, hoping these backward people even had a stable.

Vordon found himself walking around the outside of the castle with no idea how he'd gotten there. He was inside the castle talking to Zap and Savorne. He didn't even remember taking a step when he was just here. These dreams weren't just dreams. They were getting real. Damn Turbatius! Damn Havlo. The man could not take control of his mind. But he had, and Vordon didn't even know what was happening until it was over. But he knew it wasn't over, and he trembled.

He turned and went back into the castle. Zap and Savorne stared at him.

"Where'd you go?" Savorne asked.

"Nowhere. I just stepped outside for some fresh air. This castle is stuffy, don't you think?"

Loby looked around. "Well, there aren't any windows in here. You might get a breeze down in the fire pit."

They looked unconvinced. Clearly Havlo had done something to make them think he needed more than fresh air. Maybe if he acted like it was no big deal, they would forget about it—whatever

it

was. "Zap, what I was saying is you're the heir the undines have been guarding that pond for centuries for. But you can't approach Nexa from a position of weakness. You must master your elements."

"Elements!" Zap gulped. "As in more than one."

"Fire and water."

"But I'm just the water mage's apprentice. I can't jump from apprentice to master, and I know nothing of fire. Maybe you should talk to Loby about that."

"Talk to me about what? What are you trying to do, Vordon?"

Vordon rolled his eyes. "Nexa wouldn't listen to Loby no matter how skilled he was. He wasn't a son of Zelfor." Vordon knew what the boy needed. He went to the shelves against the wall and took down an empty fire cube.

Loby rose to stop him. "What are you doing?"

Vordon raised a calming palm to Loby. "Don't worry. I know what I'm doing."

"This is my castle."

"And it's made of stone, so I'm not likely to burn it down." He walked out of Loby's reach and turned to Zap. "Come with me."

"Where?" Zap stepped back suspiciously as Vordon headed for the fire pit.

"Just come with me." He grabbed Zap's hand and pulled him into the pit. Then he turned and welded the door shut with a blast of fire. He descended the steps as banging sounded from the other side of the door.

"What are you doing?" Zap stumbled after Vordon, barely keeping his footing on the steep stone steps.

"You will see. Sons of Zelfor don't whine. They watch and learn." He pulled Zap close to the fire until he could reach out and touch it. Sparks alighted in on his face and in his hair but did not burn him.

Sparks fell on Zap, too. But he was so busy being afraid of the fire that he didn't notice.

"Reach out your hand, take the fire, and put it in the fire cube."

Zap drew back toward the steps, shaking his head. "You're mad. You're working for Turbatius. Did he tell you to torture me? Or will you take me back to him so he can torture me?"

Vordon caught him before he could go back upstairs and pulled him back to the fire. "No. you're my son. This has nothing to do with Turbatius. Trust me. I'm showing you what you can do. Something you never dreamed of."

Indeed, the one element he did know something about, he was afraid of. And Zap trembled with terror before an element totally unknown to him. But he reached out. He was so close, he had to know if it was going to burn, he'd be burned already.

"Focus." Vordon projected the encouraging tones of a father. "Tell the fire it is cool, and you have come to play."

Zap closed his fist around a pocket of flame, and when he drew his arm back, the fire was still in the palm of his hand. He put it into the fire cube and smiled. "Amazing!"

"Yes, it is." Vordon reached out his hand to give the fire a loving caress, but Havlo drew back in horror and screamed. "What are we doing here? The man will get us killed." He turned and raced up the steps two at a time, and the heat from the fire followed him as if it had a special hatred for him—for cowards who ran. For cowards who stayed alive. Call it what you want. Fear would keep him alive. He had always tried to make zap understand that, but the boy was a boy.

He reached the top and slammed into the door, but it wouldn't open. He pulled at it and pushed. Frantically, he banged on the door. "Help! Let me out of here!"

Voices sounded from the other side of the door. Havlo stepped back, almost stumbling back down the steps, as the edges of the door began to glow. The door was wrenched open, and none too gentle hands pulled him inside.

"I didn't know you were a fool, Vordon." Loby shoved Havlo against the long table. "I told you not to go down there."

Havlo pushed Loby away. "You don't understand. I don't understand. Leave me alone." He wanted to get away from these people. Then he remembered that Zap was still down there.

Hell spawn! Fire is where he belongs

.

"What have you done with my child?" Savorne pulled the door open. To Havlo's horror, she started down the steps. Her element was water. She hated fire.

Havlo pulled her back. "You can't go down there."

"That's my son you took down there and left." She jerked out of his grasp and started down the steps again.

But before she could go far, Zap came out staring at Havlo with eyes of reproach. "Why did you leave me down there?"

Vordon didn't know where the question came from or how they got upstairs in the laboratory. They were enjoying the fire when . . . Havlo. What mischief has he done? He has the boy scared and blaming Vordon for fear he should have overcome. Maybe if he just explained—just told him about Havlo and hoped the boy would understand. No. Then he'd put himself in a position of weakness—something he'd told Zap not to do. "What are you talking about? You weren't in any danger. Look, you have the fire cube in your hand. I wouldn't have left you if I'd thought you couldn't handle it."

Both Zap and Savorne looked at him. Savorne shook her head. "But why did you leave? This isn't the first time you've done this."

"Done what?" Vordon could see from the faces around him that he was losing his audience—the very people that he needed to plant the seeds for Zelfor. "Look. I can't explain what I'm doing in simple terms." He looked at Prenda. He might as well be trying to explain this to her unborn child. He'd be the next fire mage after his father. But Vordon wanted to get rid of mages entirely. If he didn't do it in Loby's generation, what chance would he have with Loby's son? "It's not simple. But I know what I'm doing. You just have to trust me."

His lovely queen Cintella looked worried, but Jawan looked like he was about to laugh. "Is that why you came running up here screaming for help. Yeah, you know what you're doing after you get burned a few times."

Vordon sighed. He couldn't win them over with arguments. But that wasn't even necessary. He had what he and Zap needed from the fire pit. Time to move on. "Now I will show you how to invoke the power of fire."

"I told you, I'm the water mage's apprentice."

"And where is the water mage?"

Zap winced. Vordon took note that was a sore spot.

"Son, I know what happened to your master. I'm sorry, but we have to move on." This was why they needed to return to the ways of Zelfor. If magic weren't confined to a single mage, Lacus's death wouldn't be such a calamity. The boy had no idea what to do and no way to remedy his situation. Curse the mages. Magic was for everyone. "You got power over water from your mother. Now that you no longer fear water . . ." He paused and gave Zap a pointed gaze to make sure the boy understood he'd passed that phase and was ready to move on. "You can move beyond apprenticeship."

Zap blinked in puzzlement. "How can I learn more without a master?"

Vordon smiled. He often smiled. "I will show you what you need to know about fire, and Savorne will show you what you need to know about water. But to master them, you need to invoke the symbols."

"Wait a minute." Loby jumped back in Vordon's face. "You're not the fire mage. I am. And Savorne is a nice woman, but she's not the water mage. We have a process for replacing a mage. And I doubt very seriously if the other mages will select an undine."

"And maybe it's seriously time to change that." He took the fire cube from Zap and held it up like a prize. "This is living fire. Zap needs living water." He turned to Zap. "Come. We must go outside."

"Outside!" Zap yelped. "What about Alecto?"

"What about her? Have you not mastered that fear? We must go."

"Where are you taking my son?" Savorne pulled Zap behind her.

Vordon pushed Savorne aside and pulled Zap to the door.

"Hey!" Jawan and Loby advanced on Vordon, but he created a wall of fire between them.

"We are only going to the pond. He's been there before." He gave Zap the fire cubes, put his book in his pocket, and they took a flask to head down to the pond. When they reached the portcullis, Alecto was high in the clouds, waiting and watching, but Zap held his head up to show he was not afraid. Alecto frowned and hissed but did not come close. They filled the flask with pond water.

Using the fire cube, Vordon turned a stick of wood into charcoal and found a clear space near the pond. He drew a circle to represent spirit. Then inside the circle he drew the symbols for fire and water. He directed Zap to put the fire cube on the symbol for fire and the flask on the symbol for water.

Chapter 28

Zap put the fire cube in the very center of the triangle that symbolized fire. Then he took a minute to realize that fire looked just like a triangle. No matter what burned, the flames were always wide at the base and shooting up in the middle.

He put the flask in the center of the upside-down triangle that symbolized water. He shook his head trying to remember something about water that resembled an upside-down triangle—but couldn't.

Vordon took out his book and turned the pages until he found what he was looking for. "Say these words."

Zap looked where Vordon pointed. It was just a silly rhyme—but no sillier than the mantra of the Holy Order of Mice.

Fire and water, the two be twine

And then the twine be one

Fire and water, you both are mine

Until this world be done

Now what? He sat back on his heels, waiting for something to happen. He shot a glance at Vordon, who only smiled encouragingly. What was supposed to happen? The items were in the center of their symbols. He guessed that was how he was supposed to do it. Vordon would have said something if he'd done it wrong.

"Look up." Vordon pointed at the sky.

The stars moved. They ran across the sky like a river—splashing, eddying, cascading toward the Earth. Zap gaped in wonder. The stars were putting on a water show. They were the color of water, and he thought he could hear it gurgling across the sky.

Other stars began to glow—shooting up in fiery triangles. To Zap's dismay, where the fire and water met, they annihilated each other. The water boiled and turned to steam, and the fire was just extinguished.

"Is it supposed to do that?" But Zap saw from Vordon's expression that it wasn't. "What went wrong?"

Vordon studied his book again—frowning at what obviously weren't answers. He turned what seemed like the last page and sighed with relief. "Here you have to separate the atoms in the water."

Zap gulped. It was one thing to separate the hydrogen and oxygen atoms in rainwater. "How can I make the stars in the sky act like water and obey me?"

"Are you going to start doubting yourself now? Say this."

Zap memorized the short line in his mind, closed his eyes, and recited it with all his willpower focused on making the hydrogen separate from the oxygen.

An electric current sizzled through the celestial water, and it broke into its component parts. The fire flared up, but to Zap's dismay, the water didn't flow.

"It's not water anymore. This isn't working." He didn't see how it could work. Fire and water just didn't mix, so what was Vordon trying to do? Whatever it was, Zap couldn't do it. He hated the thought of disappointing his father, but he just couldn't do what Vordon wanted.

Raindrops started to fall. dampening his mood. Storm clouds gathered over the pond. Alecto cackled. "I will always be here for you, little boy. Whatever you think you're doing, you'll never get away from yourself and never, ever from me."

"You've overcome your fear before. Don't give in to it now," Vordon warned.

Zap swallowed his fear. He'd show her he wasn't afraid. Raising his fist, he yelled into the threatening storm. "I'm not afraid of you. Leave me alone."

Thunder rumbled and Alecto shrieked. "Fool!" The word flashed across the sky like lightning. Wind pushed Zap to his side and nearly toppled Vordon.

Vordon covered the fire cube and flask against the storm, but the drawing had already been damaged. "Anger is just as bad as fear. You're only making her stronger. Relax. Ignore her. Ignore your source of fear."

Zap relaxed. He sat still until Alecto could find nothing to energize herself with. The storm abated. To strengthen his resolve not to invite Alecto back, Zap used the fire cube to make more charcoal and redrew the sigils as he had seen Vordon do. Then he replaced the fire cube and flask and smiled up at Vordon.

"Watch." Vordon flashed Zap a mysterious smile.

Thunder rumbled again, and Zap thought Alecto was still trying to destroy him. But it was just the hydrogen and oxygen coming back together. With over a billion molecules in every drop of water, it made a lot of noise. In a sonic blue flash, the water flowed, but once again the fire was doused.

"This isn't going to work."

"You have to keep doing it until they dance. Say the rhyme and send the electric current again."

"How often do I have to do this?"

"I don't know. Just keep doing it until something happens."

"Until what happens?"

Vordon smiled but not before Zap detected a moment of doubt. "Something wonderful."

It didn't sound to Zap like Vordon knew what would happen or if anything would happen. He expected Zap to keep doing this all night, like a dummy who had nothing else to do. But he didn't, really, and he'd come this far. He closed his eyes again and concentrated. He said the rhyme and short line over and over as fast has he could.

"Open your eyes and see what you're doing."

Zap opened his eyes. The fire and water did seem to dance—steam and electricity, fire and water flashing in and out of existence over and over. Then the moon set below the horizon, and something changed.

Before Zap's eyes, the symbols for fire and water moved together to form a new symbol, moving the fire cube and flask of water together. "How could they move like that? They were just lines drawn in the mud."

"Nothing that you see is just what you see. Keep watching."

"What is this symbol now?"

"That's a hexagram. It's the symbol for magic. And it's your symbol, for in you fire and water come together. You are a living hexagram."

Mist rose from the pond. And Zap winced, expecting to see his dead brother Ziph. Instead, triumphant singing flowed across the water.

And the king of the undine with all his court appeared. Fifty resplendent undines clothed in water that flowed like blue silk marched behind the father and king of all pond undine. Their voices reverberated off the water and filled the sky with the most beautiful harmony Zap had ever heard.

The courtiers hovered above the water. Their singing mellowed down to the soft hum of anticipation. Zap felt that something was about to happen—the something that Vordon had told him would happen if he kept the magic going.

Vordon nudged him. "That's Nexa, the king of the undines."

"I know he is a king. What else could he be?"

Nexa and another undine marched up to Zap. The undine held a wooden box. Like the undine who had emerged from the pond, the box was not wet. On the lid was a hexagram that looked exactly like the one Vordon had drawn except the red triangle crackled like fire, the blue triangle flowed like water, and the white circle emanated the spirit of magic. Zap just stared, not knowing what he was supposed to do. He dared not speak and wasn't sure that he could. All he could do was gaze into Nexa's blue eyes and think of water. The one element that had terrified him stood before him in the form of a man, and Zap felt no fear.

"The box, Abri." Nexa put his hands out for the box, and with great ceremony, Abri handed it to him. Nexa opened the box and took out a crown of gold. Red, blue, green, and yellow gems sparkled on the crown like stars in a golden sky.

Vordon drew in his breath. "The crown of Zelfor!"

Zap knew this was what Vordon had been longing for, and he was captivated that it was happening. His father, his mother, Nexa, and the undine.

Nexa regarded Zap. "We have waited for you, son of Zelfor, for countless generations of mortal men. I had not expected you to be so young. But here you are, and this crown is doubtless yours."

"Mine?" Zap gulped with bewilderment. "But what about my father? Vordon is the one who knew all about this."

Vordon shook his head. "I knew to bring you here, but the crown is yours. You are the true son of Zelfor. Through you, the magic flows and will live again for all people."

Nexa held the crown with the tenderness of a dear friend and placed it on Zap's head.

The undine danced and sang to a melody Zap had never heard before and would never forget, as if the whole universe were accompanying their song with its own celestial music. A shower of stars fell to the earth.

Even Vordon danced. "You did it! Magic is no longer confined to the mages."

Then Nexa raised his hands, and a solemn quiet fell over the universe. "But it is not time yet. Trouble is still very close. We must wait and keep the crown in the safe care of the undine."

"But . . ." Zap sputtered in bewilderment.

"What trouble?" Vordon asked.

"A powerful trouble—not of this world. Under no circumstances can we allow the crown to fall into the hands of the one who has come before and will come again."

He had to be talking about Turbatius. When will the world ever be safe from him? "How will you know when the trouble is gone?" Vordon asked.

"It is for the undine council to decide when the world is safe enough to release the crown." Nexa removed the crown from Zap's head and placed it carefully back in the box, then he and his court sank back into the mists of the pond.

Zap frowned and gazed at the sky. "I thought we were through with trouble."

Vordon followed his gaze. "Apparently, we've only just begun, but whatever you do now, don't invite Alecto back into your life by worrying or being afraid."

Chapter 29

Jof was a man—a hard-working man—whose wife should appreciate him for all his hard work. It didn't make sense. Ever since that Vordon scoundrel had come around, his wife had been going around the house sighing like a love-sick lass with moons in her eyes. It made him sick to watch it.

"Can't you sweep the floor without dancing and carrying on like a silly woman?"

Like she didn't have a house to care for and an impressionable son watching, Maylee hugged herself and sighed again. "Oh, it ain't nothing, Jof. I just feel good. Don't you ever feel good?"

"Woman, I don't have time to feel good. I knew I shouldn'ta let you go off like you had any sense."

His boy looked up from throwing knuckle bones at the wall. "Pa, you ain't no kind of man—putting up with being cuckolded in your own house."

"You watch your mouth. I ain't no cuckold. She's mooning over a witch. I knew that man was a witch. He's put a spell on my wife."

"And there ain't nothing you can do about it. He may be a witch. But he's a man." He got up and headed for the door.

"Where do you think you're going?"

"Oh, it's a wide world. I'll find somewhere to go."

"And some trouble to get into. Why don't you mend that fence if you're such a man?"

"Mend it yourself." And the boy was gone.

Can't get no respect around here. Good-for-nothing boy. Probably doesn't know what a mended fence looks like. Jof sighed. If he didn't do it, it wouldn't get done. That was the rule around here. He thought that as the man of the house, he should make the rules. But it didn't work that way. He went out to the shed and got the tools he needed to mend the fence, then set to work, wondering just what it meant to be a man.

He noticed all the stars on the ground. What were they doing on the ground? They belonged in the sky. But they were on the ground in all shades of blue, red, green, white, and yellow. Every color he could think of.

"Hey, Jof! Look at what I can do with these things." Rin, his next-door neighbor, ran up waving one of the stars like it was the secret to eternal life. "Put those tools away, chum. See what I did to my house. Did it overnight and didn't lift a hammer or touch a saw. The star did it all."

Jof looked at Rin's house and was surprised to see the cracked mud bricks, moldy thatch, and broken door were gone over night. Instead, a shiny coat of paint covered what seemed like wood. On the roof were real shingles. He looked at Rin, whose wife and children respected him. A man who got things done. A man. "That's witchcraft. You let the devil mend your house. Now your house belongs to the devil."

Rin gaped in astonishment. "But these are stars. The devil doesn't make stars."

"Whoever heard of stars on the ground? I don't know what they are. But they're not natural, and you're in league with the devil." He left Rin sputtering and turned on his heels.

When he got to the market square, he went straight to the constable's office.

"Witchcraft!" The constable jumped to his feet. "I knew there was something evil about this. None but the devil would bring stars down from the sky. None but the devil has the power."

Jof nodded—vindicated. "And now the devil is giving his power to my neighbors."

"To all Romatica! I have to put a stop to this. Go home, gentle Jof, and don't you be tempted by the devil's wiles."

Jof returned home to find Rin holding court.

"There are enough stars for everyone."

"I don't know, Rin." A neighbor shook his head. "I've never seen anything like these stars, and I've seen a lot."

"No, but you saw my house yesterday, and look at it now. Why let creaky joints and Uncle Arthur keep you from fixing up your house, too?"

"Make way for the constable! Make way for justice and the righteous dispense of the law!" The town crier ran through the streets, shouting the constable's approach as imperial trumpets sounded.

The constable had taken time to don his robes of office, so the people drew back in fear as he approached Rin on his makeshift soapbox. "Are you the man who has sold his soul to the devil?"

"My sole? No, sir. Me and the misses favor flounders and catfish." Rin didn't seem to know the trouble he was in. "Fishing's easy. Don't know why anyone would buy it."

To his disappointment, nobody smiled at his levity. Instead, the constable scowled and slapped him. Guards pulled Rin down from his perch as the constable glared at Rin's house.

"So, this is the work of the devil, to tempt you to live above your station. The law requires that I give you a chance to speak for yourself. Though for such a crime, I can't think of what you could possibly say. Beg for mercy, perhaps."

"Mercy?" Rin growled as if he thought himself above the notion. "You hypocrite. You'll probably use the magic your own self."

"Silence, you child of the devil. You shall be stoned until you are dead." The constable turned to Jof's neighbors. "Let the people gather stones and rid the earth of this miscreant."

This wasn't quite what Jof had in mind, but Rin had sealed his own fate, bad-mouthing the constable, whose very word was law. So, he gathered ten stones and joined his neighbors as they encircled Rin.

Rin glared defiance. "Chud, didn't I help you when your wagon broke down?"

Chud was the first to cast a stone at Rin.

A trickle of blood ran down the side of Rin's head. "And Saluy, didn't I help you? And you? And you?" He looked around at all his neighbors as if they each owed him and couldn't seriously be thinking of stoning him.

The constable actually chuckled. "The good you did yesterday pales under the evil you've done today. Stone him."

Rin continued to sneer as a rain of stones broke his body. "Jof, we were neighbors. Is this how you treat a neighbor?"

Jof was horrified to hear his name on the lips of the condemned man. He threw the last stone at Rin to prove to the constable that he hated witchcraft.

The neighbors melted back into their homes as the guards dragged Rin's body away. Jof turned away. For some reason, he couldn't look. He didn't feel particularly proud of the day's work. "He wasn't a bad man." He thought he'd said it under his breath.

But the constable grasped Jof's arm. "Don't you be fooled by this man's seeming goodness. Once a man sells his soul to the devil, he belongs to the devil, and everything he does after that will be in the service of the devil." He shook his head as his guards gathered up the stars.

There were so many stars. Jof didn't see how they could get them all. "What are you going to do with them?"

"That's not for you to worry about. We have a special place for the relics of the devil. We'll keep them safe, so others won't be tempted to witchcraft."

The guards filled ten big sacks, and still there were so many more, as if all the stars in the sky had fallen to Earth. The constable looked longingly at the stars that still lay on the ground and put one in his pocket. He looked back to see if Jof had seen him, but Jof didn't meet his eyes. So, Rin had been right. The constable was a big hypocrite. Jof thought it must be all right to use the stars and secretly picked one up and slipped it into his pocket.

The constable was so worried about keeping his own secret that he didn't notice the slight bulge in Jof's britches. "We can't get them all right now, but we'll be back. I'll trust you to keep an eye on your neighbors and report to me any who let themselves be tempted by the devil."

"Sure, you can trust me. I feel the same way about this as you do."

"Good." And with a clasp on Jof's shoulder, the man was gone.

Jof went into his house. His son hadn't returned yet, so Jof set the star on the table.

"What's that?" His wife hadn't been out there. She hadn't seen what they did to Rin, but she'd know soon as the gossip mill turned. And it didn't turn as slowly as the mills of the gods.

"It's what you've always wanted." He started to say something Vordon can't give you , but he didn't want to mention the man's name. "But you have to keep it secret. Don't let the neighbors know you have it, or they'll get nasty with jealousy."

"That doesn't look like anything I want. What am I supposed to do with it? Hang it on the wall?"

"No, I'll show you as soon as the sun goes down."

When night came, he took Maylee outside. But it wasn't dark. The stars on the ground shone bright as day. And they weren't alone. Their neighbors cast sheepish smiles at one another as they each patted the star in their pocket.

The same hands that had picked up rocks to condemn Rin had picked up those stars, but there was nothing Jof could say. He took out his star and set it on the fence post. "Watch this." He didn't know what to do. He'd never used magic before. But he'd watched Myrlo do his work, and it seemed like the mage had done little more than think about what he wanted, and the magic just happened. So, he closed his eyes and put his hand on the star and pictured the fence as he wanted it. When he opened his eyes, the fence was mended without a trace of where it had been broken. Well, if the devil works like that . . . Then all the neighbors started using their stars.

Jof's son returned. He had several stars of his own and a beautiful lass on each arm. "This is Jilly, and this is Lorne. They know what a real man can do for them." He looked around the house. "And from the looks of things, you do, too—at last, Pa."

Chapter 30

"Jawan!" Cintella screamed.

Jawan put the brakes on his feet, but the rest of him kept going, stopping inches from plunging into Vordon's fire wall. Good thing Loby was beside him. If he'd bumped him from behind . . . "Loby? You're the fire mage. Get rid of this."

"What makes you think I haven't tried? This isn't natural fire. It's some kind of magical fire. I don't know how to get rid of it."

Jawan backed away. "Magical fire? But I thought you used magic."

"I do use magic on fire, but the fire is not magic. I use magic on natural fire, and this is not natural."

"No, it's not," Savorne said. "I feel no aversion to it as an element. There's no way I could be so close to so much fire and not feel terror."

Loby just stared at the conflagration. "It doesn't even burn like natural fire. Look. It's not burning anything. Fire has to burn something. This fire is just there, and it's not spreading."

Prenda shuddered at the flames. "But it's still hot, and we can't pass through it. I feel the baby reacting to it as if it knows this isn't its true element. It's something over which the fire mage will have no power."

"You know the baby will be a fire mage?" Loby came close to smiling. "Then I will have my apprentice."

Crisp hissed at the fire but didn't approach it.

Jawan headed for the fire pit door. "Well, if it's not spreading, it's only blocking one way out of here. I'm going to the pond to get Zap and have a talk with your friend Vordon."

"He's no friend of mine."

The five of them went down to the fire pit and took the tunnel outside.

"I'll go around to the library and see if I can't find something about this kind of magic."

"Is it safe? Are you sure it won't spread?" Savorne asked.

"Not with all that stone. I just hope it doesn't find anything that it
can
burn."

"What's that on the ground?" Jawan stepped carefully around what looked like stars on the ground. Impossible. "What are they?"

"I don't know, but maybe it's the same kind of magic as the fire. I'll have to study it."

Jawan laughed, remembering how he'd thought ill of his master, Myrlo, for studying a problem instead of just getting rid of it.

Loby and the women headed for the portcullis.

As Jawan walked toward the pond, the green earth stars called to him, but he didn't recognize them as the kind of earth magic that Myrlo used.

"Jawan! It's Jawan! Ooh, come and see what we've done."

Jawan was glad to see Zap, but the idea that he and Vordon had brought the stars troubled him, though he didn't know what the stars were.

"Hello, Jawan." Vordon smiled like all was well in his world, and these stars were the answer to his dreams. "Welcome to our little tea party. Sorry about the fire, but we had to go, and you seemed not to understand that. At any rate, you found a way out. Good."

The man was mad. "This is not natural magic sanctioned by the mages."

Vordon smiled. "It's the magic of Zelfor. The mages are no longer needed because magic is available to all people."

"No." Jawan shook his head, backing away from the mad man. "This is wrong." He turned to Zap. "Come with me. We'll go back to the castle and find out what this is all about. It's not what you seem to think."

But before Zap could move, Vordon used a wind star to blow Jawan back toward the trees. Wind and earth—opposite elements, evenly matched. But he was just his master's journeyman. He was no master of earth magic.

Myrlo, the great earth mage, would know how to stop this madman. Or would he? Like Loby, Myrlo worked with the natural world. He might have no more power over this unnatural magic than Loby had. Jawan felt like a useless journeyman who would one day be a useless master.

"Use us," the green earth stars whispered to Jawan again. "We'll give you all the power you need to beat the madman."

Jawan felt tempted, and that was what stopped him. If they were honest, why did they need to use temptation? They wouldn't help him beat Vordon when Vordon created them. If Vordon couldn't trust them, why should he? He turned back to his master's castle.

Myrlo listened carefully as Jawan described the mysterious stars and what Vordon had said they meant. The mage's face betrayed no alarm. Jawan didn't know if this meant Myrlo didn't believe him or if he knew all about it, and like all mages, knew more than he would tell.

"Master, I think this is something you should look into. This man has some kind of magic power that isn't natural. If you'd seen the fire he created in Loby's laboratory. And if you could see all those stars."

Myrlo only nodded. "This is something all the mages have to handle."

"What about Zap?"

"Clearly, this Vordon has Zap under his spell. I will talk to him."

"Talk to him? How? Vordon has him kidnapped."

Myrlo raised an eyebrow. "Zap's not a little boy anymore. He may be under the man's influence right now. But he'll come to his senses once he sees which way the wind is really blowing."

Jawan went off by himself, away from his master's over-awing presence. He couldn't wait for Zap to come to his senses. It was up to the Holy Order of Mice to save Zap.

Chapter 31

Vordon sighed silently as Jawan disappeared into the trees. The crown would have been the perfect evidence for Zelfor and its magic. There was no help for it now. "We must go back and tell the others about the wonderful news."

Zap frowned. "Do we still have any news to tell? All we have are these stars, and I don't think Jawan liked what you did with them. And I don't think they liked your parting gesture with the fire. They'll probably be mad."

"Yes, we do still have news to tell. Nexa said to wait. He didn't say it was over. Besides, they're out now. They'll be so happy to be free from the fire, they won't be mad.

But as they walked back toward the castle, they rounded a bend in the path and ran into none other than Loby and company.

"You!" Loby raised a hand toward Vordon.

Vordon winced. There was no telling what the fire mage might release from his hand before he remembered that he was supposed to feel grateful. Vordon couldn't help their anger. What was done was done. He picked up a star to show Cintella. "This is the magic of Zelfor. This is what has come down to you as the last queen."

Suddenly, the queen wasn't sure. She glanced at Jawan and Loby as if she needed their approval to be who she was. "But I'm the apprentice of the fifth element.

Loby nodded. "And you don't want to give that up for some pipe dream about being the queen of a kingdom no one ever heard of."

Vordon regretted not having the crown to show them, but he wasn't going to despair. "Why be an apprentice when you are

159

already a queen. Take your place. The universe gave its blessing by sending these stars."

"What did I tell you, Jawan?" Loby pointed a dangerous-looking finger at Vordon. "You sent these stars. They are the same unnatural magic as the fire."

"I didn't send the stars. They came from above, and magic is magic. Who are you to say what is natural when the universe has given its approval?"

They stared at the stars as if they wanted to make some retort but weren't sure what to say.

Zap picked up a red star. "This represents fire. And this represents earth." He picked up a green star. "And this white star represents spirit." He turned to Savorne. "Mother, you know about this. Your king Nexa came with all the undines to induct me in as the heir to the crown of Zelfor."

"I knew about Zelfor. But I hadn't known it would happen so soon. And I wasn't there with my king and my people to welcome you. We must return to the castle. I've been too long out of water."

"We can go to the pond."

"You can, but I can't. I must go to that thing you call a bath and fill it with water."

"Put those down!" Loby slapped the stars out of Zap's hands and marched toward his castle.

"How will we get in, Loby?" Queen Cintella asked.

Vordon wondered how they'd gotten out.

Loby pointed at Vordon. "You're going to put that phony fire out, or I'll crisp your britches with real fire."

As they headed for the laboratory, Vordon realized he didn't know how to put the fire out. He pulled out his book and thumbed for the incantation.

"You set my castle on fire that you don't know how to put out?"

"I knew it could be put out. I just wanted to make sure I have the words correct. The wrong words could make it spread."

"Just put it out."

Vordon found the words he was looking for and put the fire out. He was about to follow them into the laboratory when the chimes rang, signaling someone coming out of the portal. He stepped back just before Myrlo stepped in.

The earth mage was the last person Vordon wanted to see. No way could he make an easy case for Zelfor with this man around. It was Vordon and Zap alone against the four of them, with the queen undecided. And Prenda would, no doubt, take her husband's side.

"Loby, the mages are holding a conclave to determine what these stars are. As fire mage, your attendance is required."

Vordon thanked the stars that Loby and Myrlo were going away. If he just stood still, Myrlo wouldn't even notice him.

"I know where they came from," Loby said. "Vordon brought them."

Vordon backed farther away from the door.

Why don't they just leave?

"Vordon!" Myrlo spat his name like a curse. "He came to me before, and I turned him away. Where is Vordon? We must apprehend him and find out where he got the magic from."

"He's right here." Loby came out and pulled Vordon into the laboratory.

Myrlo flared at Vordon with green eyes that might as well have been red. "You have worked this mischief in the earth, and now all the earth is distressed because of you."

"It's not mischief. It's the magic of Zelfor."

Myrlo raised an eyebrow. "I never heard of Zelfor. There are five elements and five mages of the elements: earth, wind, fire, water, and spirit. The fifth element is sometimes called ether, but there is no element of Zelfor."

Didn't he know? Of course he knew. The hypocrite. These mages knew exactly what this was about. "Zelfor is a kingdom that existed in the very place where you now stand. In fact, it was the mages who destroyed Zelfor and deprived the people of their right to magic."

Myrlo drew in a breath as if Vordon had struck a nerve. "You don't know what you're talking about. The people don't have any right to magic. The mages protect magic from the people and the people from magic. They would abuse it, and no one would be able to protect them from themselves."

"Protect them from themselves? That sounds familiar. But who will protect the people from you when you have all the power? I've heard the mantra your journeymen sing."

Loby banged on the laboratory table, and Jawan huffed as if his best friend had been insulted. "What do you know about our mantra?"

Despite the seriousness of the matter, Vordon was enjoying watching them squirm. "Though wind and fire assail us. Though water and earthquake impale us. We are mice."

Loby jumped in Vordon's face. "You don't know what you're talking about!"

Myrlo raised an eyebrow. "What's that? I've never heard that before."

Loby obviously hadn't meant for him to hear it. "Nothing. I'm going to let Prenda know where I'm going." With that, he went up to their bedroom where Vordon supposed she'd been sleeping.

Vordon laughed. "The mages have hidden the truth of Zelfor, but now the universe has revealed it. After centuries of deceit, Cintella has been revealed as the last queen of Zelfor." He smiled at her and wanted to take her hand but knew he had to tread carefully until she accepted the truth for herself.

"What is he talking about?" Myrlo glared at Cintella.

Cintella stared at the stone floor. "I don't know."

"What do you mean you don't know?"

Myrlo clasped Cintella shoulders, gazing into her eyes as if he were her father and speaking to her as if Vordon weren't there. "Vordon is a charlatan wielding unnatural magic, and you should not be fooled by self-aggrandizing myths about a queen."

Vordon turned to Cintella, trying to get through to her with Myrlo still holding her. "We talked about this. You were happy to be queen of that great kingdom—lost though it may be—and . . ." He looked accusingly at Myrlo. "You even remembered something your grandmother told you."

Myrlo put himself between Vordon and Cintella. "This is nonsense."

Vordon stepped back. The mages had power here. He couldn't convince Cintella and Zap to take their rightful places without convincing the mages to relinquish their hold on power. They wouldn't do that on his word alone, but maybe they would listen to a higher voice. "If the magic I use were unnatural, the universe wouldn't have sanctioned it by sending the stars."

"By that logic, everything that happens can be said to be sanctioned by the universe."

"You speak of philosophy. I speak of magic that is real. The stars prove this is real." Vordon turned to Cintella. She was the queen. How could he argue for her if she would not argue for herself? "Will you let these mages keep you away from who you are while they apprentice you for something you are not?"

"And just what is she supposed to be?"

"She is a queen."

Myrlo rolled his eyes. "Queen Quila is queen in Romatica. Is there room for two queens?"

"I can't explain this to you. You think I'm talking about . . ."

Cintella stepped out from behind Myrlo. "I know what you're talking about. But it is my decision, but I will not make it alone. I will consult the spirits. If this Zelfor is real, then they will know it, and I must know it also. If it's not real, I will know that, too."

Vordon sighed. At least she wasn't a slave to the mages. Though he wasn't sure the spirits would support him either.

Chapter 32

Turbatius sat on his throne at last. He was king—no, he was lord of the Realm of Chaos. Change that. The Realm of Disorder.

Yet he didn't see disorder in his throne room. He didn't see anything. Just an empty room. He'd locked all the particles away where they wouldn't disturb him with the subtle order of chaos. But nothingness wasn't disorder either. Disorder was entropy, and entropy was the loss of energy, not matter.

He couldn't just let them out. Unless . . . he let them out . They couldn't create disorder in the Realm of Chaos. They belonged here. They could only create disorder where they didn't belong.

He opened the door to their prison, and billions upon billions of particles swarmed out. At first, he thought they might attack him for what he'd done to them. But they swept past him as if he were just another wall to be worked around.

"I am the lord of this realm. You will obey me." Then he thought about that. If disorder were controlled, it wouldn't be disorder. He couldn't control disorder, but he could create it.

He opened all the gates of the Realm of Chaos and blew the particles out into Nanosia.

They flitted about here and there—up and down, right and left, diagonally and zigzag. To Turbatius's delight, the normal movements of his children disrupted the orderly orbital movements of the quanta.

"You're not supposed to be here."

"You're not supposed to go there."

Turbatius laughed. What did his children know about supposed to?

"Move. You're in my way."

"You're occupying the space that I want to occupy."

That took care of the hidden order in chaos. This was pure disorder, and Turbatius loved it. He couldn't wait to see what this was doing to his arch enemy.

***

"This is highly irregular."

Particles from the Realm of Chaos disrupted Nano's efforts to send quanta through the nanotube. They zoomed in and out of the tube themselves, danced with Muto's charmed lambdas, and kept the W bosons going in such circles they didn't know a positron from a photon.

Nano's nine bosons tried to push the particles back into the Realm of Chaos, but Turbatius closed the gates, leaving them with nowhere to go and nothing to do. The particles danced around the bosons and zipped away in all directions. The hidden order of chaos had been hidden even to the particles, so they didn't miss it or see the difference between the law of chaos and pure entropy.

Muto saw a sight he'd thought he'd never see—particles from the Realm of Chaos dancing with his charmed lambda and even with regular quanta. So, Turbatius let them out. The particles were turning all Nanosia into one big Realm of Chaos. Nano must be going out of his mind. This was beautiful.

Among the careening quanta, he saw his first creation Amaki.

"What's the matter, dear? You don't look happy. Aren't you enjoying the fun?"

"You!" She shrieked and took off running.

Well, when the lambda run like prey, there's nothing for a wolf to do but give chase. So, wolf that he was, Muto chased her right through a portal and into Hadley Town.

The first thing Muto noticed was the storm was gone. Alecto hovered in the distance, but Vordon had done something to keep her at bay.

Instead of water, the ground was covered with stars—hundreds, no, thousands of stars covered every inch of ground. Muto wasn't sure he could walk on them. But Amaki had no trouble running on them, so he stepped out of the portal into a new kind of chaos.

Vordon stood by the pond with the boys from Nano's dungeon. Vordon picked up a yellow star and pointed it at one of the boys. The boy must have done something to vex Vordon, because he was blown back into the trees.

What are these stars? This is some kind of magic Vordon has stumbled on. He could play with Amaki anytime. For now, he had to tell Turbatius about this.

Turbatius looked like such a picture of bliss basking in the chaos of this new Nanosia that Muto hated to be the bearer of bad news. And whatever

Vordon was doing, Muto was sure Turbatius would take it as bad news. He wasn't wrong.

"The man has given me nothing but trouble. Now I will give him trouble." Turbatius glared at Muto as if remembering some trouble Muto had given him, too.

Muto backed away, glad that he hadn't mentioned the boys. One more piece of bad news and no telling what Turbatius might do.

"Come with me." Turbatius pushed through the cloud of particles and quanta.

"I think I'll stay here and keep an eye on things—make sure everything stays the way you want it."

Turbatius looked back at Muto with amusement. "You have no idea what I want." He stepped through the portal, not waiting to see if Muto was following.

Muto shrugged. He was getting to be a veteran of inter-dimensional travel. Oh, well. He followed Turbatius back into Hadley Town.

Turbatius glared around—disgusted. He must know what all those stars on the ground mean. Muto thought that if he hung around, he'd know, too, and he wasn't sure that would be a good thing. He just followed Turbatius, trying to look inconspicuous.

What looked like all of Hadley Town was milling around picking up stars and gazing at them with greedy eyes as if someone had dumped gold on the ground.

"Do you see this?" Turbatius swept his arm at the people. "This is not what I told Vordon to do. Where is Alecto?" He spotted her and scowled. "Why are you hiding in the glare of a clear sky? Where is your storm? Where is your fury?"

"My fury is for the wicked and the cowardly. But the boy is not afraid. I will attack him when his fear returns."

"Boy? What boy?"

Muto cringed. He wanted to back away, but that would mark him as guilty. All he could do was stand there and hope Turbatius didn't take his anger out on him.

Turbatius looked around. Many boys joined the crowd picking up stars. Muto had seen the stars' power. But was it so simple that even a child could wield it? He didn't see the two boys from the dungeon, but Turbatius would find them now that Alecto had mentioned them. Muto felt sorry for them.

"Why are you focused on a mere boy when it was Vordon who summoned you?" Turbatius demanded.

"But this is not a mere boy," Alecto said. "He is the last of the Zelforeans, and he has been acknowledged as such by the undine who guard the sacred pond."

Muto couldn't believe the boy was all that. He seemed like just a normal boy. If he'd do a little spin, even Nano might say he's regular as they come—in this world anyway.

Turbatius's eyes glittered. "I had the boy. I had him," he muttered. "Where is the boy?"

"He has gone into yon castle."

"How did he escape?" Turbatius glared at Muto as if he'd helped the boy escape himself.

Muto stilled his face to not look guilty or protest innocence too much. He just tried to not be there.

"What are they doing with those stars?"

Muto shrugged again. "Looks like they're working some kind of magic."

A homely lass held a blue star in one hand and a green star in the other. She smiled, and the features of her face flowed together like water, then solidified into a pretty face. A boy in homespun rags picked up a star, and they transformed into the raiment of a prince. Then the girl and the boy pranced off together.

"This is not entropy. This must stop."

"You want entropy?" Alecto cackled. "Then let me take some of these people to my home in Tartarus. They are wicked enough."

"Tartarus?"

"The underworld of the underworld. The door of absolutely no return."

"Taking these greedy townsfolk will not create the level of disorder I crave. Take the whole pond."

Alecto cackled again. "That will create disorder indeed. That will mess up somebody's plans."

Turbatius smiled, and Muto wondered.

Chapter 33

Cintella didn't like Myrlo making her decisions for her. If Vordon was a charlatan, she could find out by consulting the spirits.

"The spirits know a lot," Myrlo said. "But they don't know everything. You're just an apprentice. If you won't listen to me, then at least ask Quintessuma."

"Sure." But when she stepped through the portal to her castle, she had second thoughts about telling Quintessuma about Vordon and his magic stars. If the mages were having a conclave, she'd find out anyway. But Cintella needed to make her own decisions before Quintessuma made them for her, as mages did.

She may be just an apprentice, but Cintella knew how to consult the spirits. She'd talked to them and they to her. They may not know everything, but neither did the mages.

She went to the willow grove just behind the castle. Here sixteen rose bushes grew inside the fronds of a massive weeping willow. The willow was so huge that she could walk around inside its hanging fronds and never touch a bush.

Like walking a labyrinth, circling all sixteen bushes gave her spirit time to focus. When she came back to the first bush, she plucked one of the roses and sniffed its fragrance. Then she walked to the trunk of the tree and leaned back against it, closing her eyes. Every rose stem had one thorn on it. She pierced the tip of her finger and said the words that would bring the spirits to her.

"Spirits come.
Spirits go.
Their world is neither here nor there.
It is everywhere.
It is nowhere.
Thence we came.
Thither we go,
But no man knew where or when."

With each line of this incantation, she plucked a petal of the rose and made sure a drop of her blood touched it before she tossed it into the air. Some petals flew away—where, she knew not—and some melted into the earth. She knew this without opening her eyes.

Her spirit eyes opened, and she saw the spirits of men, women, and children in the quintessence.

"Is this Zelfor where I stand? Was there ever such a place?"

Five spirits swirled down to land within the willow. One of them came forward and touched Cintella's eyes. The willow disappeared, and she found herself floating through the streets of a village.

This isn't Hadley Town . She knew without being told that she was in a village of Zelfor. The people wore clothes like none she'd ever seen. A man entered a shop and came out carrying three stars like the ones she'd seen on the ground in Hadley Town.

So, the magic was for everyone who had the money to buy it. They couldn't pluck it off the trees or fish for it in the ponds.

She floated through the streets being guided by the same force that brought her to this place. The village soon gave way to countryside. This wasn't different. The grass was still green, birds still flew in the blue sky or sang in the tall trees. So Zelfor was on Earth.

She'd heard of Romatica but had never been there, so when she entered a large town, she imagined that it was what Romatica must be like—crowded and noisy. Every building was two or three stories high. In several buildings women hung out of the windows, calling at men on the street. She'd heard of what went on in these houses and was glad the spirits weren't going to take her inside.

She passed drinking houses and taverns on her way to the center, where stood a glorious palace. It made the mages' castles look like oversize hovels. She landed on a balcony of blue marble with gilded railings. Then she rushed toward a stained-glass door. She couldn't tell if she was coming toward the door or if it was coming toward her, and she couldn't slow down or close her eyes. She just braced herself for the crash. Instead, she floated through the door like a ghost.

The room was bigger and taller than the house she used to share with her grandmother. Women in silk gowns and men in velvet doublets mingled and chattered. A young man dressed in chainmail snatched a drink off a tray carried in by one of the many servants.

Cintella passed right through them and didn't stop until she reached a golden throne, where sat a jolly king. He looked like Vordon. No, he looked like an older version of Zap. She'd never noticed that they looked so much alike.

Beside him, ten men stood wringing their hands and whispering to each other and to the king. She could tell they were whispering, yet she could understand what they were saying.

"Your Majesty, you must protect the magic from Zelfor's enemies."

"There is naught that we must do. We need better advice than this. Don't you know the magic belongs to everyone? How can we protect it without limiting it? Shall we attack the very foundation on which Zelfor rests?"

"But, Your Majesty, forty percent of the students in the magic school are foreigners."

"Magic knows no foreigners, and neither does our school."

While the king slept that night, the spirits of Zelfor took the crown from the chamber where it was kept and replaced it with a gold crown of no magic power. Cintella had never seen a crown before. The mages wore none. Though she knew the king in Romatica wore one, she doubted it exuded as much power as the crown the Zelfor king had worn. It was marked with runes symbolizing the five elements. Then was what Vordon had said true? Was his magic no different from the magic of the mages? Then why were Myrlo and Loby so dead set against him?

In the morning, the royal valet rushed into the king's chambers near tears. "Your Majesty, the crown of Zelfor has been stolen and replaced with a fake."

The king laughed. "Someone is playing a prank on me."

Cintella groaned at his gullibility. No wonder the spirits took it. She thought she'd seen it all when he put out a reward for the crown's safe return.

When word went abroad that the crown was missing, a vast army invaded Zelfor. The kingdom had thought itself so secure in their magic that they didn't even have a standing army, so they weren't prepared for a serious invasion.

The jolly old king had always been able to talk his way out of any predicament, so he called for a parley.

Their mages met him at the edge of the battlefield, but they came to talk piece, not peace. The sergeant looked around at the empty battlefield. "Where is your army?"

The king shrugged. "We have our magic. We are a peaceful nation and have no plans to invade our neighbors. What need have we with an army?"

"You are a fool, King Saba. And since you cannot guard magic, we will guard it."

They closed all the shops and gathered up all the stars. Anyone caught with a star was put to death.

They held a conclave and elected five mages to be the masters of the five elements. But they weren't satisfied. "We must find the sacred crown of Zelfor. Then our power will be absolute."

"And we won't call this place Zelfor ever again. Henceforth the name of our land is Romatica."

But the spirits built a pond in the place in the middle of a forest where the foreign mages would never look. It was a forest far from the king's palace but still within the realm of what was Zelfor. They buried the sacred crown under the water and commissioned Nexa, the king of the undine, to guard it. The five mages built their castles near this place of power, though they never searched for the crown in the pond, and their presence only made it less likely that anyone would think to look for it right under their noses.

In their mad search for the crown, the foreign mages broke into the king's palace and killed many.

"Long live the king," their most loyal courtiers cried as they pushed the royal family into the castle's secret passageway.

This saved them from sure slaughter but left them as exiles, bereft of wealth, kin, and country.

They'd wandered here and there, doing odd jobs and farm work to sustain themselves, until they came at last to the place where the five grand mages dwelt—what was now Hadley Town.

Cintella sat back as the fronds of the weeping willow ended her vision. Vordon had been right. And what her grandmother had told her had been about Zelfor. Cintella remembered those days not long ago when she was a young lass living with her grandmother after her father passed away.

They'd come from a land far away. So far away that no map in the kingdom bore its name. Cintella remembered Vordon said far away could mean time as well as place. And of course, the Romaticans wouldn't put the name Zelfor on a map.

Hers had been a royal family with great wealth and magic. Her grandmother's whole face had come to life as she told Cintella of footmen in fine livery and maids. Oh, the maids! There'd been a maid to make the bed in the morning, and another to pull the covers down for the night.

The family belonged to a powerful and very old dynasty. But they had enemies. Just when they'd thought their place in the world was secure and their enemies were nothing more than an occasional nuisance, an army that stretched from east to west assaulted their borderlands.

"I had a brother who died who had a son named Havlo, who was lost and didn't acknowledge the kingdom because it had been lost. But I know, and now you know."

Havlo! The name kept popping up. Savorne had called Vordon Havlo, then Vordon said he'd dreamed about Havlo. Now Cintella remembered her grandmother saying Havlo descended from a royal family. What could the connection be between Havlo and all these people?

The spirits had shown Cintella more than even her grandmother had known. But the more she knew, the more questions she had. How could she be the queen if Zap is the king since the man said she would marry Jawan?

Even through the fronds of the willow Cintella could sense Quintessuma searching for her. She had to brace herself. Quintessuma would sense that she'd been in the quintessence and want to know why. There was no way Cintella could lie to the spirit mage. Quintessuma would want to know, and Cintella would have to tell her whether she was ready to do so or not.

She entered the castle and went to the chamber where her master waited. Quintessuma stood in the middle, the only focal point in a bare room with black walls spangled with stars so bright Cintella felt as if she'd stepped out into the universe. Her eyes—her spirit—were drawn to the mage of spirits. Could she stick to her decision? She wasn't sure she'd even made a decision. Vordon had been right, but Cintella still wasn't sure how to interpret that.

But she was sure that she couldn't let the mages railroad her into submitting to their authority without thinking things through.

"What did the spirits tell you?"

Cintella gulped. "They told me . . . they told me this land that we call Romatica used to be Zelfor."

Quintessuma's eyes narrowed. "Did they tell you that, or did they show you something that you interpreted as Zelfor?"

Cintella couldn't believe the mage was actually trying to discredit what she'd seen. "I asked them if we were in Zelfor, and that is what they showed me. Why would they show me that if it weren't an answer to my question?"

"Who knows why the spirits do what they do? Why did you ask about Zelfor? Do you believe that there is such a place?"

That was a dangerous question. Cintella couldn't lie to the mage. Most importantly, she couldn't lie to herself. "I don't have to believe in it. I've seen it."

"You've seen a vision."

"Are you saying the spirits lied to me?"

"You haven't answered my question. Why did you ask them about Zelfor?"

"Because Vordon told me I am the queen of that land. My grandmother told me I am descended from royalty."

Quintessuma stood still like the statue of serenity herself. Only her eyebrows moved—whether in anger or exasperation, Cintella didn't know. "I don't know why the spirits showed you that particular vision. But you can't fulfill the duties of an apprentice and the duties of a queen. You must decide what you want to be."

Cintella knew that already. Vordon had said as much. There were still too many questions. Vordon might know the answers—no matter what the other mages thought of him. It wasn't about whether she was ready to make a decision, but were they ready for the truth Vordon was determined to tell them?

Chapter 34

Jawan shook his head in reluctant disbelief. Disbelief that Vordon was telling the truth. Reluctant because he didn't want to believe that Cintella wasn't. "It's true. At least part of it is."

Vordon had no problem believing his own tale. "It's all true. Now we know the true history of Zelfor."

"Nexa wouldn't have put on a big show with all his court if this weren't true." Savorne would know what her king would and wouldn't do.

But Loby still held out. "I don't know."

For his own reasons that only a mage would know, Myrlo remained adamant. "No. This makes no sense. Cintella, did you even bother to talk to Quintessuma?"

"After the vision. But there were too many questions still unanswered."

" After the vision? Did it ever occur to you to talk to her before the vision? She could have shared the vision with you and answered all your questions. That's what an elemental master is for."

Jawan raised an eyebrow at the idea of the secretive mages answering all their questions, but he said nothing.

Vordon turned to Cintella. "Well, of course, some questions can only be answered by time, and some things are buried in the past."

"I'm not talking about the past," Cintella said. "I need to know what I'm supposed to do now. If I'm the queen . . ."

Jawan remembered the old beggar man who prophesied that he would marry a queen. He loved Cintella. The thought that she was the queen and that the prophecy was coming true right before his eyes excited and frightened him. But there was a problem. "If you're a queen and I'm to marry you, wouldn't that make me a king? The old man hadn't said anything about that, so I'd be a king only because you're a queen."

Cintella shook her head. "But they gave the crown to Zap. If Zap is the king, none of this is making any sense."

"Nexa didn't say I'm the king. He said I'm the heir."

" The heir . Yes. And if what I saw in the vision is true—and I believe it is—you are the son of my grandmother's nephew. That makes us cousins. One big royal family."

"Incredible!" Jawan said. "That makes Vordon the king if his son is the heir."

"No, in the vision, my grandmother said Havlo not Vordon." Cintella looked at Vordon. "I guess you know how that works out. Some connection between you and this Havlo."

"Yes, I know." Vordon stared off into space, then shrugged. "I'm not the king. But you're the queen. Havlo was not in the direct line of descent, but since Zap is his son, he is the closest thing you have to an heir."

Jawan wondered where his place was in all this. "But if I marry Cintella, won't that make me a king?"

"No, you can be her consort, but you can't wear the crown of Zelfor because you're not a Zelforean."

Her consort! Talk about a big-time demotion. Well, at least he'd know whose consort he'd be, but what would she be the queen of? "How can she be a queen without a kingdom?"

"Good question," Loby said.

Myrlo was quick to say, "She can't."

"No! No! No!" Vordon insisted. "It's not a political kingdom. Cintella is the queen of the magic of Zelfor. Once the danger is past and Zap takes his crown, Zelfor will be inevitable."

Danger! "What danger?" Jawan thought of Alecto and Turbatius but didn't know what they had to do with Zelfor.

Vordon said, "Don't think Turbatius is gone. We don't know what plans he is hatching even as we speak. Nexa won't relinquish the crown to Zap until Turbatius is no more."

Jawan remembered the dungeon in the Realm of Chaos and knew Turbatius wouldn't just go away. "So are we just supposed to wait for Nexa to summon us? Will the king of the undine come here?"

Savorne shook her head. "He will not leave his pond."

Jawan had heard enough from people who didn't know what to do. "Then we need to go to the pond and ask Nexa what to do about Turbatius, unless one of you has an idea."

Myrlo rolled his eyes toward heaven. "This is all very convenient. You have a magic crown that you can't get until you get rid of a magic monster. And you need the king of the undine to help you. Cintella, does any of this really make sense to you?"

"It does. And if Nexa won't come to us, we need to go to him and ask him what to do."

Myrlo threw up his hands. "Now that I know where the stars come from, I will tell the other mages and we'll determine what to do about Vordon. As for what the spirits told you, Cintella, I'll see what Quintessuma has to say."

"Do about me?" Vordon postured in front of Myrlo. "I'll tell you what to do about me—leave me alone and let me do what I am destined to do."

"I doubt we'll leave you alone, Vordon. I doubt that very seriously." He turned to Loby. "Fire mage, we must go." With that, he left the castle and Loby followed.

Cintella looked at Vordon. "Did you just tell the earth master to leave you alone?"

"He's not my master, and you know how I feel about mages. It's not like you haven't wanted to tell him the same thing."

Cintella looked away.

"Well, I guess we'll be going, too. Savorne, it's your king, so I guess you should lead the way."

Savorne blanched. "No, if you're going to talk to Nexa, then I should not be with you. The last time I saw him, he wasn't too happy with me."

Jawan stared at her. "Why does that sound like an understatement?"

Savorne shrugged. Jawan shrugged back, and he, Zap, Vordon, and Cintella headed for the pond.

When he stepped past the last tree into the clearing, Jawan stopped and stepped back. "We must have taken a wrong turn. I could have sworn the pond was down this path.

"What do you mean?" Zap stepped around Jawan. "This is the path we always take. This is . . ."

They stepped into the clearing. Where once Jawan and Zap had skipped stones and Alecto had raged, there was not a drop of water—only a hole fifteen feet wide and twenty feet deep where the pond had been.

"Jawan?"

Jawan looked around. Who could be calling him out here? The trees?

"Jawan." Out from behind a tree popped a creature from another world.

"Amaki? What are you doing in Hadley Town? How did you get here?"

If Jawan had been surprised, Zap was delighted. "Amaki!"

Cintella and Vordon turned to gaze at the little quantum from the Quantum Realm. "What is that?"

Zap glared at Vordon. "She's not a what. She's a who, and her name is Amaki."

"I don't care what it is. It's not human."

"As I said, she has a name, so she's not an it ."

"I'm afraid that today I am the bearer of bad news."

"If it brought you here, it must be very bad news."

Jawan stooped down to eye level with her. In her world, she'd be one-billionth his size. But in this world, she was as big as a small child. "What happened?"

"Turbatius, that awful spirit from the Realm of Chaos, took the pond."

"Took the pond?"

"How do you take a pond?"

They stared at one another totally dumbfounded.

Vordon asked the question that was most puzzling. "Where are the undine? They must stay with their pond, and if he took the whole pond, are they still in it, or did he destroy them? Is Savorne the only undine left?"

It was an important question—not just for Savorne but for all of them. It was their reason for coming to the pond in the first place. But nobody had an answer.

The question led Vordon to another conclusion, and he gasped. "If Turbatius has the undine, then he also has the crown of Zelfor."

Zap shuddered. Alecto gathered her clouds, and the five of them ran for the cover of the fire mage's castle. Lightning and gale force winds chased them into the portcullis. Jawan cranked up the drawbridge, and they all collapsed with exhaustion and dread.

Vordon was the first to rise. "We have to go after him."

Zap shook his head in dismay. "He's in the Realm of Chaos. I don't want to go there again."

"If we want to save the undine and your precious crown, that's where we have to go." Jawan entered the laboratory, wondering which of them would tell Savorne about the pond. She looked up at him expectantly, and he didn't think he'd be the one.

"That was quick. What did he say?"

Vordon took Savorne's hands and started to speak. "It's . . ."

Savorne pulled her hands away. "It's what? What happened?"

Staring at the floor, the table, the fire cubes—everywhere but at Savorne—Vordon tried again. "The pond. It's gone."

"What do you mean, it's gone?"

Amaki stepped forward. "Turbatius took it. He took all of it and left a big crater."

"B-but my people are in that pond! If he took it, where are they?"

Jawan, Vordon, and Cintella glanced at each other. None of them spoke.

Savorne sank under the weight of the only conclusion she could come to. "He destroyed them. He destroyed the king of the undine, and I never had a chance to make peace with him. I'm an undine without a people. I can't just go to another pond."

"We don't know that he destroyed them." Vordon held on to hope. "We'll go to the Realm of Chaos and find them."

"The Realm of Chaos!" Savorne gasped. "That doesn't sound like a place where good things happen."

Zap backed away. "It's not, and I don't want to go there."

Jawan headed for the portal. "Well, we're all going, but you can stay here. Maybe Myrlo and Loby will be back before Alecto brings the roof down. Not that they can stop her. But they sure will be happy to see you."

"No, I won't stay here by myself." Zap followed the five of them through the portal.

Jawan stepped into the mists of Nanosia and knew something was wrong.

Cintella staggered out of the portal and stepped up beside him. "This is Nanosia? At last, I get to see this place."

Jawan turned to stare at her. She wasn't supposed to be here. He remembered how she'd gotten stuck on the Hadley Town side of the portal when she'd tried to come here before. Some law kept her from being in the same world with her alias, Queen Quanta. But here she was. This was the chaos Turbatius had created. It was more than chaos. It was disorder.

Savorne tumbled out of the portal, gasping for breath. Jawan had forgotten to warn her to brace herself for the sensation of being pulled apart and put back together. "Are you all right?"

She stood up and closed her eyes to get her bearing. "I think so."

"The Big One!" a swarm of quanta surrounded Jawan and his friends.

Swarm? In Nanosia? Again, Jawan knew something was wrong. Nano never let his quanta swarm. They orbited and spun in orderly groups. Only in the Realm of Chaos did the particles swarm, and they were particles, not quanta. So, where was he?

"The Big One has come again."

"He has come with all his disciples."

"But there is no trouble for him to save us from."

"Maybe he came to join the fun. That's why he brought all his disciples."

"The more, the merrier."

Fun? Jawan looked around at all the quanta mixing with particles in pure disorder. This wasn't even chaos. Despite his misgivings about the Realm of Chaos, he had to admit there had been a beauty in the surprising patterns and colors the particles created when they danced. But here there was no beauty. Just disorder.

"It looks just like the queen." A lambda landed on Cintella's shoulder.

"It's the queen's antimatter," a proton said.

"An antiqueen."

"No, I'm not against the queen, and I'm not an it ."

"You'll just have to get used to that." Jawan twitched his nose as a neutrino alighted on it. "They mean well."

"You see!" Vordon beamed with pride. "There can be no doubt. Even the quanta proclaim Cintella as queen."

Amaki shook her head. "They think she is the queen's antimatter."

"And you should know there is no fundamental difference. Only the charge is different between matter and antimatter. A queen and her antiqueen are mirror images."

Jawan started walking. "It won't matter what the quanta say if we don't get to the Realm of Chaos and rescue the undine."

181

Cintella looked around at all the quanta and particles. "It looks like all of Nanosia is the Realm of Chaos."

Jawan sighed. "That will make it even harder to find out what Turbatius did with the pond."

"What's going on here?"

To Jawan's utter dismay, a rumpled-looking Nano and his nine bosons pushed their way through the horde of quanta and particles. Somebody had given the queen's right-hand man a hard time.

But Nano wasn't about to tell Jawan what happened to him. "You again! In the mist of all this chaos, you manage to make even more trouble."

Jawan wasn't going to take the blame for the dent in Nano's hat. Though he wondered what could have put it there. Maybe the same thing that was causing all the chaos in Nanosia. "I'm just an innocent bystander. There's no more trouble than there was when I got here. I don't understand why you're tolerating so much chaos. Getting lax in your old age?"

"The one thing I won't tolerate is you coming here pretending like you have nothing to do with this mess. You and chaos go hand in hand. Whenever there's trouble, you're somewhere around, and don't tell me some nonsense about a prophecy." He turned to his bosons. "Arrest them!"

The quanta and particles buzzed like bees.

"You can't touch the queen's antiqueen!"

"It's untouchable!"

"Touch it, and you touch the queen!"

They could do nothing against the bosons, but their sheer numbers created enough of a distraction for Jawan and his friends to get away.

They ran until they could no longer hear Nano venting his outrage. The mist shrouded them from his view, though they could still see the flashing energy of the bosons running here and there. They hadn't conjured a road to any particular place, so they had no idea where they were—just somewhere in Nanosia.

"What will we do now?" Cintella asked. "How do we get to the Realm of Chaos from here?"

Jawan shook his head. "Nanosia has changed so much. I need to talk to the queen to find out what's going on before we barge into the Realm of

Chaos." He conjured a road wide enough for the six of them, and they set off for the Quantum Realm.

"The palace is beautiful." Savorne clasped her hands together in awe. "It's brilliant like the palace of Nexa."

Jawan remembered when he'd first seen the palace of Queen Quanta. From a distance it looked like it was made of diamonds. But there were no diamonds in Nanosia. Diamonds were made up of atoms, and everything in the Quantum Realm was smaller than an atom. He hoped Savorne would not be too disappointed when she saw the unlucky quarks that made up the palace's walls.

"Make way for the Big One!"

Their escort of quanta and particles cleared a corridor straight into the queen's throne room for Jawan and his friends. Jawan cringed at the thought of big beefy bosons trying to force Vordon to prostrate himself before the queen. He just didn't see Vordon as the prostrating kind.

But the bosons were busy trying to keep order in the bedlam that had once been an orderly throne room.

Queen Quanta was on her throne, clearly not enjoying the chaos—no, the disorder—around her. Instead of orbiting the throne, protons, electrons, and neutrinos scurried about, bumping into one another, standing still, and ricocheting off the bosons. Worst of all, their spin was inconsistent. It was this lack of a spin that made Nano reject Jawan as irregular. The quanta in Queen Quanta's throne room were spinning, then standing still, then whirling at a breakneck speed before slowing to what amounted to a dirge. Jawan supposed that Nano preferred not to see this. Like his bosons, he could be in more than one place at a time. But the disorder outside must have been enough.

So Nano was one personality Jawan didn't have to worry about as he approached the queen. He looked pointedly at Cintella. "Stay here."

"No, we all came here with you, why should we stand here?"

Jawan opened his mouth to explain, but they were pushed forward by quanta and particles eager to see the queen meet her alias. Cintella stepped forward, totally oblivious to the danger, and when she and the queen met one another's violet eyes, they became locked in a mirror. When the queen clasped her hand over her mouth, Cintella's hand covered her own mouth.

When the queen blinked, Cintella blinked. Most uncanny of all, Cintella's clothes mirrored those of the queen. The entire throne room murmured in awe.

Jawan readied himself. As long as they were just looking . . . But they were matter and antimatter, and if they touched, they would annihilate one another.

"Are you mocking us? What's going on?"

Cintella was so mesmerized she reached out to see if the queen was really a mirror.

The queen was just as awestruck by this numinous meeting, and she reached out to touch Cintella's hand as it reached for hers. "We know you."

Jawan snatched Cintella's back and pushed her into the crowd of quanta. "If you love your queen, don't let them touch. You know what happens when matter touches antimatter."

"Long live the queen!"

"Not if you let them touch, she won't."

Cintella turned toward Jawan. "What do you think you're doing? She said she knows me. I'd like to know why, since I've never been here before. What kept me out the first time? Why am I the only one who doesn't seem to know what's going on?"

"I don't know how to explain." Jawan sighed. He really didn't understand how this worked. Like Vordon and Havlo, the queen and Cintella were somehow the same person, and they weren't supposed to occupy the same world at the same time as two different people. If they didn't stop Turbatius, who knew what other unthinkable things would be possible? "You and Queen Quanta are the same person. Don't ask me how that works. I don't know. But you're matter and antimatter to each other, and if you touch, you'll both be destroyed or turn into something other than what you are."

"But how does she know me?"

"This is still our court, and we do not appreciate being spoken of as if we were not present."

Jawan and company bowed deeply before the queen. "We apologize, Your Majesty. We were hoping you could tell us what's going on here. Why is there so much disorder? We know Turbatius is responsible."

The queen nodded. "The spirit of disorder. He was here, but he could only cause this much disorder if he brought something from the Big World that isn't supposed to be here."

The humans stared at each other. "The pond," they said in unison.

Queen Quanta blanched. "There could only be one pond he's interested in. Only one pond whose displacement could cause the trouble we're seeing."

"Then you know about this," Jawan said. "He took the whole pond, and as far as we know, he has all the undine and the crown of Zelfor."

"This is what we were afraid of. This is really bad." The queen's eyes fell on Zap and brightened. "But you have brought hope with you, for you have found the prince of Zelfor."

Zap stepped forward. "But I've been here before, Your Majesty, and you didn't know me."

"Because you did not know yourself. But now, you are the heir, and you must claim your kingdom. To rescue the undine and restore order, you must use the power of the crown."

Zap sighed. "Then we have to go to the Realm of Chaos anyway."

Jawan nodded. "Looks that way."

"Uh-oh." Everyone turned to Amaki, who stared at her feet. "I remember Alecto telling Turbatius to take the pond to Tartarus."

Queen Quanta's eyes grew big as moons. "That's the worst news we've heard in eons."

Chapter 35

Chapter 35

Loby followed Myrlo, feeling resentful that the earth mage walked ahead of him rather than beside him. He'd still been a journeyman when his late master died without preparing him to take up his mantle as the new fire mage. Loby had proven that he had mastery over his element, but the other mages still treated him like a junior member of their little club, and he resented it. As a father-to-be, he thought he should at least get some respect for that.

This was his first conclave, and he had no idea what to expect. Apprentices and journeymen were never allowed at these secret meetings. If only he could comport himself in a way that earned their respect. And respect was something he had to earn—not demand.

The magic stars crunched under his feet like fallen snow. He didn't want to step on them. This was a magic he didn't understand, and who knew what powers he was releasing? But between the castle and the forest, the ground was so thickly carpeted with stars that he had nowhere else to place his feet.

Myrlo bent down and picked up five of the stars. "Do you see this? It is a mockery of true magic. This is what the order of mages was created to guard against."

The order of mages?

There was still so much Loby didn't know. His late master had been too busy trying to destroy the universe to teach him anything. Loby had been thrust into the position with no knowledge of the history of the mages. He shouldn't have been surprised that they had some kind of organization—and order. In time, when the other mages stop holding his hand, maybe they'd get around to telling him about it.

"What is that?" Loby pointed at something glowing blue in the forest.

Myrlo looked up from studying the stars and wrinkled his brow. "I don't know, but we need to find out."

Whatever it was, it shone as brightly in the gloom beneath the trees as the noonday sun—except it was blue.

"Help! Fire master! Help!" Four boys ran out of the forest waving their arms and yelling. They grabbed Myrlo and Loby and pulled them toward the forest.

"You've got to come quick!"

"You've got to stop this."

"We didn't mean to do it."

"Please don't be mad. Just help."

Loby and Myrlo shook off the boys' hands and dug in their heels.

"What's going on?"

"Didn't mean to do what?"

"Fire!" the boys yelled at once.

"The tree is on fire."

"You have to help."

Loby and Myrlo looked at each other and ran to the forest. But even as they ran, Loby knew there was nothing he could do about blue fire.

As bright as it was, the fire was only burning one tree. The entire tree glowed like a lantern, but the flames didn't jump from tree to tree or ignite the underbrush. But it crackled like true fire, and the heat was so intense that they could not get within ten feet of it.

Loby noticed something red sticking out of one of the boys' pockets. "What do you have?"

The boy saw Loby looking at him and turned away. "Nothing. Aren't you going to put out the fire?"

Loby hesitated. Could he just tell them that he couldn't? They were depending on him, the fire mage, to know how to do things.

Myrlo turned to the boys. "It's not fire. It's something else, and we need special magic conditions to put it out."

"What's that in your pocket?" Loby asked again.

"Nothing . . . It's just a star."

"Give it to me." Myrlo reached for the boy, but he backed away.

"It's mine. I found it. Get your own."

"You can't play with these things. They're dangerous. Give it to me."

But Loby knew that just taking the boy's star was pointless when there were hundreds more all over the ground. He had to convince them to give them up. "You couldn't control the fire. You had to run to us for help. Suppose we hadn't been there. Let us find the right magic before you play with this stuff." Loby knew he'd said the wrong thing.

"Find the magic?"

"You're the fire mage. You're supposed to already have magic."

"Why should I give you the star when you don't know how to put the fire out any more than we do?"

"Because you don't know what you're doing." Myrlo reached for the boy again, but they ran. He raised his hand to summon earth magic to stop them, but nothing happened. "The stars are blocking me from the Earth. This has never happened before." He ran after the boys, and Loby followed.

The boys swerved through the streets of Hadley Town. Loby knew the town as well as they did, so their efforts to shake his tail were futile. But he and Myrlo stopped when they saw people waving stars all over town. They'd hung stars like talismans on their doors and clothes. They waved the stars around, using magic to do every little thing. Some folks were flying on wind currents like birds. They drank from the water stars as if they were canteens.

A crowd formed around two men facing off on the street pointing red fire stars at each other.

Loby drew in a breath when he realized the people were actually placing bets to see which man would win the duel.

"Enough!" Myrlo pushed into the crowd to the men. "You will not do this. These stars are not to play with."

"Are you going to call the constable on us, Myrlo?" Catcalls and snickers enlivened the crowd.

Loby stood beside Myrlo. "You don't understand what these stars are. You're playing with power you can't control."

"We understand it well enough, fire master. The earth mage should be happy I no longer have to chop down his precious trees for firewood."

"You mages have kept magic to yourselves long enough. Now we have it, and we're going to keep it."

Myrlo shook his head and said under his breath, "I never thought the mages would have to do this again."

Loby looked at Myrlo. Was that something he wasn't supposed to hear? "Do what?" He remembered what Vordon had said about the mages stealing the magic of Zelfor. He tried to throw the thought out of his mind. That was a long time ago, done by different mages. Not the ones he knew.

As if reading his mind, Myrlo sighed. "Just something unfortunate that happened long ago."

Myrlo hadn't answered his question, but Loby knew mages well enough to know that asking again would be met with the same tacit refusal. He turned his thoughts to the people.

They wouldn't give up their magic. A standoff between the mages and the people would be disastrous. No matter who won, everybody would lose. Then an idea formed in his mind. This could be his chance to prove himself by helping them find a solution.

Myrlo glared at the people, but Loby wondered what the earth mage would do. His earth magic didn't work, so there was nothing he could do. The longer he stood there glaring at the people, the more they'd wonder why he wasn't doing anything and the bolder they'd become. If he just walked away, the results would be the same.

Loby stepped forward. "When have we ever needed to call the constable? So, you found a little magic, and now you think you're ready to go toe-to-toe with the mages. Your magic is new. Our power is ancient. Yes, you have magic, but you don't have power, and your foolishness has left us with no other choice." He let that hang as an unspoken threat, then turned ominously and headed for Quintessuma's castle. He wondered how Myrlo would extricate himself from the crowd, but when he turned, Myrlo was already ahead of him, leaving the people wondering what the mages would do.

When Loby entered Quintessuma's council chamber, Volvo, the wind mage, was already seated. Myrlo stood trembling with rage as he threw the stars onto the council table. Quintessuma and Volvo looked at the stars, then at Myrlo, patiently awaiting his explanation.

"These stars give magic to the people while draining our power. I can't connect with the Earth, and I don't think Loby can connect with fire, or he would have used it."

A frown knit Quintessuma's eyebrows. "This sounds like . . ." She glanced at Loby as if weighing whether to go on.

"We might as well tell him." Volvo sighed. "I hope we won't be pushed that far, but if we are, he will have to be a part of it."

"A part of what?" Loby felt irritated. There was something going on, and his status as a mage was still not established enough for them to tell him what it was.

"But he's so young," Quintessuma said. "He might not understand."

Loby glared at these mages whom he'd thought he knew. They were sitting on a secret so terrible that they thought he wouldn't understand. Vordon's claims seemed more and more credible, and Vordon's solution seemed more and more like the only course they could take. "I hope I'm wrong about what it is so terrible that you don't want to tell me. But still, the people have magic now and won't give it up. Maybe we could teach them how to use it properly. We could form magic guilds and have more than one apprentice."

"That is not the way we do things." Myrlo glared at Loby like he'd said something unbelievably preposterous.

"That's the way it was done in Zelfor." Loby knew he had gone too far. He didn't care. When people wanted to bury the truth, revealing that truth was always going too far.

"What do you know about Zelfor?" Myrlo bellowed like affronted authority.

"Zelfor! This is about Zelfor? Cintella came to me today with a preposterous tale about Zelfor. It seems that your Vordon told her she is the queen of this so-called kingdom. I'd like to know what these magic stars have to do with this."

"I meant to ask you what you thought of that." Myrlo turned all his attention on Quintessuma like he was about to be vindicated. "She claims the spirits confirmed her as the queen of Zelfor. Considering what these stars are doing to our magic, do you really think the spirits would sanction something against nature?"

"No, and she can't be the queen of a forgotten land."

"Assuming that there ever was a Zelfor," Volvo said.

Loby couldn't believe they were actually going to try to deny the kingdom their predecessors destroyed.

But Quintessuma saw in Loby's eyes it was too late to do that. "Yes, long ago, there was a Zelfor. But there were no magic guilds. At least none that taught the people to handle magic responsibly. I hope we can avoid the violence the old mages used to wrest magic out of the hands of the people."

Myrlo drew in a breath as if trying to calm himself. "We may not have any other choice. You should have seen Hadley Town. These magic stars are all over the ground, and they won't give them up peacefully."

Loby gasped. He'd come here to convince them to treat him with the respect he deserved as fire mage. And he still didn't appreciate being treated like an unreasonable child. He was tempted to be just that, but this was too important. This was about more than just how they treated him. They were talking about unleashing violence on the very people they were supposed to protect. He had to convince them. He picked up one of the stars. "You can use force to make things stay the way they've always been. But doing what you've always done has left you in a place where you have no good choices for what to do about Master Lacus. Are you going to appoint Zap as the new water mage? With a guild and open access to magic, we'll always have someone trained to step in when a mage dies. And if we can't keep magic away from the people, at least we can have some control over how they use it."

Volvo shook his head. "The people are like children. They cannot be trusted with power even if we taught them how to use it. They will abuse it."

Myrlo nodded in agreement. "Power corrupts."

"You have power and aren't corrupted by it." Loby wasn't so sure about that, considering what they were thinking about doing.

"I am the master of spirits. I know the hearts of men. The more people who have magic power, the greater the chance it will be corrupted."

Loby remembered the Holy Order of Mice. He'd formed the club specifically because of mages like his former master, Lord Elveston, who treated their apprentices and journeymen like lab mice to experiment on as they pleased. "Mages have been corrupted with no one to check their power. The people should have a way to protect themselves."

The mages didn't look convinced.

Myrlo spoke for them. "You still have a lot to learn."

Chapter 36

"Tartarus?" Zap shuddered. "Why do I not even want to know where that is?"

"If that's where the pond is, that's where we have to go," Jawan said.

"If that's where the crown is, that's where we have to go," Vordon said.

"If my people are in Tartarus, then we must go to Tartarus."

"Tartarus!"

"Tartarus!"

"Tartarus!"

All the quanta and particles in the throne room shuddered.

"Where is Tartarus?" Zap asked. "Is there a fifth realm in Nanosia?"

Queen Quanta raised her scepter to signal order, but there was little use when they had already been in disorder. "Tartarus is the dark child of chaos. To go there, you must enter the castle in the Realm of Chaos."

"Chaos inside chaos!" Zap backed away. "There has to be another way to do this."

The queen shook her head. "There is no other way. And disorder is not chaos. Disorder was born of chaos. But is bereft of beauty. It is chaos bereft of its intricate order. We have been to the Realm of Chaos. The dance of the particles looks like disorder. But if it were true disorder, it wouldn't be a dance. There'd be nothing to delight the eye as it did ours."

Zap shuddered again. She made it sound like fun. But he'd been to the Realm of Chaos, and it was anything but fun.

"Don't worry about the Realm of Chaos, Zap." Jawan poked him in the ribs. "Nano and his bosons will get us long before we get there."

"That's not funny."

Cintella said, "It certainly isn't. We have to go there, Jawan, and you're not helping."

"I know. I'm just tired of Zap being scared of everything."

"You weren't scared of Alecto," Vordon pointed out. "Tartarus is just another Alecto."

Somehow, Zap didn't think they were the same. But when he thought about it, he couldn't have explained why not. He'd never been to Tartarus. "Suppose we run into Turbatius? I'll take a boson any day rather than him."

They'd all seen Turbatius and looked at each other with apprehension. None of them wanted to run into him.

Vordon looked away. "We just have to avoid him—see him before he sees us."

"Easier said than done when we don't know where he is." Jawan took Cintella's hand. "Are you ready for an evening stroll through the Realm of Chaos?"

"If only that were all it is. But how do we get there? In all this chaos or disorder or whatever you call it, there seems to be no difference between here and there."

"We will show you the portal that will take you near the Realm of Chaos, though there is no portal directly into that realm."

Zap thought he'd never get used to traveling through portals. The portals within Nanosia left him just as woozy as the ones into Nanosia. They all stumbled out of nowhere into the same melee of quanta and particles slamming into one another in their woozy rush to nowhere. "So how do we get from chaos to the Realm of Chaos?"

Jawan just started walking. "You know what they say—any road you follow will eventually lead to the Realm of Chaos if you stay on it long enough."

Vordon shook his head. "We don't have time for something that will happen eventually. And we can't follow just any road. Where exactly is the Realm of Chaos?"

Jawan kept walking. "This isn't just any road. I conjured it to take us where we need to go. That's how things work in Nanosia. So, come on."

They fell in behind Jawan and followed him through the mist.

"That's them!"

Nano and his nine bosons charged toward Jawan and his friends, and they took off running.

"Get them before they enter the Realm of Chaos. I knew he was in league with Turbatius." Nano scowled as Jawan's group passed through the gates of their dubious haven. "We can't go in there.

But maybe he'll betray Turbatius like he betrayed Antipan. Let them kill each other and save us the trouble."

Zap braced himself. Jawan wasn't going to kill Turbatius. He hoped they wouldn't even see Turbatius. In the mists of Nanosia, every direction was traversable. They could go up or down, right or left, back, forth, or diagonal simply by conjuring a road or steps under their feet, and the mist would congeal into that shape.

So, they went up in a straight diagonal line to the castle. Or as straight as they could while dodging particles. The particles zipped around like unstoppable objects, but Zap knew he wasn't an immovable object, so he dodged. The portcullis was up, so they piled into the vestibule. Zap headed for the laboratory.

"Where are you going?" Jawan asked. "This is a big castle. But I think we should stay together."

Vordon shook his head. "No, it's modeled after the fire mage's castle in Hadley Town and looks to be just as big. We should split up."

"What are we looking for?" Cintella asked.

"I know where to go. You must stay here." Zap didn't know how he knew, but he knew he was walking in the right direction and dreaded where his feet were taking him.

"That's right, son. You must do what you must do." Vordon stood beside Zap as he paused at the fire pit door. "We've been here before—this very castle in another world." Vordon closed his eyes, and Havlo opened his. "What are you doing here? Have you gone mad?"

Zap looked up with his hand on the door latch. "What?"

"We have to get out of here. The man is mad. You don't have to be mad with him. I'm in charge now. I know Ziph's death wasn't your fault. I should never have sent you away. But we can go back to Romatica now and be a family."

"What are you talking about, Vordon? You know I have to do this." But this wasn't Vordon. The vision of his father, so long ago—the man who took him from the orphanage—was the same as Vordon. "Who are you?"

"You know who I am, and you don't have to do this. You don't have to do anything anymore. Come with me. I'll keep you safe. I know you always wanted to be safe."

"No one will be safe if I don't do this. I'm not afraid."

Zap opened the door.

Havlo pushed the door shut. "You should be. Haven't I always told you that fear will keep you alive?"

What Zap had always felt as fear now manifest itself as anger. "Yes, I got that from you. But Vordon believes in me. He's more of a father than you."

Havlo grabbed the front of Zap's tunic. "You don't know what you're talking about. It was Vordon who summoned Alecto."

Zap wrenched himself out of Havlo's grasp. "That's a lie!" It had to be a lie. Zap wanted Vordon to come back and tell him it was a lie. But he knew that wasn't going to happen. Vordon had been evasive when they asked him why Turbatius came after him. If Havlo was Vordon, then they both summoned Alecto. He could trust neither of them.

"You know it's not a lie. Enough of this." Havlo grabbed Zap again. "You're coming with me."

"Where do you think you're going with my son, Havlo?"

"Your son? After you left him in an orphanage, you now want him to be your son?"

"You didn't have a problem with that when you sent him back to me. Let him go, Havlo."

Havlo sneered. "He doesn't have to do anything. He's just a boy. Why can't you let him be a boy—just a regular boy doing regular boy things?"

Regular boy things. That had always been what Zap had wanted. But that fearful boy had grown up a little, and his regular world would be anything but regular unless he did what he had to do.

Savorne moved closer, pleading evident in her voice and eyes. "You don't understand. He has to save my people. If Vordon is in you anywhere, you know he has to get the crown of Zelfor. I know he's a boy, but he's not a little boy. He can do this. He has to do this."

"Forget about Vordon. Forget about Zelfor and forget your sorry people. This is what I'm trying to get Zap away from—all these nonhumans and your magic. It's not natural. It's not normal. I want my boy to be normal. Why do you think I went to Romatica? Why do you think I left you and your stupid pond and married a real woman?"

"A real woman." Savorne stared at nothing. She stared at her hopes and all that she had given up to be with this man. She stared at the life they'd had together. She stared at the death of an undine whose human lover had been unfaithful to her. "Zap, you must not fail." She put her arms around Havlo and laid her head on his chest.

"Get away from me!" He tried to push her away, but her death grip held him fast.

Death grip? His mother was dead. He'd just met her, yet Zap hadn't felt so abandoned since Lacus was taken from him. He had nothing now. Not a mother. Not a father. Not a master. But he had his mission. *No, Mother, I will not fail* . While Havlo struggled to free himself, Zap slipped through the fire pit door.

Red, yellow, purple, and orange tongues of fire licked the walls. Beneath the roaring conflagration, the flames hissed, *Little boy, little boy, do you dare?*

"I'm not a little boy." But did he dare do what he knew he had to do? Now that he was in front of the fire, it was clearer than ever. He took a handful of the fire as he'd done in Loby's fire pit. It didn't burn him. He stepped closer until the flames licked his shins and his feet felt the rim of the pit itself. It was one thing to hold fire in his hands, but to reach Tartarus, he'd have to plunge in. He couldn't walk into it. He had to immerse himself in the element. And once he fell in, he had no idea how he'd get out.

Lacus appeared in the fire. "Don't be afraid."

Ziph appeared beside him. "We would not ask you to do this if you were going to die here."

Savorne appeared between them. "Son, you are not alone, but you are the only one who can do this."

Zap held his breath as if plunging into water and jumped. He'd expected to fall. Instead, the fire enveloped him.

He landed in darkness, and he knew he was in the abode of the damned. Their howls spoke of unimaginable torment. He turned one way and heard weeping. He turned another way and heard the gnashing of teeth. He looked behind and all around him and saw fire. Nowhere did he see any sign of the pond.

"A man."

"Let me grind his bones to make my bread."

To Zap's horror, six titans rushed at him. The smallest was fifteen feet tall. They bore clubs longer than Zap was tall. He ran—stumbling as their pounding steps shook the ground under his feet. He ran until the stitches in his side nearly drove him to his knees. If he stopped, the titans would drive him farther than that.

He saw a cave and ran into it. Falling to the ground, he gasped for breath. The titans beat the entrance to the cave with their clubs until it caved in. They couldn't get in, but Zap couldn't get out.

He widened his eyes, trying to adjust them to the darkness, but the cave was black as ink. He'd give anything for one of Alecto's lightning storms. At least there were flashes of light. But here there was only darkness.

To his left, he heard the sound of wings beating and the caw of birds. There must be another way in . He only hoped it was large enough for him as well as the birds. He got to his feet and felt the wall. It was slimy and sticky at the same time, and he snatched his hand away.

The cawing faded away, and a man moaned. "There is no help. There is no help for me. But I'm not sorry for what I did."

A person. Who could it be? Zap was happy to know he wasn't down here alone. But again, this was the place of the cursed, so whoever it was wouldn't give him any help. The man sounded like the saddest human in the universe. But Zap didn't care. Anything was better than being down here alone. Icky as it was, Zap had to follow the wall by touch until he found an opening where the man was.

A short corridor led to another cave. He looked around and guessed that lichen could grow anywhere—even in Tartarus. In the dim glow of this bioluminescent organism, Zap saw a man lying on the ground that was littered with feathers.

"You have no wings," the man whispered. "You're not a vulture."

"Last time I checked, I wasn't."

"The last time you checked! Then you can turn into a vulture. What creature have the gods created to torture me with now?"

"No, I'm just a boy."

Six vultures entered and pecked at the man's stomach until his insides were exposed. Then pulled out one of his organs and fought over which of them got the biggest piece.

Before Zap could figure out which way to run, the birds turned and flew away without looking at him. The man's stomach healed until it was smooth and unblemished as a newborn baby's.

Zap sighed with relief. "They're gone."

"They'll be back. I've been down here for eons. They come, eat my liver, then fly away. It always heals. They always come back, and it never hurts any less no matter how many times they've done it."

Zap felt sick. His own stomach lurched in commiseration. He looked more closely and was puzzled. "You're not chained down here. Why don't you run away?"

"The gods put me here. I can't escape."

"How do you know? Have you ever tried?"

"The gods put me here. What's the point of trying?"

Zap backed away, shaking his head. What could this man have done? He didn't look like he could have done anything worse than what Turbatius had done. Maybe Tartarus was a different world with different gods. Or maybe the gods only punished people who believed in them—like this man. Zap was in Tartarus, but no god had put him here to punish him. Maybe they would punish him just for being here—if he believed in them.

"You better believe in ussssss, little boy."

Zap nearly jumped out of his britches when six snakes slithered across the ground with poisonous venom glistening on their fangs. They bypassed the man and came straight at Zap. Without even thinking of which way was out, he started running. At the far end of the cave was a black space without lichen. Zap thought that was an opening and ran for it.

The snakes chased him into another cave where a man strapped to a burning wheel hung suspended in midair. Zap couldn't tell what the wheel was hanging from. The wheel turned, so that sometimes the man was upside down. When he was right side up, he looked like a handsome prince, despite the shocked expression on his face.

Above the wheel hung a crudely lettered sign. "For unlawful carnal knowledge." When the flames burned his skin to blackened bubbles, it healed completely, and then burned him again.

"Never try to love a goddess, or you'll wind up like me," the man said before turning upside down.

Like him! Zap gulped.

"Yesssss, little boy. Jussssssst like him." The snakes came at him again. With two flanking him on either side and two behind, it was clear they weren't just chasing him. They were herding him.

He plunged through an opening in the cave wall and entered another chamber. Instead of stone, grass carpeted the floor of this cave. A tree top-heavy with fruit hung over a crystal-clear brook. A man reached for the fruit, but as if it had a will, the tree pulled the branch out of his reach. He tried to fill a cup, but the water ran from him.

"What are you doing?" Zap asked.

"This is my punishment—to grasp forever at that which remains out of my reach."

"Why do you keep reaching for it? Aren't there other trees in Tartarus?"

"Yes, but this is the one I want. If I keep trying, sooner or later I'll catch the tree unaware and grab the fruit. I've been doing this for so long, I can't quit now."

"How long will you keep doing that?"

"Who knows. The one I give up on may be the one I could have gotten."

That is a punishment , Zap thought. He wondered if that might be his punishment for reaching for the crown of Zelfor, which seemed to be just as much out of his reach.

"You haven't seen punishment yet, little boy. It gets worsssse and may never get better." Snakes behind him and beside him, a swift brook in front of him. If he jumped in, he'd never get to the other side. There was a time when fear kept him alive. And being alive meant staying away from water. Vordon had told him he wasn't afraid of water anymore. Why was he thinking about Vordon? If he drowned down here, nobody would know what had happened to him. So, he thought he was the heir of a powerful crown. He had no power. He was just a boy with nothing to crown his head but muddy brown hair.

"Hiss."

The water was fast moving, but it didn't have poisonous fangs. He jumped in, and the current carried him away.

The hills and trees zipped behind him faster and faster. A tree hung its branches low in the water, but it was all Zap could do to keep from being clobbered by it—never mind grabbing it.

A man pushed a gigantic boulder up a hill beside the brook. When he got near the top, the boulder slipped, and he jumped out of the way to keep from being crushed. The boulder rolled down the hill and splashed into the water just in front of Zap.

He couldn't stop. He couldn't go around it. He could only close his eyes and wait while the unstoppable object that was his body met the immovable object that was the boulder.

The brook went under the boulder, and he found himself in another cave. He saw a pond and knew it was his pond, but he had to get out of the brook. He could throw himself against the ragged rocks of the bank. Ahead of him, a dragon emerged from the brook and opened its maw to swallow him. Zap grabbed one of the dragon's fangs and swung out of its mouth just before it clamped down on what would have been his legs. The dragon's eyes were as big as a cave entrance, and it glared at Zap as the boy tried to pull himself up on the dragon's snout. But the leg of his britches was caught in the dragon's teeth. He held on precariously to the dragon's snout and pulled as hard as he could, but they were stuck. With one hand, he loosened the cord that held his britches and shimmied out of them.

Zap felt the heat from the dragon's nostrils. It drew in its breath, and Zap felt himself being drawn in with it. He clambered up on the dragon's head and climbed down its neck just as it released fire and burned the britches he'd left behind.

The dragon reached up a claw to slap Zap off its neck, but Zap jumped—landing hard on the rocky bank. The dragon roared and breathed fire. Zap scrambled away. The fire kept coming. Zap kept scrambling until he fell into the pond.

Chapter 37

Nexa hated being called before the undine council. He racked his brain for an answer the eleven members of this somber assembly would accept as an answer to their inquiry.

"We've been made to understand the undine are celebrating because the reason for our guardianship has been fulfilled. The heir of Zelfor is now with us, and the magic has confirmed him."

Nexa stood before them, trying not to betray his discomfort, but his trembling lips and unstill hands betrayed him.

Jonlin, the council's speaker, rolled his eyes. "So we'd be interested to know why the crown still remains with us."

"There is a problem." Nexa knew his stalling would only make them more suspicious of what he would tell them. But he still wasn't ready to just come out with it.

"Do you think we don't know that there is a problem? In fact, there are several problems. What we really want to know is why you allow celebration of what couldn't possibly be the heir to Zelfor. Not only is his mother a traitor to the undine, but his father is an untalented human."

Nexa exhaled half the breath he'd been holding. It was bad enough that they knew about Savorne and Havlo, but at least they didn't know about Turbatius. Maybe he could think of some way to . . .

"And we don't know if it was fortune or misfortune that a spirit of disorder threatened the crown, since you saw the threat and had enough sense to take the crown back after placing it on the imposter's head."

He couldn't win for losing. Even if he could get rid of Turbatius, which he doubted, the problem of Zap's dubious parentage remained. "They don't celebrate because I let them. As you said, the magic confirmed him as heir. I could do nothing to prevent that."

"Yes." Jonlin scowled. "The magic confirmed this imposter, and you don't seem to see this as a problem."

"I don't see why you continue to call him an imposter when the magic says he is the true heir."

"He isn't, you idiot!" Jonlin roared and banged his fist on the table. "He has somehow manipulated the magic to make it seem to confirm him."

Nexa raised an eyebrow. How far were they willing to stretch incredulity? "But that is impossible. No one can control the magic."

"But they can control our perception to make us think it is the magic. You have created a problem for us. The people want to know when this Zap will conquer the spirit of disorder and take his throne. Fish feathers! You will tell them that there has been a mistake. That the true heir of Zelfor is yet to come."

"How am I to do that? They saw the magic. Am I to deny it?"

"We don't care how you do it. Your negligence and permissiveness caused this problem. You figure out how to resolve it."

The other council members nodded in agreement and glared at Nexa, daring him to contend with their decision. They had spoken. Jonlin was only expressing what they'd already agreed on. There was no court of appeals.

Dismissed, he made his way back through the citadel, wondering how he was going to recant what he had said and deny what the people had seen. Why couldn't they leave well enough alone? It wasn't like Zap was charging into the pond demanding his crown. The boy would wait until Nexa told him the trouble was over and the crown was his. That would never happen. So, what was the harm in letting the undine celebrate?

He stopped to look out one of the windows in the long corridor of the citadel. The calm water of the pond relaxed his nerves and helped him think. Occasionally, one of the few schools of fish in the little pond would swim by and trigger his thoughts into a new direction. But today, the fish swam by in a state of frenzy. The floor beneath him swayed, and he had to grab the windowsill to keep from falling.

The emergency siren wailed through the citadel. Nexa had never heard it before, but he knew what it was. Undine ran everywhere.

An undine stumbled down the corridor and grasped his arm. "What's going on?"

He wished he knew. He wished that as king, he could tell her it was all under control. But he had no idea what was happening and would not offer false hope.

Undine scouts ran down the corridor and saluted him. "King Nexa, you must come to see this!"

"What is it?"

"The pond, sir. It's no longer in the forest of Hadley Town. We went to the surface, and all around us is darkness."

"Darkness? Is it night? Did the sun go down?" But Nexa knew it wasn't that. The siren didn't go off when the sun went down.

He swam to the surface and gasped. They seemed to be in a cave. The trees and grass were gone, and in their place was nothing but rock. He started to ask how this could happen, but he didn't want his scouts to think he was clueless and depending on them for answers. Especially not Abri, his protégé. He was clueless, but they needed to be able to look up to him. "It seems the whole pond was moved." There. At least they could feel he wasn't completely at a loss about what was going on.

"How could someone move the whole pond?"

"You assume that a person did this. This has never happened before, so we can't make assumptions." At least he wouldn't have to tell the undine not to celebrate. What would he have to tell them?

"What's that?" One of the scouts pointed at something floating in the water.

Nexa went to investigate and gasped again. It was Zap!

"It's a human."

"Is it dead?"

Nexa sighed with relief. They didn't know it was the heir they'd been celebrating. If he was dead, they needn't ever know. If he was dead . . . but he might not be dead. There was a way to revive humans who took in too much water. As an undine, he couldn't throw the boy's life away for his own convenience. "We must take him to a dry place. Grab his arms and legs."

They hauled him up on the rocks, and Nexa pumped the water out of him. Nexa felt ashamed to feel mixed relief when Zap coughed and opened his eyes.

"Nexa, king of the undine! You're just the man I came to see. I came here to help."

"Came here? Then you know where this place is."

"Yes, we're in Tartarus. I came to help you get back to Hadley Town, but I need the crown."

Nexa narrowed his eyes. "You sneaky human. Need the crown, do you? And why should I give you the crown when you brought all this trouble on us and on yourself? Not to mention, Turbatius is still out there."

"He looks more like he needs britches to me," one of his scouts said.

Zap shuddered. He should shudder, the little rascal.

"Why does he want the crown?" a scout asked. "Is he the heir?"

"I think I recognize him," another scout said.

"No!" Nexa couldn't let them think that—not until he figured out what he wanted to do. "He's just a human boy who thinks we should feel grateful after he saved us from the trouble he brought on us."

"It's not like that," the boy pleaded. "I really came to help. I went through a lot just to come down here and help you."

"Is that how you lost your britches?" Nexa sneered. "Or were you in such a hurry to help us you forgot to put them on. How are you going to help us? You can hardly help yourself."

"I really can't help you without the crown. Give it to me, and I can get you out of here."

One of the scouts started scratching himself. "I feel so dry out here. Even in the forest, there was moisture in the air. But this place is as dry as dead wood."

"King Nexa, we need to get back in the water. But what are we going to do about him?" The scout pointed at Zap. "Maybe we should take him to the council and let them decide. We can't just leave him here."

Nexa didn't see why not. His first responsibility was to the undine scouts. If the air was moist enough, an undine could survive more or less comfortably outside a body of water. What had the boy called this place? Tartarus. A fitting name, he supposed. The dry air was sucking his energy. He had to get them and himself back in the pond. "He got here by himself. He can stay here by himself."

Zap sat up. "You don't have to leave me here. I can swim."

Nexa rolled his eyes. No way would he take the boy to the council half-naked. If they were in doubt about him before, the sight of this half-drowned bedraggled boy would leave them without question. Nexa had nothing else to do or say here, so he jumped in the water. It wasn't as cool and refreshing as it had been in the forest, but it was still water, and he drew in its energy.

The scouts caught up to him and passed him to scout out any more dangers. Who knew what had made its way into their pond here in Tartarus? Maybe something here objected to them calling it their pond. They had to get back to the forest at all costs.

He felt the boy's presence in the water behind him. The idiot. Let him follow if he can. He entered the citadel and turned to watch. Zap's eyes bulged as he strained to keep the air in his lungs. Nexa counted to see how long the boy would last. Not long. He was still in double digits when Zap turned back to the surface. Nexa shook his head. No way was this the heir.

He went back to the council. The scouts were already there, giving their report.

"What is Tartarus?" one of the scouts dared to ask.

The council members frowned at one another. This was one of those questions they felt they had to answer delicately—if at all. "Tartarus is the underworld under the underworld. It is the place of those who were truly evil on Earth."

Jonlin glared at Nexa. "Do you see what you have brought upon us, Nexa? The very gods are punishing us for tolerating this false heir of yours."

"He's no heir of mine."

"We saw him just now when we went to the surface," a scout said.

Nexa glared at him. "Abri."

"That was him—the heir of Zelfor. But he was in trouble. We had to save him because he couldn't breathe the water."

Jonlin looked at Nexa. "Can't breathe water?"

"We should give him the crown," Abri insisted. "I saw the magic come down to him. The crown is his."

"Is it?" Jonlin raised an eyebrow. "Then let him come and be crowned. Let him stand before me right here, and I will place the crown on his head with my own hands."

Nexa sighed inwardly with relief. "That will never happen. Why are you so upset about something that just isn't going to happen?"

Jonlin stared at Nexa. "Our beloved pond is in the bowels of hell, and you see no reason to be upset? If the gods did this to us for merely tolerating this imposter, I shudder to think what they would have done if we'd actually left the crown with him."

Abri frowned. "You have no intention of crowning the heir to Zelfor?"

"I will crown him when I see him."

"When you see him?"

"Do you have a problem with that?" The warning in Jonlin's voice was unmistakable.

Nexa cleared his throat before Abri could open his mouth and dig himself into more trouble. "Crowning the heir is a point of contention, and it's not something we have to worry about right now. The people need our leadership. As king, it's my job to give it to them. So, if you will excuse me, I will be on my way." He turned to Abri. "Come with me."

"But I . . ."

". . . are coming with me." With that, Nexa ushered him out of the council chamber and out of trouble.

"Where are we going?"

Nexa said nothing—just marched to the top of the citadel with Abri in tow. He entered the command tower there and activated the voice blaster that would broadcast his message to everyone in the pond.

Abri closed the tower door and confronted Nexa. "So, you're just going to let those old water-logged prigs deny the heir his crown?"

Nexa looked at him. He could only protect Abri so much, but not if he spoke foolishly to the wrong people. "You have colorful names for our council. They are the ones who make the decisions. That's why we have a council. Not because we agree with everything they decide but because we gave them the right to make those decisions."

"Well, if we gave them the right, we can take it back."

"If we did that, we might as well not have a council."

"We'd be better off without one if they won't even listen to the universe when it speaks."

Nexa couldn't number how many times he'd thought they'd be better off without a council, if for no other reason than that they scared him senseless. But that was no reason to actually do away with them. "Don't talk foolishness. I will speak to the people. Then we'll go among them and offer whatever comfort is needed."

Abri rolled his eyes. He wasn't convinced, but he'd learn sooner or later—hopefully sooner rather than later.

Nexa pulled the mouthpiece of the blaster to him and began to speak. "Good evening, people. In the wake of our recent disaster, some of you may be wondering what's good about it. Well, we still have a lot to be thankful for. The pond is no longer in the forest, but we are still in the pond. And, except for those who were slain, we are still alive and able to restore life in the pond. We are undine, and that is what we do. I will organize restoration parties who will take responsibility for the health of our pond."

Abri plopped down in a chair and shifted his feet. He needed something to do.

"Get your scouts together and organize the restoration parties."

"This evening?"

"Since there's no sun down here, evening is a matter of opinion. There's enough light coming from the citadel to enable you to organize around the clock."

Nexa went out to talk to the people and survey the damage. Moving the pond to Tartarus had shaken their world like a land temblor. There hadn't been anything like that in their forest. Families stood outside their demolished homes. Nexa only wished the damage had been limited to their little bubble-shaped domiciles.

A woman saw him looking and ran to him. Falling to her knees, she wailed. "My daughter was asleep when it happened. How much safer can a child be but asleep in her own bed?"

There was nothing he could say. With his finger, he wiped a teer from her cheek and put it on his own. She smiled bravely, rose to her feet, and hurried back to her surviving family.

"What's that?"

Everyone looked up and murmured as glowing streaks shot across the surface of the pond. The water grew warmer as Abri and his scouts descended.

Abri swam ahead to the surface, then came back quickly. "There's a fire-breathing monster heating the pond with his breath."

"A monster?"

"Where did it come from?"

"Help us, King Nexa!"

Nexa closed his eyes. They called on him—not the council—in times of trouble. But this wasn't normal trouble. "This was that boy. He'll do anything to get that crown."

Abri scowled. "You can't blame him for everything."

"Who else should I blame?"

Nexa wasn't going to let himself be convinced that it was a coincidence that Zap showed up just when the trouble started. He rose to a spot where the water wasn't glowing and caught his breath. The monster towered over anything he'd ever seen. It was a dragon—that fairy creature from long ago. They didn't even exist in the world where their pond had been. They were in another world.

Zap hid behind a rock like the coward that he was while the dragon bathed the surface of the pond with fire. What could he do against such a creature? If he didn't stop the dragon, they'd cook like those potatoes the humans eat. But there was nothing he could do.

To Nexa's consternation, Abri rose in a cool spot not far from him, bearing the crown, and walked toward Zap. What does he think he's doing? The idiot is going to give Zap the crown . "Oh no you don't!" Nexa jumped out of the water and grabbed Abri by the throat. "Have you lost your mind?"

"Have you lost yours? Only the power of the crown can fight this dragon."

He was right, but he couldn't give that power to the boy. He was a king. If anyone should wield the power of the crown, he should. Nexa grappled Abri to the ground and wrestled the crown out of his hands. The jewels in the crown glowed in the darkness of Tartarus. With this crown, he would master all the elements—not just water. He placed it on his head and strode toward the dragon, ready to do battle. "This is my pond and my people. Trouble us no more."

The dragon opened its mouth and fire poured out. Nexa felt the heat but didn't flinch. He was wearing the crown, and nothing could harm him. Those were his thoughts—his last thoughts while he burned until he thought no more.

Abri watched in horror as his king burned. This wouldn't have happened if he'd stayed in the citadel. Nexa wouldn't have dared challenge the dragon if Abri hadn't brought him the crown. True, he hadn't brought the crown for Nexa, but he should have known the king would fight him for it. He glared at the heir cowering beside him behind a rock. The human for whom the undine king had died. Was he worth it? Then he felt ashamed. Of course the heir of Zelfor was worth it. It was for him the undine had been guarding the crown for centuries. The universe had confirmed him, and if the undine didn't give it to him, then their guardianship was for nothing. It was for his disobedience Nexa had been consumed. In fact, his own arrogance—not dragon fire—had consumed him. To his horror, the dragon picked up the crown and put it on its head.

Chapter 38

Cintella watched Zap and Vordon disappear into the castle's laboratory and shuddered. She wasn't sure why she was shuddering. Being in the Realm of Chaos was reason enough. But under the fear, she felt excited. She'd met her alias in the Quantum Realm and knew that everything Vordon had told her was true. She didn't just look like a queen. Cintella was a queen.

As if reading her mind, Jawan caressed her hair. "My queen."

Queen Quila was still the queen of Romatica, so Cintella didn't know what she'd be the queen of. She just knew that she was much more than she'd ever dreamed of being.

"What are they doing?" Savorne turned toward the laboratory. "I hear him. That's not Vordon. That's Havlo." With that, she went after them.

"Havlo?" Cintella didn't understand. Who was Havlo? She looked at Jawan, but he just shrugged.

"Where do you think you're going with my son, Havlo?" Savorne was yelling, but who was she talking to?

Cintella and Jawan stared at the laboratory door, unsure what was going on.

"Your son? After you left him in an orphanage, you now want him to be your son?"

That was Vordon, but it didn't sound like Vordon, and Cintella had no idea what he was talking about. Vordon never had a problem with Zap being Savorne's son, and he'd never said anything about an orphanage.

"You didn't have a problem with that when you sent him back to me. Let him go, Havlo."

Cintella and Jawan exchanged looks. "Didn't we just introduce her to Vordon. She just came in out of the rain and didn't know any of us except Zap." Then Cintella remembered that Savorne had called Vordon Havlo when she first met him, and Cintella thought she was mistaken. What was going on? Who was this Havlo speaking with Vordon's voice?

Havlo sneered. "He doesn't have to do anything. He's just a boy. Why can't you let him be a boy—just a regular boy doing regular boy things?"

"You don't understand. He has to save my people. If Vordon is in you anywhere, you know he has to get the crown of Zelfor. I know he's a boy, but he's not a little boy. He can do this. He has to do this."

"Forget about Vordon. Forget about Zelfor and forget your sorry people. This is what I'm trying to get Zap away from—all these nonhumans and your magic. It's not natural. It's not normal. I want my boy to be normal. Why do you think I went to Romatica? Why do you think I left you and your stupid pond and married a real woman?"

No, that was not Vordon.

"A real woman."

"Get away from me!"

Then there was silence that told Cintella something was wrong more than all the yelling. She and Jawan went into the laboratory in time to see Zap slip into the fire pit door.

"Zap!" Cintella ran forward. "Savorne, why are you letting him go into the fire pit?" But when she touched Savorne, the undine didn't respond. She looked at Vordon and blinked. Where was Havlo? Did he go into the fire pit? "Vordon, you've got to stop Zap. Why are you just standing there?"

Vordon blinked and shook his head as if he'd been in a trance. "Vordon? I'm not . . . I am Vordon." He stared at Savorne as if he had no idea what she was doing in his arms. "She's dead! Oh my god! She'd dead."

Jawan tried to pull Savorne away from Vordon. "She's so stiff."

Cintella was horrified. She reached out to help Jawan. Then she stopped. "Zap!" She had to help Zap. If the boy was chasing after this stranger Havlo, no telling what might happen. She opened the door to the fire pit. A blast of heat knocked her back.

"What are you doing?" Jawan reached for her, but she shook away from him, braced herself, and dashed down the fire pit stairs.

Cintella shuddered again for a different reason. She was in the Realm of Chaos, but she could still remember when Lord Elveston brought her down into his fire pit in Hadley Town. Everything was just the same. In the crackling inferno, she could still hear the roaring and hissing voice of Fuego, the spirit of fire to whom she had, unwittingly or not, given herself. Lord Elveston had promised to make her his queen. He had loved Queen Quanta, but his love came with a price. Cintella was a different kind of queen than the one he'd promised, though she still wondered what that meant.

"Zap!" She didn't know if he'd heard her or how he could stand so close to the fire without being scorched. Havlo was nowhere, unless the man had jumped into the fire. Never mind him. She had to pull Zap back to safety. She had to . . . To her horror, he plunged into the flames. "Zap!"

She raced toward the fire, screaming, "Zap! No!" But the heat held her back, and she collapsed to the floor.

"Cintella." Jawan lifted her to her feet and held her. "It's all right. It's all right." He looked around. "Where is Zap? Did he take the tunnel outside?"

"N-no, Jawan. He jumped into the fire." She pointed to the flames, sobbing.

Vordon stood beside her, looking shocked. "He did what?"

Through her tears, Cintella glared at Vordon. "It's because of you Zap is dead. I don't know what's going on between you and this Havlo. You put all that magic nonsense into his head." She lunged at Vordon, ready to throw him into the fire, but Jawan held her back.

"Cintella, calm yourself. Vordon didn't do anything. Calm down and tell us what happened."

"I-I told you. He was just staring at the fire, and then he jumped in." She wanted to slap Vordon. "All that nonsense about being a queen."

"You are a queen." He stared into the fire. "And Zap isn't dead."

The man was insane. Why hadn't she seen it before? The way he acted. But insane or not, he was the reason Zap had given himself to the fire, and she hated him.

Jawan shook his head. "If he jumped into the fire, he's dead."

"No," Vordon said. "He came here to go to Tartarus. Apparently, that's what he did."

"And Tartarus is the place of the dead." Jawan bit his lip and headed up the stairs.

Chapter 39

The more Zap tried to convince him that he needed the crown, the more suspicious Nexa became.

The undine grew uncomfortable in the dry air of Tartarus. With little concern for Zap, they jumped back into the pond. Zap looked around him. Suddenly, the cave was a shade darker when they left, as if they had taken some of the light with them. Zap thumped his own head. After all he'd been through, why was he now afraid of the dark? Anyway, whatever had made Nexa act like an idiot didn't change the promise Zap had made to his mother. He had to get that crown and save her people. He held his breath and jumped into the pond after the undine. He knew how to swim. He moved his arms and legs like the fins on a fish. But he wasn't a fish. He had lungs—not gills, and long before he reached the underwater castle where the undines had gone, his lungs burned for air. He really could drown down here, and this time, there'd be no one to revive him. He couldn't help his mother's people if that happened. Feeling like a coward, he turned and swam back to the surface. Pulling himself up on the rocky bank, he sat down to think of some other way to help them. If he couldn't follow Nexa into the underwater castle . . . Zap looked at the pond. It was no bigger than it had been in the forest. No way could a castle be down there. But it was, and there were smaller buildings, too. So, the undine had their own magic.

Zap felt the thump of heavy footfalls treading nearby. He looked up and saw the dragon approaching the pond. It had seen Zap fall in and must be coming back to retrieve its lost prey. If the dragon turned just a little, it would see Zap. If he ran to hide in the still air of this cave, the movement might draw the dragon's attention. He had to move carefully. He saw some rocks he could hide behind but decided the first place he saw would probably be the first place the dragon looked if it became suspicious.

Another rock beckoned him. He tried to move silently, though his footsteps thundered in his ears. As he wedged himself behind the rock, he turned to see if the dragon had heard him. But it went straight to the pond. Fire shot out of the dragon's mouth across the surface of the pond. Anything near the surface would have been cooked. If it kept that up, the whole pond would heat up. Were undines hot water spirits? He tried to imagine undine children frolicking in a geyser but couldn't picture it.

To Zap's horror, Nexa broke the surface of the pond where there was no fire. Did the idiot think he could fight a dragon? He must have come up here with no idea what was heating the pond. There certainly hadn't been any dragons in the forest of Hadley Town.

If he could see Nexa, the dragon probably could, too. Zap shuddered at the thought of the dragon engulfing Nexa in flame. The dragon was so intent on the pond that it hadn't seen Nexa—yet. At least Nexa had enough sense to watch the dragon and not move.

Another undine surfaced not far from Nexa and started walking toward Zap. Was he out of his mind? He'd draw the dragon's attention. Nexa ran at the undine and yelled something at him. The undine yelled back. Nexa wrestled the undine to the ground and took something shiny from him.

It was the crown of Zelfor! Maybe the undine had planned to give it to Zap, and Nexa hadn't wanted that. Nexa put the crown on his head and walked toward the dragon. But the crown wasn't for him. He wasn't the heir. Could he use the power of the crown anyway to defeat the dragon? Would it work for him? If it did, then Nexa could rescue the undine, and they didn't need Zap.

Fire poured from the dragon, and Nexa went up like a piece of kindling. A man burning was a horrible sight, but Zap couldn't turn his eyes away. He watched until Nexa was a pile of ashes.

The undine scrambled away and joined Zap behind the rock. He glared at Zap as if Zap had summoned the dragon specifically to kill his king. Then the undine looked ashamed of his own anger. Zap didn't know which emotion would win out in the end—the anger or the shame.

With more dexterity than Zap thought possible, the dragon picked up the crown and put it on its head. No! Zap thought. That was his crown. It wouldn't empower the dragon any more than it had Nexa. But it would help Zap, and he couldn't bear the thought of something so priceless in the dragon's mindless possession. Zap knew from reading fairytales in the orphanage that dragons hoarded gold, and once they took something, they'd never let it go.

"What are you doing? Where are you going?"

The undine must have thought Zap was mad running up behind the dragon, but he couldn't stop to explain. He ran up the dragon's back. The dragon bucked, snorting fire and smoke. Zap slipped but grabbed one of the dragon's bony horns to keep from falling. The crown was in reach, but to get it, he had to release his death grip on the horn with at least one of his hands. He closed his eyes, let go, and reached.

His fingertips touched the crown, and it slipped away. He opened his eyes. It was still on the dragon's head but a little further away. He stretched as far as he could while still holding the horn and grabbed the crown. Once he put it on his head, it seemed like everything in the world was right again, even in a cave in the heart of Tartarus.

Slowly, the dragon quieted down. Its head drooped as it let out one last puff of flame and fell asleep. Zap climbed down its back and walked over to the rock where the undine trembled.

"You are the heir! You're alive, you got the crown, and no doubt you are the heir!"

"Yes, I am. Now it's time to do something about it. Let's go save your people."

"If anybody can, you can. By the way, my name is Abri."

They stepped out from behind the rock, and Abri froze. "The dragon!"

Zap walked right up and patted it on its snout. "Magic put it to sleep, or at least there was some kind of magic when I put on the crown. Maybe it recognized me. It will probably take magic to wake it up as long as I don't lose the crown."

"You don't want to do that."

With Abri glancing gingerly at the dragon, they entered the pond. The water clothed Zap. "I don't need britches!"

"You're the heir of Zelfor. The water is your britches, and your tunic, too, if you want."

At first, hitting the water felt like sinking into a hot bath. Maybe a little hotter, but without the dragon's fire heating it, the water soon cooled, and they swam to the citadel in comfort. Zap remembered when he was a little boy with his mother the undine. Before Havlo, before the orphanage, he swam through water like it was his natural element. It was, and even the fish envied him.

Abri grasped Zap's arm. "Wait. The prince of Zelfor should have a proper entrance. A triumphant entrance." He ran off, leaving Zap wondering what was going on. Soon Abri's voice reverberated through the whole citadel. "The prince is here! The crown the undines have guarded for centuries has been claimed by its heir. Come one! Come all to the first gate and render a proper welcome to the heir of Zelfor!"

Abri rejoined Zap at the gate and ushered him through crowds of cheering undines. Carpenters dropped their tools, mothers herded their children, and undines of all ages blew bubbles as what must have been every undine in the pond rushed to honor their prince.

Zap flushed. "They know me."

Abri smiled. "They've been waiting a long time."

Another voice caught their attention. "Well, well. The prince is here. Let him come to the council chamber that we may honor him as well. There can be no proper welcome without the council."

Abri frowned. Something about the way the speaker said proper made Zap frown, too.

Chapter 40

Cintella stared at the two men. They were both mad. How could Jawan just leave, and how could Vordon stand himself? "It's your fault." She turned and ran toward the fire.

"My queen, no!" Vordon's hands pulled her back. He turned her to face him and wrapped his arms around her. "Cintella, you are the queen of Zelfor. Trust me, there really is a Zelfor, and Zap isn't dead."

She pushed him away. "Don't talk that nonsense to me. Zap is gone because he believed that nonsense." Turning back to the fire, she gazed into its dancing contours that seemed to beckon her as it must have beckoned Zap. It must be alive. The spirit of Fuego must still live. But she was apprenticed to the mage of spirits. She knew all about them—had talked to them. This was different. The spirit of fire was nothing like the spirits in the quintessence—the spirits of the dead. Dead. Zap was dead. A hand touched her shoulder. "Get away from me! Don't you understand? Zap is dead."

"It's me. Calm down." Jawan's fingers caressed her hair as if to apply a salve to her mind. "Come with me. There's nothing we can do here." He turned her away from the fire towards the stairs. "Let's go home."

Yes, they had to go home. They had to leave Zap in the fire and go home. She moved on wooden legs as Jawan led her back to Hadley Town.

She was vaguely aware of Vordon following them. But she didn't forget he was the reason Zap was dead. She didn't forget his nonsense about the boy being alive. When they stepped into Loby's laboratory, she turned and pushed Vordon back through the portal. "If Zap isn't dead, then I don't want to see your face until I see him."

Loby looked up when the portal chimed. "Where did you go? I looked all over for you."

Jawan answered. "We had to go to the Realm of Chaos. Turbatius took the pond to Tartarus, and that's in the Realm of Chaos."

Loby's eyes went big. "Took the pond? What do you mean took the pond? And what is Tartarus?"

"I don't know how he did it. We went down to ask Nexa what to do about Turbatius, and the whole pond was gone. There was just a big hole where it used to be. So, we went to Nanosia and Queen Quanta told us we had to go to the Realm of Chaos."

"We?" Loby met Cintella's eyes. "Where are Zap and Savorne? Why did you push Vordon back into the portal?"

Cintella opened her mouth to speak, then stopped. Loby was a mage just like Myrlo, Volvo, and Quintessuma. If she told him, she'd have to explain to all of them that Zap was dead. How was she going to do that? They wouldn't just blame Vordon. After she told Quintessuma that she was a queen, they'd blame her, too. Cintella didn't want to think about it. She'd been as much a sucker for Vordon's fantasy as Zap. Except she was still alive, and somehow that made her an accomplice rather than a victim. She tried to speak again but couldn't get the words out.

Again, Jawan answered. "Zap is dead. He jumped into the fire pit in the Realm of Chaos because he thought that was what he had to do to retrieve the crown of Zelfor. Vordon says Zap is still alive."

Loby shook his head. "The man is crazy, and I was beginning to believe him myself."

"We all did. I feel like such a fool believing I was the queen of a land that doesn't even exist. But we're still here. Zap's the only one who paid the ultimate price for following a fool."

"But why would he say Zap is still alive?" Loby asked. "How could he expect you to believe that?"

Jawan slapped his forehead. "Wait a minute. We don't have to take Vordon's word for it. Cintella, you can see if Zap's spirit is in the quintessence."

Cintella shook her head. "Why go through all that. I saw Zap jump into the fire pit. What more proof do we need?"

"So, you're just going to tell yourself that Vordon is a fool, then spend the rest of your life not knowing for sure?"

"There's no way he could still be alive." Cintella knew she'd seen what she had seen, and there was just no way. But that meant the spirits had shown her a false vision. They'd shown her what she wanted to see. She'd wanted Myrlo to be wrong. She'd wanted the mages to not know what they had been talking about for once. And if she went back to the spirits, would they again show her what she wanted to see? "I don't see the point. Jawan, we were supposed to study together." There. That would take her mind off Vordon and his madness.

"Yes, we were. And I came here to get some fire cubes for Myrlo. I could use them to show you how he makes volcanoes. Then you could show me something about the spirit world."

That wasn't what she'd had in mind, but at least she'd be with him.

Loby gave Jawan some fire cubes, and he and Cintella stepped through the portal to Myrlo's castle.

Jawan took Cintella's hand as they stepped into his master's laboratory. "You are my queen. That old blind man who could see with more than his eyes said so long before we ever heard of Vordon. Zelfor or no, you are mine."

She squeezed his hand back and knew that somehow things would work out. But she wasn't sure just how. Vordon had said that Zap was her heir. Without him, she'd be the last in her line unless she had another child with Jawan. Then that child would be the prince or princess, and Zap would be out. She bit her lip. Zap was already out, and she was already thinking his life wasn't important and his death was a convenience. Dammit! She loved Jawan, and they would have a child. But she loved Zap, too, and didn't know how she was supposed to feel.

"Where have you been?" Myrlo's brown-robed figure confronted them when they entered the library. "The conclave was over long ago. Where did you go?"

Cintella and Jawan glanced at one another. Neither of them was ready to tell Myrlo the bad news about Zap. She held up their clasped hands. "We went for a walk."

"With all those stars on the ground, you went for a walk?"

"Yes." Her voice sounded a little too bright, so she quickly changed the subject. "How was the conclave?"

Myrlo raised an eyebrow, obviously not buying her sudden interest in the mages' conclaves. But he didn't press the matter. "I'm not sure what to think about it. Loby surprised me by championing that idiot Vordon's ideas about magic for all."

"That is odd." Cintella was glad to be off the subject of where she and Jawan had been but wasn't sure talking about Vordon was any safer.

"It's beyond odd. It's insane. That Vordon has you telling everyone you're some kind of queen and Loby thinking magic should just be passed out like candy. Jawan, you're my journeyman, and I hope the man hasn't turned your mind as well."

Jawan just shook his head. "No, sir." He headed for the bookshelves. "I'll just get the textbook about fire. I'm taking Cintella out to show her how we make volcanoes."

Myrlo sighed. "I'm afraid you can't do that. Something about those stars separates us from the Earth's power. None of the mages can use their power now."

Cintella slumped into a chair. This was bad. Zap was dead. Savorne was dead. Lacus was dead. The pond and the undines were trapped in Tartarus, and the mages had no power. Things couldn't get worse. Famous last words.

"I've been thinking about Zap." Myrlo returned to that dreaded topic. "He's still a child. We can't let him stay in that castle alone without a master. Bring him here. We'll put a bed in one of the upstairs rooms for him until we find a new water mage."

"Bring him here?" Jawan gulped.

"Do you have a problem with that?"

"N-no, sir."

"Then go find him and bring him here. He wasn't at Loby's when we came back from the conclave. But he couldn't have gone far with all those stars on the ground. I hope he's not out there playing with them."

Cintella gripped the hand she had been clasping as if for dear life. What could she tell Myrlo? If they told him Zap was dead, he'd want to know how it happened. She couldn't tell Zap's story without revealing her own foolish contributions to it. She glanced at Jawan. He wasn't ready to talk about this either. But she couldn't lie to the earth mage. He'd know she was lying the minute she opened her mouth. So she kept her mouth closed and willed herself down in Tartarus where she wouldn't have to deal with any of this.

Jawan walked toward the door. "I'm sure he's not playing with any magic stars. Come on, Cintella. We'll ask around."

Ask around? She followed him out of the castle hoping he didn't mean what she thought he meant. When they entered the grounds of Quintessuma's castle, she wondered. "Where are you going?"

"Cintella, we can't keep dodging around the subject like this. Sooner or later the mages will notice that Zap hasn't been seen for a while, and they'll want to know why. We'll have to answer them when they start seriously asking where he is."

Didn't he know she knew that? "I know that, but I'm just not ready."

"Me neither. But we'd better get ready while the situation is still in our control. Once they start asking questions, it'll be in their control."

"How can anything be in our control? We can't bring Zap back to life."

"No, but we could find out if he's really dead."

"Aw, don't bring that up again."

"Why not? Suppose Vordon is right. You can go to the quintessence and find out once and for all."

Cintella looked toward the willow tree. It stood there behind her master's castle full of answers that made her shudder.

As if reading her mind, Jawan touched her cheek. "Don't be afraid, Cint. Whether he's there or not, we need to know."

Yes, they needed to know. And part of her wanted Vordon to be right. But if she went to the quintessence and found Zap's spirit frolicking around with other departed souls, she'd know Vordon was wrong. She'd just have to deal with that. Then again, if Zap wasn't there, then Vordon was right, and she really was a queen. She'd have to deal with that, too, because she still didn't know what she was the queen of. She pushed aside the draping fronds of the willow and began the summoning ritual.

The willow, the castle, Jawan, the world disappeared, and Cintella found herself in the quintessence. She knew right away that Zap wasn't there. Then where was he? Only Vordon knew the answer. She and Jawan would have to go back to Loby's castle, drag Vordon out of the portal, and make him tell.

Chapter 41

The undines moved to form a living corridor for Zap to reach the council chamber.

The eleven council members greeted them with anything but cheer as Zap and Abri entered the chamber. Zap felt like he'd come to be executed rather than honored.

What appeared to be the leader glared at Zap. "How did you steal the crown? You shouldn't have even known where it was."

Zap started to flinch. He could have been standing under the disapproving gazes of all five mages in Hadley Town. He'd never done anything to warrant that gaze but imagined that this must be what it would feel like. Then he saw the scowl on Abri's face and remembered that he was the heir—the prince of Zelfor—and the council was just a bunch of sour bluenoses. "How can I steal what belongs to me?"

The leader scowled. "Belongs to you? Your mother is a traitor to her people, and your father is a mere human with no magical talent whatsoever. How do you imagine that the heir to Zelfor could possibly come from such stock?"

The other members of the council nodded in agreement and glared at Zap in collective disapproval.

Zap winced at the mention of his mother. She'd been no traitor. "If she'd turned her back on you, I don't blame her. But she'd never betray her people."

The council members murmured angrily. "How dare he?"

"Imposter! How dare you speak to me as if you have a right to open your mouth in this chamber. Not only are you not the heir, but I cannot release the crown from the care of the undine as long as the spirit of disorder threatens mayhem.

"The crown is mine because I have it, not because of what you can and cannot do."

"I will remedy that right now."

The leader walked up to Zap and plucked the crown off his head.

Zap grabbed for the crown, but the leader held it out of his reach. Zap turned to Abri, but even he didn't dare raise a hand against his council.

Without action but with plenty of bluster, Abri railed at the leader. "Do you think that makes a difference?"

But it did. Zap breathed out and found that he couldn't breathe in. His eyes bulged, and his face contorted. He could no longer breathe the water. He swam for the chamber door.

Abri called after him. "No, don't let them run you away."

But Zap had to get to the surface. He had to have air. The leader's mocking voice was the last thing he heard. "Looks like our prince is having trouble breathing."

The next thing he heard was water gushing out of his mouth and Abri pleading for him to live.

"You're still my prince. You've got to live. Damn you."

Damn him. He was damned. He heard snakes hissing in his ear. "Punishment. Punishment." Tartarus for those who reach for what doesn't belong to them.

But if he was damned, then Abri was damned, too. What had the undine done? What had the whole undine community done that they all wound up here? It wasn't making sense. Zap sat up slowly. How many times could he do this? Temporary drowning? A gift from his mother? Everything looked the same in the cave except the dragon was gone. "They took the magic along with the crown. Look, the dragon woke up."

"We've got to get out of here before it comes back."

"I have to get the crown back. But I can't go down there. Maybe you could talk to the people. They know I'm the heir. The council has to listen if they all . . ."

"No. As much as I hate to admit it, the council is right about the spirit of disorder. We can't endanger the crown."

"It's not just any old crown. It's the crown of Zelfor. It has power." Zap knew Turbatius had to be defeated, but how could he do it without the crown?

"The magic is in you—not the crown. The crown didn't help Nexa."

No, it didn't. The power was in him, and crown or no crown, he had to use it. "You're right." Zap took in a deep breath. "Turbatius has to be defeated, or your people will have to stay in Tartarus." Though he had no idea how he could do it, no one else would or could.

"Wait. You need to take water from the pond to make a connection the undines can follow between here and the forest. Let me get a flask to carry it in." Abri dove into the pond.

Zap sat on a rock, then jumped up as the thud of heavy footsteps shook the ground beneath him. The dragon came straight at him. He couldn't hide behind a rock this time. He couldn't jump into the pond. The dragon was close enough to burn him before he reached the water.

Before Zap could think what to do, the dragon grasped him in one of its claws and placed him—not in its mouth—but on its head.

Abri broke the surface of the pond and screamed. "Oh, no!"

"It's not here to harm me. I think it's here to help. It remembers me. It remembers the magic."

"Help you? After you put it to sleep."

"Well, if it was going to eat me, I'd be eaten already. So it couldn't be just any sleep. It was a magic sleep. Give me the flask."

Abri shook his head in horror, put the flask on the bank of the pond, and disappeared back into the water.

Zap climbed down from the dragon and picked up the flask. He filled it with water from the pond and climbed back onto the dragon's head. When they left the cave, the titans came at them, but the dragon's fire kept them at bay. It walked toward the fire that surrounded Tartarus. Zap flinched as they walked into it, then he remembered that he hadn't had the crown when he came down to Tartarus in the fire. He just closed his eyes and felt the harmless lick of the flames. When he opened his eyes, the dragon sat him down on the floor of the fire pit in the Realm of Chaos.

Zap ascended the steps of the fire pit and entered the laboratory. No one was there. He wondered how long he had been gone. Vordon/Havlo and his mother were gone. He went out into the foyer, but it was empty. He was alone in the Realm of Chaos facing a task that no one but he could do—even if there had been anyone here. Where had they gone? Why had they gone? The creaking sound of the portcullis echoed down the halls. Zap cast around for somewhere to hide. He stepped back into the laboratory and peered around its door to see who or what was coming.

His father stepped into the foyer, but whether it was Vordon or Havlo, he didn't know and wasn't sure it made a difference.

"Zap! Thank goodness you're back."

"Vordon? You are Vordon." It was Vordon. Havlo wouldn't be glad to see him.

Vordon grasped his shoulders. "Yes, I'm Vordon. Cintella thinks you're dead. You just jumped into the fire."

"You know I have power over it. You told me so."

"I didn't know you had that much power. And do you think they'd believe me if I told them that?" He looked down, astonished. "And where are your britches?"

Zap groaned. So, the water only clothed him when he was in it. "That's a really long story. I didn't stay in the fire pit. I went to another place. Another world."

Vordon nodded. "Tartarus. We knew it was here, but we didn't know you had to go through the fire to get there."

"I just looked into the fire and knew that's what I had to do. Sorry I scared you."

"Oh, I wasn't scared. We came here so you could go to Tartarus and get the crown. So when Cintella told me you'd jumped into the fire, I figured that must have been what you had to do to get there. But where is the crown? Where are the undine? You couldn't have gone through all that to come back with nothing."

Was that all he cared about—the crown? He'd fought dragons, snakes, and giants, and all he could think about was the crown. "The undines still have the crown. They're in that other world, and they won't give it to me until I defeat Turbatius."

" Defeat Turbatius! How are you going to do that without the crown? And who says you have to do it?"

"Are you going to do it?"

"I . . ."

Zap rolled his eyes. He was half hoping his father would volunteer to take the task on himself. But Vordon had no power to beat Turbatius. He couldn't even hold his own against Alecto. He could ask the mages. Then he remembered how Antipan had nearly killed Myrlo. Turbatius was far worse than Antipan. This was something that Zap alone could do. He hoped he could.

"We don't even know where Turbatius is. I've been coming to this castle every day and haven't seen him. But you know that, since I'm still alive."

"With disorder all over Nanosia, he doesn't have to stay in his castle. We'll probably find him somewhere between here and the Quantum Realm."

"You sound like you're eager to see him."

"The faster I get rid of him, the faster I can get the crown. You do want the crown, don't you?"

They walked out of the Realm of Chaos, and Zap conjured a road to the Quantum Realm.

He felt like he was walking through soup. Particles and quanta no longer careened through the mists of Nanosia. They moved sluggishly and were so far apart that they no longer collided into one another.

Zap saw Nano and gasped. "He's always had nine bosons. Now there are only seven."

"And when I am done, he will have none."

"Turbatius!" The monster he'd been looking for. What was he going to do?

"Nano and his obscene order will be no more when my plan is complete."

When his plan is complete? He'd already thrown Nanosia into disorder. What more did he want?

"There will be complete entropy in the Quantum Realm. No difference between here and there. I will be everywhere, as a spirit should be."

"Complete entropy?" Zap gasped. "What does that mean?"

Vordon glared at Turbatius. "It means all energy will be lost. The whole universe will be frozen in time." He lunged for Turbatius. "All my hopes for Zelfor will be lost."

But he never got close to the spirit before it batted him away. If they'd been on solid ground, Vordon would have crushed his skull. But the conjured road of Nanosia was still mist. Vordon sank into the mist as if it were water.

"What have you done to my father?" Zap ran over to the place where Vordon had landed. He saw one hand reaching up and pulled on it. Vordon rose slowly. Zap strained with all his strength. He had to get his father to his feet before Turbatius destroyed them both. Not that Vordon would be any help against the spirit.

"Your father? So he knew that, too. All that knowledge made him useless. Not that it matters now. I will destroy the traitor and you. But before you die, I want you to see how futile your plans have been. I want you to watch as I recreate the world in my image—the image of disorder." He touched one of Nano's bosons, and it flew away into space.

Nano shrieked. "What's happening? Energy isn't supposed to be lost this quickly." He turned to face Turbatius. "You! I cast you out once. I will . . ." But he was slow.

Turbatius laughed again. "You will what? You think you cast me out? No, I went off to gather my strength. And now you will never get your bosons back. They are gone—lost forevermore. Energy lost through entropy can never be recovered." He took the cap off Nano's head and slapped him away. "He thought there was power in the number nine. But there is more power in disorder where there are no numbers." Then he crumpled the hat and threw it in the air. It floated away—just another particle without enough energy to do much of anything.

Zap shuddered. How could he defeat a spirit that slapped Nano and his father away like flies? He had no crown, no weapon, and his movements were as slow as Nano's while Turbatius moved with ease. But he had promised his mother. The undine were depending on him. Even Nano needed him. His bosons were gone. Gone? They're pure energy. How can they be gone? "That can't be." It had to be a lie. Why should he trust the spirit of disorder? What did disorder have to do with the truth? "I've been to Tartarus. There's nowhere you can hide the bosons that I can't go." But even as he spoke, his words came slower. His movements took more energy. "What's happening?"

Vordon lay at his feet, coughing mist and glaring impotently at Turbatius. "I hate to tell you this, Zap. But he's right. Those bosons and the energy they carried are gone irretrievably."

"Nothing is irretrievable. Those bosons have to be somewhere. All we have to do is find them and get them back."

Turbatius touched another boson and it vanished. "Oh yes, they have to be somewhere. And while you search all Nanosia and Tartarus, I will go on with my plans. Don't feel bad, little boy. Enjoy the wonderful chaos I've created."

234

Zap looked around in horror. "This isn't chaos. Chaos has its own beauty. This is just disorder." Not that it made a difference what he called it. Zap still didn't know what to do about it. And he had to do something. He was wasting time. Only five bosons left.

As if reading Zap's mind, Vordon whispered, "Use your magic."

His magic? If only. "I wish I had the crown."

"You had the magic before you got the crown. Remember."

Was this the same Vordon who thought he couldn't defeat Turbatius without the crown? Parents! Phooey! But Vordon was right—magic first, then the crown. But that still didn't tell him what to do. Or did it? Zap took out the flask of water he'd taken from the pond in Tartarus. "This is all I have, but what could I do with it?" And how could he use it? He needed the water to bring his mother's people out of Tartarus.

"That's more than you need." Vordon's eyes were bright, but his words floated out one at a time like he was falling asleep. In slow motion, he reached into his pocket and pulled out his book. You know what water is, and you know what you can do with it."

Water was hydrogen and oxygen. But before Zap's sluggish mind could complete the thought, Turbatius touched another of Nano's bosons, and it disappeared. He had all the water he needed. If only he had that much time. With just four bosons left, Zap had just enough energy to reach for the book and flip to the page he needed. He took a drop of water on the tip of his finger and recited the magic words that would separate the hydrogen from the oxygen.

There were only two lines. When he said the first line, Turbatius touched two of the bosons. The second line came out like a sleep-walking snail, and before it was half out, Turbatius touched another boson. One more. If he didn't do this before the last one was gone, there'd be no energy to do it.

"Do you think I don't know what you're doing?" Turbatius's own words were coming in a faraway dream. "Do you think I will let you?" He jabbed at the last boson just as billions of hydrogen and oxygen atoms separated. After a nanosecond of excitement, the electrons drifted to the lowest energy state. Then everything stopped. The universe went from torpid to frozen. With nothing moving in space, time ceased.

From the lowest energy state, billions of electrons emitted photons, filling Nanosia with the energy of light. Zap felt a bang—a big bang—as quadrillions of particles and quanta shook off their sluggishness and soared through space faster and faster.

"This isn't supposed to happen!" Turbatius's screams echoed through Nanosia. "You can't reverse entropy. Nano's bosons are gone."

Zap smiled. "This is a new generation of energy. There will always be a new generation."

"And I will destroy it." Turbatius's powers of entropy drained energy from the orbiting atoms, and they slowed to a crawl one by one.

Zap blinked. Turbatius couldn't still be here. I must destroy him. But how?

Zap held up the flask of water. It had helped him before, and it still had work to do. He took another drop on the tip of his finger and blew it onto Turbatius. The water formed a bubble around the monster. Separated from energy, Turbatius's movements slowed to a stop.

"I destroyed you!"

But Vordon shook his head. "No, he is just asleep. The universe needs energy, and where there is energy, there will be entropy."

"I guess so. But isn't there a difference between entropy and Turbatius?"

"Not really. Turbatius is the spirit of disorder. Is there a difference between a thing and the spirit of the thing?"

"Maybe. But for now, we have to get the crown before he comes back."

"And where will we put the undine?"

Zap held up the flask of water and knew what he had to do.

They returned to the castle in the Realm of Chaos, and Zap headed for the fire pit door.

"Where are you going?" Vordon asked.

So far, Vordon was still Vordon. But Zap had been here before—standing before this very door—and knew Vordon could turn in an instant. Havlo would try to stop him, but he wouldn't follow him into the fire pit. All he had to do was open the door and step through. He handed Vordon the flask of water. This was barely enough for a libation, but according to Abri, it would be enough.

Vordon nodded and put the flask in his pocket. "Cintella will be angry if I come back without you. You're the only one who can prove you're still alive."

"I'll be back as fast as I can. But I won't come back until they give me the crown." Without another word, he opened the door and descended into the fire pit.

To Zap's astonishment, the dragon was still there. It bowed low, and Zap climbed onto its head. Zap blinked but didn't cringe or close his eyes as the dragon plunged into the fire. The titans kept their distance when they saw the dragon, and the snakes slithered out of its way as it lumbered to the pond.

But when he reached the pond, he wondered how he was going to get to the citadel. Without the crown, he couldn't breathe underwater, and if he couldn't breathe underwater, he couldn't go down to get the crown. He looked up at the dragon, knowing no help would come from there. He should have made an arrangement with Abri. But should have was always too late.

He sat down and stared into the water and saw a little boy swimming in the pond of an orphanage. People called for the boy, but he didn't want to be found. So, he dived under the water and swam unseen until he thought the people had gone away.

Then the boy that had been Zap came near the surface and stared at him. Zap shrank back. Another ghost! Was he now a ghost like his mother, Lacus, and Ziph? He looked down at himself. Nothing had changed. No ripple from life to death. No greeting from Quintessuma as he entered the quintessence. He pinched himself. Ouch! He was alive.

And he was in Tartarus looking at a boy who wasn't afraid of water. Zap reached out to touch the boy that he had once been. But all he felt was water. The pond of the orphanage became the pond of the undine. It was the same water. It had never changed. The boy had changed. No, Zap hadn't changed. The boy who'd hidden in the water and then become afraid of water—that same boy stared back at him. And he didn't have a crown. It was the same boy. He was the same boy.

Zap jumped to his feet. He didn't need a crown. He had the watermark from his undine mother long before he ever knew anything about a crown. He dived into the water and swam toward the citadel.

Something was very wrong. Zap looked around to see what it was. That was when he noticed the smell. It permeated Tartarus, and he wouldn't have noticed it except it was so different from the original aroma of the pond. And the water was much darker than he remembered. The undines meandered about as if in a fog rather than water.

"It's the prince!" The undines came to life as they gathered around him.

"But where is your crown?"

"The prince should never appear in public without his crown."

"Why do I need the crown? You know who I am. The dragon knew me. Now I even know who I am, and that's more important than some dumb crown."

Abri came forward out of the crowd. "Because only you can use the power of the crown; it's proof for those who don't know that you are the true heir of Zelfor. If it wasn't important, why is the council trying so hard to keep it from you?"

That was a good question. As if Abri had summoned him, who should barge through the crowd but Jonlin himself.

"You! I should have known wherever there was trouble you'd be in the middle of it. Except you should be dead or half-drowned by now. How are you breathing, you half human?"

"There's no trouble here. The people came to honor the prince of Zelfor." Zap glanced at Abri, except his friend was gone. He stood alone before the council head and a strange crowd of undines. No, they weren't strange. They knew him. He looked the council leader in the eye and dared him to object.

"Honoring the prince of Zelfor? And where is this prince? All I see is a half human whose mother is a traitor."

"Yes, and my father is human. You need to come up with something better than that. It's not working for you."

"How dare you!"

The crowd muttered. "What does he mean?"

"We weren't saving the crown for an undine. But were we saving it for a human?"

"Who else could be the heir of Zelfor?"

"Councilman Jonlin!" Abri's voice echoed throughout the pond. "On behalf of all the undines, I thank you for your generous offer to place the crown of Zelfor on the head of its heir who stands before you now."

"Now wait a . . ."

But the cheering of the crowd drowned out whatever idiocy he was about to say.

Chapter 42

Vordon emerged from the portal in Loby's laboratory wondering if Cintella was still angry at him. She'd said she didn't want to see him until she saw Zap, and Zap wasn't with him. There was no help for that. He had to do what he came to do. If Cintella was still mad, she'd just have to be mad.

But when he entered Loby's castle, he only saw Loby about to step out of the laboratory. "Where is everyone?"

Loby turned back and stared at Vordon as if amused by his mere presence. "I wouldn't think you'd want to see Cintella right now. She sure doesn't want to see you."

Vordon grimaced. So she'd recruited everybody to share her anger. "No, I guess she wouldn't. but I had to come back here."

"Without Zap?" Loby pushed Vordon aside as if the boy might be hiding behind him.

Vordon shrugged. "I had to come back. I have something to do."

"Something to do?" Loby peered into Vordon's eyes. "So you found out you couldn't raise the dead after all. Was he too deep in the pit for you to reach him?"

"No. And he's not dead. He's fine. He'll be back as soon as he gets the crown."

"The crown. You are amazing."

"I am that, and I'm gone." Vordon patted the flask of water in his pocket. "I have a task to complete," he said over his shoulder as he exited the castle.

Vordon stepped into the clearing in the forest. Alecto growled impotently in distant clouds. He didn't see the point in pouring the little bit of water into the hole where the pond had been. But it had something to do with the undine, and the undine had the crown. So, he unstopped the flask and poured its contents into the hole. Nothing happened.

What did you think was going to happen? Havlo sneered. To Tartarus with all this magic nonsense.

No! You can't have my body. You should have gone with Turbatius.

Turbatius created you, so you're the one who should have died with him. I was born in this world.

But you rejected Zelfor. You rejected your heritage. And now I reject you
. Vordon delved into his mind with the strength of the incumbent spirit.

Havlo cast him out like a projectile. He jumped back in and wrested
control of his hands long enough to pick up a fire star. He pulled the fire into
his body. He felt the heat, but Havlo burned.

Exhausted, Vordon sat down and stared into the empty hole. It was still
just a hole, and the water he'd poured into it had long since absorbed into
the ground. But as he shifted his weight, his hand brushed the book in his
pocket. He took it out and turned to the pages about water. He kept turning
the pages—looking for something that might help. In frustration, he turned
to a section about travel and began to read.

"No!" Alecto blew the book out of his hands.

He picked it up and held on to it, but Alecto blew the pages so much he
couldn't read it. but he'd seen the words he needed to recite and knew from
the monster's reaction that they were the right words. He said them, and the
water began to rise. Alecto blew her wind, but Vordon didn't give her enough
energy to bring up a storm.

The water reached its full height, and undines rose out of it, creating a
singing corridor for none other than Zap. The boy marched across the water
with regal splendor, and to Vordon's delight, he wore the crown. Now if they
could just get him some britches.

"Nexa gave you the crown. Where is he?" Vordon didn't see how the
undines could hold such a glorious procession without the king of the
undines.

Zap stopped in front of Vordon and shook his head in dismay. "Nexa
tried to keep the crown for himself and met with a bad accident."

"An accident?" Vordon stared at Zap, then at the crown that fit his head
so perfectly. Would it grow as the boy grew? Vordon knew that it would.

The song of the undines rose to a crescendo. "Long live the prince of
Zelfor!" And they bowed low before disappearing back under the water.

Vordon saw his dreams coming true. The stars were everywhere. People
could step out of their doors and pick magic up off the ground. No longer
would the mages keep power hidden away in their castles.

"I need to talk to the mages," Zap said.

"Why?"

"We still don't have a water mage. Now that I'm no longer afraid of water and have so much mastery over it, they'll have to appoint me. Why else do I need the crown?"

"Why do we need a water mage? Why do we need any mage? Magic is for everyone."

But Zap was already headed for Loby's castle.

Cintella and Jawan came in. She ran to Zap and embraced him. "Zap! Thank goodness, you're all right!" But her eyes were full of reproach when she looked at Vordon, as if he'd thrown Zap in the fire pit for a prank. "Where are your clothes? Why do you have this boy running around outside half-naked?" She marched Zap to one of the upstairs bedrooms and rummaged through the closet until she found a pair that wouldn't fall off him.

They went back to the laboratory and sat down.

"You're decent enough now, but where'd you get the crown?" Jawan asked.

Zap touched the crown and beamed. "It's proof that I've been accepted by the undines."

"The undines?" Loby raised an eyebrow.

"Like Savorne." Cintella beamed back at Zap.

Zap drew in a breath. "Yes, like my mother. I'm no longer afraid of water. I have mastery over it like Master Lacus."

"I don't know, Zap." Cintella shook her head. "There's a difference between not being afraid of something and being its master."

Jawan looked amused. "You'll have to talk to the other mages if you want to be the new water mage."

This wasn't what Vordon wanted. This wasn't what he had been fighting for. "We don't need a new water mage, Zap. Your crown has all five elements on it. Not just water. It symbolizes a new age of magic for all. As the prince of Zelfor, that's what you symbolize. Don't you see that?"

Zap shifted on his feet uncertainly. "I'll talk to the mages and see what they say."

What they say? Vordon knew what they would say.

Loby nodded. "I've been thinking about this, Vordon. Maybe you're right. Things are different now. So, maybe it's time we changed the way we did things."

"That's right." Vordon smiled. With one mage on his side, maybe he'd have a chance to convince the others. Maybe he didn't have to write them all off as a lost cause. "How many mages are there anyway?"

"Five elements, so five mages."

"Five mages holding magic for the whole world. Maybe if we both go to them, they'll listen."

"They won't." Jawan shook his head. "And they're not going to let Zap jump from being an apprentice to being a master."

"Hypocrisy!" Vordon banged his fist on his thigh. He wished he could bang it on a few heads. "By not having a water master they have already broken with tradition and might as well accept free magic for all."

"We can't just turn magic over to the people," Jawan said. "They'll abuse it unless the mages teach them to use it properly."

"That's what I told them at the conclave. They don't want to teach the people, and they're the only ones who can."

Zap touched his crown. "Are they? If they won't let me be the water mage and no one else can, they'll be too busy trying to figure out what to do to keep me from teaching the people."

"They'll still try," Vordon said.

"They can't keep the people from using magic. If they have something against me teaching them to respect it, they've come a long way from the lessons about magic they tried to teach me."

"A long way." Vordon knew that he himself could never sway the mages. But maybe Zap could.

Zap and Loby stepped toward the portal.

"Wait." Jawan took the crown off Zap's head.

Zap reached for the crown he'd worked so hard to gain and regain. "What are you doing? I need that to win the respect of the mages. It's proof I have power over water."

"No, it's not. Trust me, you'll be better off without this."

Zap narrowed his eyes doubtfully as Loby pulled him through the portal.

Chapter 43

Zap and Loby slipped through the portal in Quintessuma's castle. "Wait." Zap paused in the foyer. Quintessuma didn't know they were coming, and they hadn't thought about what they'd say to her. If they just came out with the request to teach the people or make Zap the water mage, her mind was already set to say no.

But she already knew what she wanted to talk about. "There's been a lot of unfortunate goings-on lately—none of which concerns you. It's high time we considered what we're going to do about a new water mage. You need a new master to complete your training."

"I . . ." This could be the right time to bring up his ideas.

But before Zap could speak, she went to the table beside the portal and rang the summoning bells for Myrlo and Volvo. After some time, the two mages stepped through the portal one after the other as if they'd been waiting for this long overdue discussion. All Zap could think of was how to get his point across without letting them cow him under the sheer weight of their authority. What was he worried about? He'd beaten Turbatius and Alecto. He'd outwitted the council of the undine and won their crown. Let the mages do their darndest. He was ready for them.

They gathered in the council chamber, and Loby took his place behind the table with the other mages. Zap hoped that meant Loby was still on his side.

Quintessuma cleared her throat. "I can't remember a situation where a master died before his apprentice was fully trained to take his place. Without a precedent, we're at a loss for what to do."

"Didn't Lacus leave written notes?" Volvo asked. "We could use those notes to teach Zap what he needs to know until he completes his training."

Loby said, "If there's no precedent, then we're free to do things a little differently."

The other three mages cast suspicious eyes on Loby. They knew where he was going before he got there. Still, Zap was glad to have someone on the council bring this up before he did.

Ignoring the mages' looks, Loby plowed on. "Zap has been through a lot and has learned things that even master Lacus couldn't have taught him."

Myrlo shook his head. "How could you be a mage yourself and say something like that? Do you have any idea . . .?"

"In fact, my master hadn't taught me how to be a mage. So we do have a precedent."

"That's not the same. You were a journeyman, not an apprentice, so you did have some training in fire."

Loby gave Zap an opening. "Tell them about the undine."

Where to start? "My mother is an undine. Through her I have power over water that doesn't come from reading books. Don't misunderstand. I have nothing against books. I will continue to read master Lacus's vast library. But I'm way ahead of mere apprenticeship." He thought about telling them how he'd divided water into hydrogen and oxygen. No mere apprentice knew how to do that. But then he'd have to tell them about Turbatius and explain what he was doing in Nanosia in the first place. Simple would be better. He was glad he hadn't worn the crown.

"That is as may be," Myrlo said. "But it's no substitute for the rigor of being under a mage, and it's no shortcut to magehood."

Quintessuma nodded. "It certainly is not. The three of us will take turns giving you the lessons that Lacus would have given you."

Zap sighed. There was nothing he could say. They weren't going to listen. "What is a mage?"

"You don't know what a mage is, but you want us to make you one. This isn't even a real conclave where we make decisions, or you wouldn't be here." Volvo scowled.

"Have we made a decision for what to do about the magic stars?" Loby asked.

Quintessuma, Myrlo, and Volvo looked at Zap and said in unison, "No."

"Myrlo and I saw that the people aren't going to give up those stars, but Zap can teach them how to use them responsibly."

"We've been here before, Loby. The answer is still the same."

Myrlo rolled his eyes. "What makes you think the people will listen to him if they won't listen to us?"

"That's just it. Because he's not a mage, the people will listen to him."

"You don't understand the depth of the problem, Loby." Quintessuma stood up. "Have you seen how mad the people have become? she gestured to the wall, and a vision appeared.

Quintessuma pulled up a vision of Hadley Town. What they saw was not what any of them had expected.

The constables' deputies were everywhere. The ground was clear of stars, but the deputies held them like weapons, while the people cowered behind their doors and windows. But the deputies were dragging some people away.

"This can't be." Quintessuma's eyes bulged.

"But it is," Loby said.

"Not if we can help it." Volvo rose to his feet and headed for the door.

Everyone followed him to the laboratory, but Quintessuma turned to Zap. "You stay here. Let the mages deal with this."

Zap didn't think the mages could deal with this, but he said nothing. He just let them go through the portal, then he went after them.

He couldn't let them see him come out of the portal, so he waited in the foyer for ten minutes—enough time for them to move away from the portal, but hopefully not enough time for them to get in trouble. He came out near Hadley Town at the edge of the forest and hid behind a tree so that he could see without being seen.

He saw no one and heard nothing. He'd have to find them. He crept down the streets looking this way and that. People peering out of their windows would see him. But Zap doubted that they would run out to tell the constable he was coming or sound an alarm that brought as much attention to themselves as to him. So, he walked on but hugged the corners whenever he came to an intersection.

As he neared the town square, he heard Volvo yelling. "You can't get away with this."

The constable and five of his deputies were holding the mages at bay with stars. Each deputy pinioned a mage with a star of the opposite element. Quintessuma had no opposite element, but the white spirit star held her in place. And there was nothing any of them could do. Zap wondered what he'd thought he could do.

The constable looked at the deputy with the fire star. "Where's the water mage?" he looked around suspiciously. "It doesn't matter. He has no more power over these stars than you do. It's criminal the way you mages hide in your castle and let these townsfolk run amok. And you know what I do with criminals? I lock them up."

Zap watched in horror as the deputies marched the mages into the jailhouse. Zap waited, but the deputies didn't come out, and he had no idea how many deputies were already in there. There was no way he could sneak in.

When the sun went down, he snuck around to the back of the jailhouse and peered in at the window where the mages were being held.

"You!" Myrlo grabbed the window bars like he was going to rip them out. If only he could. "It's your fault we're in here. You and that renegade magician brought those stars and started all this trouble."

"Who are you talking to?" one of the deputies banged on the bars of their cell.

"It's probably that missing water mage. Go round back. We might as well have the lot of them in here."

Zap melted back into the shadows. He climbed a fence and snuck back into the forest. He dared not walk on the path but kept it in sight. The deputies had cleared all the stars from the path, but a few had made their way through the tree foliage and lay strewn about in the underbrush.

He picked some up—one for each element and just stared at them. What did he think he could do with them? They were useless to the mages, and Myrlo was right. He and Vordon had brought them. He raised his hand, ready to cast them away but stopped. They'd come down from the universe to confirm Zap as the heir of Zelfor. This meant everything to Vordon—his father. It meant something to Zap, too. If he got rid of the stars, what else would go with them? He didn't know what he'd be giving up, but he had to help the mages.

He returned to Loby's castle, where Vordon, Jawan, and Cintella still waited to hear news about his meeting with the mages.

"In jail!" the three of them said in unison. But while Cintella shrieked, Vordon chortled. Jawan and Cintella stared at Vordon.

Vordon shrugged. "It's not like I've got their love to lose."

"This is serious. We have to help them. Look, I brought these stars. We can use them."

"How?" Jawan asks.

But Vordon regarded the stars with wonder. "Oh, you have no idea how powerful these stars are. There's nothing we can't do with them."

"Then we need to go. The mages need us." Zap headed for the portal. "We should go to the pond. I think the magic will be stronger there."

Moonlight reflected off the surface of the water, and Zap thought about what he had to do. "Give me the book. I think I saw an incantation in it that will help us."

Vordon gave him the book. "I'd still like to see the mages' faces locked up in a jail cell. They're so used to always being in control. They won't like it now that I'm the one in control."

"Sorry you'll miss the show. We need to be here." Zap flipped the pages and started reading. The stars in his hand shimmered, vibrated with power, and disappeared. "It's done."

"What did you do?"

The night lit up like the day as millions of magic stars flew up into the sky.

"What have you done?" Vordon repeated.

"They're gone."

Vordon glared at Zap. "What do you mean gone."

"I mean all the stars have been returned to their place in the river of heaven where they belong. Now the mages can use their own power. They won't be too happy with the constable."

"You knew what those stars meant to me. You knew what I was trying to do." He knocked Zap down and reached for the book. "I've got to bring them back."

The new king of the undines rose out of the pond and took the book. "I'll keep this. The stars won't come for you. They were to herald the coming of the heir to Zelfor. That is done, and you don't need this. What you were trying to do was never the intent of the universe." With that, he plunged back into the pond, taking the book with him.

Chapter 44

The mages stared at one another. None of them knew what to do.

"This is what happens when power is given to the wrong people." Volvo held his breath as if the very air of the jail cell affronted him.

"Don't blame it on the power," Loby said. "The constable is using the stars the way he'd use any tool. It's because the people don't have power that he's been able to put the whole town on house arrest."

"Haven't you had enough of that?" Myrlo closed his eyes and concentrated with all his might to summon that one earth star hanging just where he could see it, but it might as well have been hanging in the sky.

"Look at the earth mage. He wants the star."

"Why not give it to him? He can't do anything with it."

"Except use it to blow his sniveling nose. Poor baby."

The deputies laugh at him. Myrlo couldn't believe it. The idiots were laughing at the earth mage. It was like laughing at the very Earth on which they stood. Didn't they know how much power . . . but he had no power. The Earth was his master now—not the other way around. The way it should be. The way it had always been. He wanted to bang on the window bars but wouldn't give those rogue deputies the satisfaction.

Something hissed outside. Only a human voice could make a sound like that, so Myrlo peered out the window. Zap stepped into the moonlight. What is he doing here? If the deputies catch him . . .

"You! It's your fault we're in here. You and that renegade magician brought those stars and started all this trouble."

A deputy banged on the cell door. "Who are you talking to?"

"It's probably that missing water mage. Go round back. We might as well have the lot of them in here."

Myrlo didn't dare look out the window again. Let them think it was nothing. If the boy had any sense, he'd be long gone before they went around to see anything. But if Zap had any sense, he wouldn't have come here in the first place.

The other mages cast him a questioning look. Should he tell them it was Zap and give them something else to worry about? He just shrugged and sat down on the bench. They looked tired, and he felt tired. Those stars! They weren't just put there to tantalize them. The stars with opposing elements were steadily draining their strength. He wanted to lie down. Quintessuma and Volvo were leaning on each other to keep from lying down.

Myrlo's eyes drooped closed. He was climbing the sky—grabbing handholds and footholds on the stars. All the stars were yellow, and the higher he climbed, the weaker was his hold on them. He reached the windswept top of the sky and collapsed. The Earth lay far below and out of reach.

"They're gone, Myrlo. Wake up. Can't you feel it?" Quintessuma shook him like a gentle earthquake.

"What? What's gone? The deputies?" Myrlo hadn't realized he'd been asleep, but he was glad to be back on Earth.

"No, the stars. Get up, man. Our power is back."

Myrlo sat up. He wasn't just on the Earth. He felt the energy of his connection with it. He looked up, and Loby was right. The stars were gone. He had no idea how that happened and could only hope it was by some good agency.

"What's happening?" The deputies ran around in an uproar over the vanishing stars.

The constable grabbed the bars of their cell. "You! You did this. I don't know how, but don't think I'm letting you out of here. This is my town, and you're staying put."

Myrlo touched the bars. Iron was as much a part of the Earth as any rock or grassy hillside. "I don't think so."

The constable was still grasping the bars when the cell door swung open and banged against the back of his head, knocking him unconscious.

"Those mages are crazy. Let's get out of here." The deputies ran to the front of the jailhouse, but unfortunately for them, the locks on the doors were made of iron, too.

The mages filed out of their cell and glared at the deputies.

"Going somewhere, boys?" Loby gestured toward the recently vacated cell. "There's only one door you'll be passing through tonight." He caused little sparks of fire to dance at their feet and herded them into the jail cell.

One of the deputies smirked. Myrlo remembered he was the one who had locked them in. He did a quick little twitch. "Don't look so smug. The key you have in your pocket won't work anymore. Maybe the town smith will find a way to let you out."

"You're going to leave us at the mercy of the people?"

Volvo smiled. "That's really not our problem. The people will barter in the coin in which you yourselves tendered."

Someone banged on the jailhouse door. Loby went to see who it was. "Do you mind?" He opened the door when Myrlo released the lock.

Loby backed away as dozens of deputies swarmed into the jailhouse.

"What happened to our stars?"

"Where's the constable?"

"What's going on?"

The mages let all the deputies come inside, then stood between them and the door.

Loby pointed. "The constable is right there on the floor, sleeping like a baby. Shh. Don't wake him."

In the confusion, the mages slipped out the door and Myrlo tweaked the lock again.

The sun rose without the normal bustle of early morning town life. The constable had had the people so afraid that normal life was impossible. Quintessuma sent a spirit of calm through the town. Soon, a few brave souls ventured out. Then more and more. When they saw that the deputies were gone, they filled the town square.

"It's the mages!"

"We saw your boy down by the pond."

"Zap?" Quintessuma looked alarmed. "What's he doing here? He's supposed to be in my castle."

Myrlo was glad to know Zap was all right. "Since when are boys where they're supposed to be?"

"Well, we have to go get him," she said.

"To the pond!" the people shouted. They lifted the mages onto their shoulders and marched them through the streets of Hadley Town, through the forest, and to the pond.

Once there, Quintessuma ran to Zap. "Are you all right?"

"I'm fine."

Myrlo confronted Vordon. "I want to know what you're doing here."

"Minding my business. And you?"

More insolence. Myrlo had had enough of it. He was going to say something, but the man turned away, staring at the pond like all his dreams had sunk to the bottom. Myrlo suspected the missing stars had something to do with that. He didn't see the need to cut Vordon down any further.

Some of the townsfolk came forward.

"Thank you, sir. Thank you."

"You saved us!"

"You got rid of those nasty deputies."

"Did you take the stars away from them?"

The people looked around.

"Where are the stars?"

The mages glanced at one another. This was it. They braced themselves for facing an unhappy crowd.

Myrlo cleared his throat. "The stars are gone."

"Gone?"

"Did he say gone?"

"What do you mean, gone?"

"I mean the stars are back in the sky where they belong. Now Hadley Town can get back to normal."

"Normal? I'll give you normal!"

"The mages are up to their old tricks—keeping all the magic to themselves."

It amazed Myrlo how people could go from gratitude to outrage in the blink of an eye.

"We want our stars back."

"Magic isn't just for you anymore."

"We want magic!"

"Give us magic!"

The mob surged toward the mages with single-minded intent.

Myrlo pointed at the ground. And it quaked under the people's feet. Volvo blew his breath, and a whirlwind swirled around them until they could hardly breathe. Then Quintessuma struck them with the spirit of fear, and they ran until there was no one in the clearing but the four mages, Zap, and Vordon.

Loby just stared at them. "I can't believe you would use magic against the people."

"And you think you're the only ones who can use magic without abusing it," Vordon said.

Volvo narrowed his eyes. "They were attacking us. What did you expect us to do?"

"You could have saved yourselves without attacking them back. You needed a shield—not a weapon," Loby said.

Volvo shook his head. "A shield has to be used over and over until it wears out. But a weapon only needs to be used once. They weren't hurt, and they won't bother us again."

Myrlo knew this was wrong. It went against everything he believed was the proper use of magic. Maybe that was all he had—untried beliefs. At the end of the day, he acted on the same fears, anger, and desires as the people in Hadley Town. "If we'd had time to think it through, we would have responded differently."

"What was there to think through?" Vordon asked. "If you had special powers of goodness, your response would have been automatic."

Myrlo and Quintessuma looked away, but Volvo sucked his teeth.

Zap looked thoughtful. "If you want things to stay the way they've always been, you'll always have to use magic as a weapon to keep them that way."

Vordon beamed as if Zap had given him an opening. "Time, like entropy, cannot be reversed."

"But it can be guided," Loby said.

Vordon turned to Loby. "Perhaps you and I can work together."

"I'd like that. We can . . ."

Myrlo thought, Oh no. I'm ready for a few changes. But this is going too far too fast . "Vordon cannot be a mage. There can be only one mage for each element."

"That could change," Loby said. "Meanwhile, he can be my journeyman."

"Your journeyman?" Vordon looked skeptical.

"For now."

Chapter 45

Vordon couldn't believe what Zap had done. His son—the boy he trusted—had betrayed him. "You knew what those stars meant to me. You knew what I was trying to do." The boy knew and had deliberately betrayed his father.

Zelfor? Queen Cintella? Zap the heir? His dream? The book. The stupid undine king swam off with his dream! Vordon ran toward the pond. "No!"

Zap pulled him back. "Father, you must not. Didn't you hear what he said? The stars were just to confirm the heir. They weren't for the people to misuse the way they did."

"But the magic. The stars brought free magic."

"Did they? The magic—the real magic—was here before the stars. Just like I had the magic before I had the crown."

Vordon started to protest, but the boy was right. "Are the mages really in jail?"

"Of course. I said they were. And the stars kept them from using their magic."

Vordon wanted to say the mages didn't need any magic, but he knew that wasn't true, and Zap knew it, too.

But the people wanted their magic back. When the mages failed to produce the stars, the people congealed into a mob.

Vordon didn't know what the mages would do. They hadn't taken the stars away and couldn't bring them back even if they wanted to, which Vordon was sure they did not. To his dismay, the mages started using magic against the people. Earth, wind, and spirit assaulted the mob until it dispersed.

This was what Vordon had been fighting against. "And you think you're the only ones who can use magic without abusing it."

Loby stared at them with disbelief. Myrlo and Quintessuma had the grace to look ashamed, but Volvo held his ground as if unaware just how shaky that ground was.

Then Loby offered to make Vordon his journeyman. Was he mad? "Journeyman?" As if Vordon were a boy eager to put himself under a mage.

Loby thought about what he'd said, then amended his offer. "For now."

For now. It was a start. A foot in the door that had erstwhile been closed to him. He'd accept that cracked door and see what he could do with that foot.

Myrlo, Volvo, and Quintessuma headed off to their castles, while Vordon and Zap followed Loby to his.

Jawan looked from the portal to the laboratory door and back. "We thought you were in Quintessuma's castle. Why'd you go outside?"

"With no cloak," Prenda noted. "What happened?"

"Another long story. The short answer is that the mages have agreed to let Vordon be my journeyman."

"Well, that's a big change. How'd you manage to get that much out of them?" Jawan asked.

Prenda and Loby looked at one another. She smiled. "Now you will have two apprentices."

"If that doesn't make the older mages respect me, nothing will."

Vordon chuckled to himself. It was a big change. But not anywhere near big enough. "You know, I think one of the first things we should do now is start a magic guild."

"Whoa! The mages are going to let you show the people how to use the stars?" Jawan's eyebrows shot up.

Vordon winced. He was trying to make the best of this disaster. But it was still a disaster, and it still hurt. "No, the stars are gone. Zap sent them back into the sky to help the mages.

"Why do we need a guild? The stars are gone. We don't have to worry about people abusing magic anymore," Cintella said.

"True, the stars are gone, but there've got to be people out there who have magic talent that needs to be trained. And among them may be the only person who can replace Lacus," Vordon said.

Loby shook his head. "I don't think the other mages will want to take the time for such a big endeavor. But you can start a club like the Holy Order of Mice. Call it the Holy Order of Magic."

Cintella pursed her lips in thought. "We'll need a mantra."

Zap lit up. "Yeah! Magic. Magic everywhere."

"No, that will remind people of the stars. How about 'Somewhere over that hill, somewhere behind that tree. Magic flows like water.' Help me. What's the next line?"

"It flows through you and me," Vordon ventured to add.

"Well, we don't have to settle on a permanent mantra right away," Loby said.

"No," Vordon agreed. "What's important is that we think about what our guild will stand for."

Jawan raised a questioning eyebrow. "Well, it was your idea, so I guess you have a reason in mind."

"In fact, I do. If what the undine told me is true, the spirit of Zelfor isn't about the wild use of magic. Our guild will be to teach people to respect magic whether they have a talent or not. And to train apprentices and journeymen." He picked up the crown and put it on Zap's head. "You'll be the first crown prince of the new order." He looked at Cintella. "Don't think I've forgotten you, my queen."

Cintella blushed. "How can I be the queen of Zelfor when Zelfor is still Romatica, and Queen Quila is the queen."

Vordon clasped her shoulder and looked into her eyes. She had to understand. "Queen Quila is not the queen of magic. Spirit is the highest element. You can be the dean of the new guild, and when you become the spirit mage, you will be the queen of all elemental mages."

Vordon sighed. If the mages made the concession of accepting him as fire journeyman, he'd have to make the concession that mages were useful. They had their place—as long as they remembered that place and there was a balance of power.

A horrendous scream echoed down the corridors outside the laboratory. No human voice could penetrate the stones of the fire mage's castle. They ran to the portcullis and looked out, dreading to see what could have produced such a sound of anger and anguish.

In the dark sky, they saw Alecto fading into black nothingness. "She's going back to Tartarus," Zap said.

"Wherever that is. As long as she's going and won't come back anytime soon," Cintella said. The stars appeared. But Vordon had never seen such stars. "What is that?"

Cintella smiled. "That's a five-point star with the fifth element pointing up."

Chapter 46

"Can I do this now?" Zap asked in the morning.

"Sure. Why not?" Jawan pulled him toward the portcullis.

Zap was still a boy in the mages' eyes, and they wouldn't hear of him staying in a castle alone without his late master.

"But I'm . . ."

"An apprentice. And I'm a journeyman. If I'm not too old for it, then you certainly aren't."

As they went down the path to the pond, Zap braced himself. But the dread he usually felt when he entered the forest wasn't there. The trees were still tall, but they soared to the sky rather than loomed over him. The pond was so placid, he could see his reflection in the water. He was ready to believe that Abri, the undine, and their king had been a dream, except he wore the crown. The pond looked the same, but the eyes of the boy he saw in its water didn't dart about fearfully. He was alive, and it wasn't fear keeping him alive.

He picked up a stone and flicked his wrist to make it skip across the water. It skipped three times as a regular stone should. Zap watched the rings spreading out from where the stone sank into the water and thought it was perfectly normal.

Connect to Rhonda Denise Johnson

I hope you enjoyed. Below please find information about connecting with Rhonda Denise Johnson.

Email:

connect@rhondadenisejohnsonauthor.com

Twitter:

https://twitter.com/Rhondauthor

Facebook:

https://www.facebook.com/rhondauthor

mailing List:

https://lp.constantcontactpages.com/su/T74BR9T

As a reader and an author of fantasy and science fiction, I created this mailing list to share with all you lovers out there a weekly round of reading recommendations, interviews with various authors, science facts, quotes from various authors, and more.

Occasionally I will let you know about special coupons for my own books available only to subscribers as well as a free short story or flash fiction piece

Don't miss out!

Visit the website below and you can sign up to receive emails whenever Rhonda Denise Johnson publishes a new book. There's no charge and no obligation.

https://books2read.com/r/B-A-AWWS-FZLHC

BOOKS 2 READ

Connecting independent readers to independent writers.

Also by Rhonda Denise Johnson

Bedtime Stories
Prince Alarming: A Short Story
The Listening Heart: A Short Story
Sticks: A Short Story
The Tale of the Western Crocogator: A Short Story
Dinner is Served: A Short Story
On Target
Stuporman to the Rescue: A Short Story
The First Nine: A Short Story

Nanosia Fantasy Series
Queen of the Quantum Realm
Fire Master: Book 2 of the Nanosia Fantasy Series
Mage of the Black Hole: Book 3 of the Nanosia Fantasy Series
Chaos in Nanosia

Orisha Series
Two Women Two Roads One Future

Standalone

Speaking for the Child: An Autobiography and a Challenge - Bonus Edition

Watch for more at rhondadenisejohnsonauthor.com.

About the Author

As a reader, I'm fascinated by well-written fantasy novels. As a writer, I find that magic naturally works its way into my stories.

An idea percolates in my head telling me a story is there, and I must write it. I imagine you, the reader, smiling, laughing, hollering at my characters, or remembering something in your life, and I get a good feeling. It's like when you know what your purpose is in life, and it's something that affects people in a good way.

When the reader in you meets the writer in me, there is MAGIC!

Read more at rhondadenisejohnsonauthor.com.